Sweet Devotion

MAE & TRISTAN'S STORY
(A WATCHER NOVEL)

BY

INTERNATIONAL
BESTSELLING AUTHOR

S.J. WEST

CONTENTS

COPYRIGHTS

Cover Design: Stephany Wallace, all rights reserved.
Interior Design & Formatting: Stephany Wallace, all rights reserved.
Proof Reader: Kimberly Huther.

Published by Watchers Publishing November, 2017.
www.Sjwest.com

BOOKS IN THE WATCHER SERIES

Lucifer
Redemption

The Dominion Series
Awakening
Reckoning
Enduring

Watcher Books
Sweet Devotion, Mae & Tristan Story

OTHER BOOKS BY S.J. WEST

The Harvester of Light Trilogy
Harvester
Hope
Dawn

The Vankara Saga
Vankara
Dragon Alliance
War of Atonement

Vampire Conclave Series
Moonshade
Sentinel
Conclave
Requiem (Coming Soon)

ACKNOWLEDGMENTS

I would like to express my gratitude to the many people who were with me throughout this creative process; to all those who provided support, talked things over, read, wrote, offered comments, allowed me to quote their remarks and assisted in the editing, proofreading and design.

I would like to thank Lisa Fejeran, Liana Arus, Karen Healy-Friday, Misti Monen, and Erica Croyle, my beta readers for helping me in the process with invaluable feedback.

Thanks to Kimberly Huther, my proofreader for helping me find typos, correct commas and tweak the little details that have help this book become my perfect vision. Thank you to Stephany Wallace for creating the Cover Design as well as the Interior Design of the books, and formatting them.

Last and not least: I want to thank my family, who supported and encouraged me in this journey.

I apologize to those who have been with me over the course of the years and whose names I have failed to mention.

Time has a way of playing with our memories. Moments you thought would be unforgettable grow hazy as new experiences press them to the furthest reaches of your mind. Yet those small fragments of our past aren't entirely lost to us forever. They're simply woven into an intricate tapestry of distant remembrances, pushed so far out of our grasp that they teeter on the edge of forgetfulness. It's only when something within the present overlaps a strand from the past that we recall what was all but lost to us.

I can remember mornings when I would crawl into bed with my big sister, Caylin, and snuggle up against her warmth, finding comfort in the knowledge that she loved me and always would. My big brother, Will, would never say no when I asked him to play, making me feel like I was someone special in a way only a brother can. Both of them did their best to shield me from all the hidden dangers that lurk within our strange world of angels and demons, providing me with their wisdom and always encouraging me to be brave and live my life to its fullest potential. When my mother gave birth to the twins, Xavier and Ariana, I readily accepted the mantle of protector, just like Caylin and Will did for me.

The unconditional love and support of my family is something I know I can always count on, no matter how hectic our lives might get. The strong bonds that tie us all together are anchored by the firm foundation of my parents' devotion to one another. It's a love that's never wavered or even known one moment of weakness since the day they pledged their lives to each other. I've known from a very young age that if I ever need their support, my family will always be there to help me find a way to overcome any obstacle the world tries to place in my path, and even if I fall I know those who love me most will help me back up.

"Pumpkin pie, pumpkin lattes, pumpkin muffins, my mom's caramel-spiced pumpkin trifle with homemade whip cream, your dad's bourbon chocolate chip pecan pie..." Ella sighs as she wilts into the brown leather passenger seat of my Jeep Grand Cherokee, looking completely dejected. "I swear, Mae, Thanksgiving is determined to doom me to failure!"

I can't help but laugh as I briefly take my eyes off the road to glance in Ella's direction.

"You have more willpower than you think you do," I tell her confidently. "You're one of the strongest people I know."

"Not strong enough when it comes to good food, though, or I wouldn't have this extra padding clinging to my body."

"I think you're perfect the way you are, but if you want to stay on your diet this week I'm here for you. In fact, while we're with our families, I'll make sure you exercise every day and stay away from all the sugary goodness that awaits us. Did you tell Aunt Tara that you're on a diet?"

"My mom's been able to eat anything she wants to her whole life and not gain a pound," Ella laments. "I'm not sure she even understands the concept of a diet, much less my need to be on one during the holidays."

"You just wait," I say, keeping my eyes on the heavy traffic as we head to downtown Denver, where one of Caylin's art galleries is located. "I think your mom will come through for you. She always does."

"I just wish I had some of your angelic DNA running through my veins."

"What does that have to do with anything?" I ask, perplexed.

"Do you know any fat angels?" she asks in a voice that doubts such an anomaly exists in nature. "No. You're all good-looking and don't gain a lick of weight unless it's muscle. Me, on the other hand?

The only thing being part fairy does is give me the supernatural ability to sniff a cookie and magically gain ten pounds."

"You do not," I protest, unable to stop myself from giggling at her exaggeration.

"I swear to the good Lord above that I believe it's true. Maybe not ten pounds, but at least half of one. You just don't know how lucky you are not to have to worry about your weight."

"There's one thing that you'll never have to worry about," I tell her. "I'll always love you and be there for you, no matter what."

"Girl, I know that," Ella says with a smile. "I just want to feel better inside my own skin, is all."

"Did I mention how gorgeous you look in that dress?" I ask, giving her another brief sideways glance. "I certainly can't pull off wearing a lime-green and purple outfit like that."

"Mae Cole, you could wear a dress made from crumpled old newspapers and still look hot," Ella declares with a roll of her eyes. "Which reminds me of something I've been meaning to ask you about. Why did you say no to a date with Danny Raye?"

"How did you hear about that?" I ask in surprise, since that particular incident only happened that afternoon.

"When the quarterback of your college's football team takes an interest in a girl on campus and she turns him down flat, word gets around pretty fast. The question is, why didn't *you* tell me about it? And why did you say no to him?"

"He comes with too much baggage," I reply with a small shake of my head. "I don't need the drama, and I definitely don't need people watching me too closely. You know how hard it is to date someone who isn't a part of our world. My family lives on the down-low. I don't need to start developing feelings for someone who might end up being a world-famous football player one day."

"As usual, you're overthinking things," Ella protests with a wave of her hand, as if such an action can push away my real-world concerns. "One date wouldn't have hurt anything. Besides, you know him. He's been in a couple of your classes. I thought you said he was nice."

"He *is* nice," I sigh with a pang of regret, "which is part of the problem. I don't want to end up liking him and then breaking up with him later on. I've been down that road once. I would rather not do it again."

"Ahh, yeah, Clay," Ella says, nodding her head in understanding. "I remember that. You cried for a solid week after you broke up with him. I still don't understand how you knew he wasn't the one for you. Your brother married outside our circle of friends. Why can't you?"

"That was different. Will found the person he was meant to be with. I haven't yet."

"But, how did you know Clay wasn't your Mr. Right? How do you know Danny isn't either if you don't give him a chance?"

"I'll know when the right guy comes along," I say, hoping she leaves it at that but knowing she won't.

"Mae," Ella says knowingly, "please tell me this doesn't have anything to do with what happened when you were three years old. I thought you had finally let that go after Uncle Malcolm told you that Tristan would probably never be able to see you again."

"He only said that Tristan had to deal with some family issues before he would be able to keep his promise to come back and see me," I clarify, feeling slightly defensive for some reason.

"And he also said that if you tried to contact Tristan, it would put you both in danger. You're not thinking about going back on your word to him, are you?"

"If I wanted to do that, I would have by now," I reply more testily than I meant to. "I could have found a way to follow Uncle Malcolm or even Jered to where Tristan lives, but I haven't, have I?"

"Only because you don't know what the fall-out would be. It's been years since you saw him. Why haven't you been able to get him out of your head yet?"

"It's not my head that's the problem. It's my heart," I confide. "Besides, it's been thirteen years since Uncle Malcolm had that talk with me. Surely Tristan's close to solving his family problems by now."

"You're talking about a Watcher family, and a bad one to boot," she reminds me. "He left them in order to protect you, and then he went back to give them misleading information to help Caylin and the others take down the princes. For all you know, he might end up spending the next thousand years trying to work out his issues with them."

"I don't think that'll be the case," I say confidently.

"How can you possibly know that?"

"I just have a hunch. Can we leave it at that?"

Ella huffs agitatedly, but she doesn't ask any more questions or try to push the matter any further. We've discussed Tristan a handful of times over the years, and always end on the same thorny note. She wants me to forget about him. But, try as I might, I just can't. The years have made my memories of him fuzzier, but sometimes, especially when I dream, I can see his face so clearly and remember exactly how it felt to be with him.

Ella once asked me if I thought Tristan was my soul mate. My mother and Caylin found theirs, so it wasn't outside the realm of possibility that I would, too. Honestly, I don't know if he is or not. I was too young to understand what such a connection meant or should feel like. All I know is that I can't fully commit to anyone until I stand face to face with Tristan again. Then, maybe I can move on— either with him or without him.

When we reach Caylin's art gallery on Santa Fe Drive, I'm lucky enough to find a parking space directly across the street from it. Caylin, Aiden, and their children split their time between the home Aiden built for them here in Colorado and the townhouse they own in New York City. Caylin operates three different art galleries in three cities: Denver, New York, and Paris. Not long after they were married and he became human, Aiden opened up his own security firm in New York City, which caters to high-profile celebrities and international dignitaries. Their kids, Kate and Andrew, both attend the same private school in Lakewood that all us kids graduated from. Even though it was partially destroyed during the fight with the princes when I was younger, the Watchers of the world pulled together and helped rebuild it in record time. Since Uncle Malcolm continues to teach there, it's considered a safe zone.

"What's the name of the artist Caylin's pimping this month?" Ella asks as I shut the engine off.

"She wouldn't tell me," I say with a shrug. "For some reason, she wanted it to be a surprise."

"That's weird. Maybe it's someone famous! Let's get in there before she sells everything they have."

When Ella and I walk into Caylin's spacious split-level gallery, the sound of laughter and congenial chit-chat fills the air as dozens of people travel from one painting to the next. Several canvases of abstract artworks hang on the smooth white walls, filling the well-lit space with their vibrant colors.

"Ohh," Ella croons as she glances at the paintings we can see from the doorway. "I like this artist already!"

"I should hope so," we hear Aiden say as he walks over to us through the crowd. When he reaches us he holds out his hands, indicating he intends to take our coats.

"Why?" I ask as I slip my brown wool coat off and hand it to my handsome brother-in-law. "Do we know the painter personally?"

Aiden smiles, looking almost bashful before he says, "I would say so, since the painter is me."

"Get out of here!" Ella practically shouts, causing some of the stuffier clients of my sister's to look in our direction with raised eyebrows. "I didn't know you could paint like this, Aiden."

"I usually leave artwork to the true artist in the family," he says, "but she convinced me to do a few pieces for her to show off and sell."

"They're gorgeous," I tell him truthfully. "And I expect to have my pick waiting for me underneath the Christmas tree at Mom and Dad's house this year."

Aiden chuckles. "Then you'd better hurry up and choose, because we've already had offers on quite a few of them." Aiden reaches for a small sheet of red stickers on the glass entryway table with the number 40 printed on them. As he hands it to me, he says, "Just place one of these stickers on the card of the painting that you want, and we'll hold it for you."

"Ahem." Ella crosses her arms over her ample bosom, and gives

Aiden a look indicating she expects a painting for Christmas, too. "Just because Mae and I share an apartment, doesn't mean I don't deserve to get my own painting."

Aiden smiles and reaches for another sheet of stickers that are yellow with the number 41 printed on them.

"You're absolutely right," he says apologetically. "Feel free to put a sticker on any painting still available. All of them are for sale except for the one titled *Andrew*. Caylin just wanted to display that one because it's her favorite."

"Why isn't it for sale?" I ask, intrigued by its exclusion from the event.

Aiden's cheeks turn a shade pinker before he replies, "You'll have to get the answer to that question from your sister."

Ella grabs my arm and tugs me toward the paintings. "Come on, Mae! I see a woman looking at the painting I want. I need to claim it before she does!"

I hear Aiden laugh behind us as my best friend pulls me away from him.

I fear Ella is going to trip on her high heels as she practically dives toward the painting's card to slap her sticker on it before the woman standing in front of it can.

"Phew!" she says in relief. "I thought I was about to miss out on it."

"You're hilarious," I tell her as I loop one of my arms through hers. "Come on, let's go find this painting Aiden mentioned. Maybe I'll find the one I want along the way."

Aiden's artwork is a unique blending of Picasso's cubism with Monet's impressionism. Almost all of the paintings use vibrant colors, paying particular attention to the warmer hues of red and orange. One painting in particular catches my eyes because it doesn't seem to fit in with the rest. Its colors were applied more chaotically, without rhyme or reason. Yet every patch of paint seems to complement the other. When I look down at the card to see what the picture's name is, I discover that it's the one titled *Andrew*.

"Do you like that one, Mae-Mae?" I hear my sister ask.

I feel her arm lay across my shoulders even before I have a chance to turn my head and look at her. I find it hard to believe that Caylin is in her mid-thirties now with two children of her own. She doesn't look any older than twenty-five, but I know she has my parents' good genes to thank for her youthful appearance. Even though my folks are in their fifties, they still look and act young. They continue to teach at Southeastern College, which probably helps them maintain their young at heart outlook on life. Since my dad is quickly approaching the age of sixty I asked him if he had any plans to retire, but he quickly shot that idea down. He said he still enjoyed teaching his art classes and discovering new talent. Caylin had even represented a couple of his best students and helped them gain a footing in the art world. As long as my parents are happy, I don't care what they do to fill their days. Plus, they have a couple of rambunctious teenagers still at home who keep them busy.

"I do like it, but Aiden told us it wasn't for sale," I reply. "He said you would tell me why that is."

Caylin's cheeks become slightly rosier before she answers me.

"This is one Aiden and I painted together," she says before turning her head to look at me to finish her explanation. "We did it the day Andrew was conceived."

It takes me a minute, but I quickly catch on to what my sister is insinuating.

"The two of you had sex on this canvas!" Ella blurts out, ever the restrained one in a crowd of strangers.

"No," Caylin whispers back, as she vainly attempts to hold in a laugh at Ella's outburst. "It actually started out as a tickling match that quickly led to other things."

"So..." I say, thinking this through, "the two of you covered yourselves in paint and rolled around on the canvas, tickling each other?"

Caylin nods as she returns her gaze to the painting with a distant look in her eyes.

"It was one of the best days of my life," she whispers, smiling as she allows herself to fully remember the moment this particular painting was made. "Where is Aiden by the way?"

"He met us at the front door," I tell her. "He took our coats to the back room, I think."

Caylin leans in and gives me a quick peck on the cheek. "I'll find you again in a little bit. I think Uncle Malcolm is in the back section of the gallery. He was hoping to see you tonight."

"Does he have his usual Barbie doll on his arm this evening?" I ask, sincerely hoping that my uncle didn't bring his latest conquest to the event.

"Not the one you're thinking of," Caylin says with smile. "He brought JoJo with him so she could see Aiden's artwork."

Ella claps her hands together excitedly. "Oh, JoJo! Let's go find her so she can see how pretty I look in the dress she made me."

"I'll catch up with the two of you after I find Aiden," Caylin promises, walking away to no doubt make out with her handsome husband after mentally reliving the fond memories she has about the day Andrew was conceived.

Ella and I walk towards the back of the gallery where we find my uncle and JoJo quietly discussing the painting they're standing in front of. I immediately smile when I see Uncle Malcolm, but that's not an uncommon occurrence when I see him. In fact, I can't remember a time in my life when seeing him *didn't* make me smile. He's always had a way of putting me at ease and making me feel like someone special, even if we're in a crowded room. He's one of my favorite people in the world, and I'm luckier than most because I know I'll always have him in my life.

He's dressed rather dapperly in a well-tailored dark blue suit with a crisp white shirt peeking out from underneath his jacket, setting off his sun-kissed skin. He's left the first three buttons undone, which is something he does when the temperature begins to drop as we approach winter. He has his long dark hair pulled back into a ponytail and hanging straight down his back. As we approach the pair, I notice he's leaning on his wolf-head cane a bit more than usual tonight. He told me once that the cold tends to cause his hellhound bite to ache more, causing him to rely on his cane.

As if sensing my presence, Uncle Malcolm stops speaking to JoJo in mid-sentence as he turns his head to look at me.

"There are my girls," he says to us as his lips stretch into a welcoming smile. "We were wondering when the two of you would show up to this shindig."

When JoJo turns her head to look at us, her eyes light up when she sees that we're wearing the dresses she gave as part of our fall wardrobe. For some reason, JoJo loves to dress all us girls up in her clothing. Since they're one-of-a-kind creations by a world-famous designer, none of us finds a reason to complain about her pampering.

"You both look so beautiful," she says proudly. "Not everyone can wear that particular color of green, Ella, but I knew it would look gorgeous against your perfect complexion, *mon cheri*."

"Aww," Ella says, looking embarrassed yet pleased by JoJo's praise. She waves a hand at JoJo as if swatting her compliment away, like she doesn't deserve it. "It only looks good on me because you cut the dress to hide my figure."

JoJo looks slightly confused by Ella's words. "Your figure is not hidden, simply accentuated."

"Either way," I say, "she does look gorgeous in it. It's a beautiful dress, JoJo."

"*Merci*," she says, with a slight tilt of her head in acceptance of my compliment.

"Your mom and dad should be here soon," Uncle Malcolm tells me. "Lilly said they had to drop Xavier and Ariana off at a party one of their friends from school is having this evening."

"Speaking of school," I say, "how are your classes going this year?"

"As well as can be expected when dealing with human spawn, I suppose," he replies. "If I can ever get Xavier to think about something other than the girls in class, he might be able to get a passing grade this term."

"What else do you expect from your namesake?" JoJo asks with a small shake of her head, as if my younger brother is doomed to follow in Uncle Malcolm's womanizing footsteps.

"I expect him to have enough sense to pass his English Lit final," he complains.

"Since you mentioned womanizing," I say, directing the conversation away from my little brother before my uncle allows his disappointment in Xavier's academic work to darken his mood, "where's Carolina this evening?"

"In Budapest, shooting some romantic comedy," Uncle Malcolm replies off-handedly. "It doesn't really matter. I called things off with her a few days ago. She was beginning to get too clingy for my taste."

"Can you blame her?" I ask. "It's been a year since the two of you started dating. Most women expect to at least see the promise of a ring by this point."

"Which is exactly why I called things off," he replies. "I have no intention of ever marrying anyone, much less some Hollywood starlet."

"Uh, didn't she win an Oscar this year? I think that makes her a *star*, not a starlet," Ella says in Carolina's defense. "I hope you didn't break her heart by dumping her like a bag of trash. I like her movies!"

"I always leave my women on amicable terms, and feeling more satisfied than when I found them," Uncle Malcolm replies. "Trust me. She's probably already transferred all of her affections for me to her latest leading man in this new movie of hers. I seriously doubt Carolina will be on the market for very long." Uncle Malcolm looks over at me, as if he's decided it's time to change the subject. "Lilly told me you plan to help Kallie at her clinic during your Christmas break."

"That's my plan, as long as nothing happens to change it. I need all the hands-on experience I can get if I want to be a great veterinarian. Plus, Kallie is such a patient teacher. I've always loved working in her clinic. Not a lot of people would have taken a nine-year-old under their wing like she did me."

"I still think she's too good for Chandler," Malcolm grumbles.

It doesn't happen very often, but every once in a while Uncle Malcolm gets put in his place by a feisty JoJo Armand.

I can't hold back a smile when she gives him an admonishing slap on the arm.

"Don't you dare talk about Chandler in such a way!" she tells him heatedly. "He's a good man and deserves all the happiness he can find in life."

Unfazed by JoJo's scolding, Uncle Malcolm sighs heavily. "All I said was that he didn't deserve someone as good as Kallie. I assumed he would settle for some supermodel to have perfect little babies with to perpetuate his self-delusional rock-god complex."

"You are such a buffoon sometimes," JoJo says despairingly, with an exasperated roll of her eyes. "Jess chose the perfect woman for Chandler. Even Mason said as much."

Uncle Malcolm shrugs his shoulders. "I still stand by what I said. Kallie is too good for him, but even I have to admit that he's not as annoying as he used to be since he met her. At least she and the kids keep him grounded."

"Don't all children keep their parents grounded?" I hear a familiar male voice say behind me.

When I turn around, I see my mom and dad. No matter how old I am or where we are, I always feel a sense of home when my parents are close by.

"How are our college girls doing this evening?" my mom asks as she leans in to give me a kiss on the cheek before giving Ella one, too.

"We're doing fine," Ella tells her, looking behind my mom as if she's searching for something. "I thought my mom and dad would be coming with you."

"Actually, Tara's busy with a project at home," my mom says, somewhat mysteriously.

Ella tilts her head, and narrows her eyes suspiciously. "What kind of project?"

"I'm sorry, sweetie, but I've been sworn to secrecy," my mom answers with a helpless shrug of her shoulders. "I think she wants it to be a surprise. I'm sure you'll find out what it is when you go home later."

"Oh, Lord," Ella says in dismay. "I can't even imagine what that woman is up to now."

My mom laughs. "Don't fret so much. I'm pretty confident you'll like it."

Both of my parents turn their attention to me, and begin to ask all about my week and how my classes are going. It strikes me as funny that they sometimes act as though they don't see me every Sunday for lunch. It's a tradition that was started not long after Caylin went off to college. We've always been a tight-knit family, and when the first of their children left home my parents decided that we should all come together at least once a week in order to prevent us from losing that connection to one another. Plus, I was so young when Caylin left, I didn't quite understand why she didn't live in her room anymore. There were mornings when I would phase to the apartment she lived in near Yale and crawl into bed with her. Of course, she would snuggle with me for a little while before phasing me back home and staying with us for breakfast. I don't remember my parents admonishing me too much for leaving home without asking for their permission first. Secretly, I think they didn't mind because it brought Caylin home to them, even if it was just for a little while.

I end up spending most of the evening by my father's side. I've always loved hearing him explain his interpretation of paintings. When we come to the one titled *Andrew* I steer him away from it since I know exactly what the inspiration behind it was, and see no reason for my dad to extrapolate a deeper meaning from it for me. He does, however, help me choose the painting that will ultimately be my Christmas present from Aiden. It's one of the happier and brightly-colored abstracts.

"I think this one was meant for you," my dad tells me, studying each stroke of green, peach, and blue paint. "It flows freely across the canvas, like your spirit, and will brighten any room just like you do."

"You are *so* my father," I say as I loop an arm around one of his, secretly pleased by his words.

"I admit my opinion of you might be slightly skewed due to that fact," he concedes half-heartedly, "but it doesn't make my words any less true, Mae. I'm not the only one in this world who sees you like that. You've always had this special gift of making the people around you happy."

"You think so?" I say, wondering if my dad is right.

"I know so," he tells me readily. The smile and look of pride on his face as he peers down at me automatically causes me to return his smile.

"Brand!" I hear my mom call out.

My dad looks down at the other end of the room, where my mom is impatiently waving him over to where she's standing with Uncle Malcolm and JoJo.

"I should probably go see what your mother wants," he says to me.

"Go ahead," I tell him as I let go of his arm. "I'll join you in just a minute. I need to claim this picture so Aiden knows I want it."

As my dad walks away, I happen to catch the high-pitched lilt of Ella's laughter. I look for her in the crowd and find her talking to a blond-headed man near the gallery's front door. From the way my best friend is laughing, the stranger must be funny since he seems to have her in stitches. I quickly peel one of the red stickers from the sheet Aiden gave me and place it on the card beneath the painting that I want. It's only then that I notice what the artwork's title is: *Sunrise*.

I make my way through the crowd until I reach Ella's side.

"Care to tell me the joke so I can laugh, too?" I ask Ella, while she attempts to catch her breath over something the man said to her before I reached them.

When I look over at the stranger, I automatically feel a sense of déjà vu about him. I know I've never seen the young man standing in front of us before, but a corner of my mind is convinced that I have. He's tall, at least six feet, with short blond hair and deep-set dark-blue eyes. He's dressed semi-casual in a black sweater and slacks.

Ella takes in enough of a sobering breath to introduce me to her new acquaintance.

"Mae Cole, this is Jay...I'm sorry. I didn't catch your last name."

Jay smiles beguilingly at us both before saying, "That's because I didn't give you one. I like to remain mysterious for as long as I can."

"Are you a friend of my sister's?" I ask him. "She's the owner of this gallery."

"Actually, no, I'm not. I heard there was going to be a show here this evening, and I thought I would check out the artwork. Whoever the artist is, he or she is quite talented."

"The artist is Mae's brother-in-law," Ella informs him.

The ringtone from a cellphone interrupts our conversation. Jay pulls out the ringing phone from his pants pocket to answer it. From hearing only his side of the conversation, it seems like the caller is asking him to be somewhere else.

"I'll be there as soon as I can," Jay tells the person on the other end before ending the call.

"I'm so sorry, ladies, but my father needs my help with something," he apologizes. "I need to go before he ends up having a heart attack. I hope to see you both again someday."

"Do you go to Colorado State?" Ella quickly asks. "That's where Mae and I go to school."

Jay shakes his head. "No. I don't go to college. I work for my father, and he's something of a taskmaster. I really do apologize, but I have to go. I hope the two of you enjoy the rest of your evening."

Jay heads out the door, and is rushing down the sidewalk determinedly before Ella can ask him anything else.

"Did he seem familiar to you at all?" I ask her, still unable to shake the feeling that I've met him before.

"Nope." Ella sighs before she says disappointedly, "And it will probably be my luck that I'll never see him again, but if we do I call dibs. That boy was hot!"

I can't help but laugh at Ella. "He's all yours, if we ever meet him again that is."

"Did your dad help you find a painting?"

"Yeah, he did. Come on. I'll show you what I picked out."

As I turn to show Ella the painting I chose, I can't help but feel a sense of foreboding about our encounter with Jay. Something was off about him. I just don't know what.

E lla and I stay at the gallery for another hour before we decide to head out.

"We have your room all ready for you," my mom tells me. "Just come on over after you take Ella home."

"Aunt Lilly," Ella says hesitantly. "I need you to be straight with me. Is this surprise my mom is working on going to be a good one or a bad one? I need to know if I should mentally prepare myself for the worst."

My mom laughs. "All I'm allowed to say is that she's worked really hard on it. I'm pretty confident you'll appreciate what she's done."

Ella's shoulders relax a smidge, but I can tell she's still nervous about the surprise her mother has waiting for her.

"I'll see you two at home," I tell my folks as Aiden hands me and Ella our coats.

"Don't forget that we're all supposed to go to Cypress Hollow tomorrow night for their annual candlelight hayride," Caylin reminds me. "Jess and Mason are expecting us all to be there."

"I didn't forget about it," I reply. "Kallie told me that Chandler composed a special song to sing to us this year. No one else in the world has ever even heard it except for her."

"Wonderful," Uncle Malcolm grouses, "we get to listen to his caterwauling the whole way. That'll be relaxing."

"I could sing for you if you want," Aiden offers.

In unison, everyone says a definitive 'no' to his offer, even JoJo. I love Aiden dearly, but singing is definitely not one of his better qualities.

"You are a doll," JoJo tells him to soothe his feelings after our somewhat harsh rebuke, "but even you know that you cannot hold a tune, *mon ami*."

Aiden smiles. "Oh, I know. I was just joking about me singing a solo, but I at least made Malcolm realize having Chandler sing isn't the worst thing that could happen tomorrow night."

I notice Uncle Malcolm rub his injured leg, but I'm not even sure he realizes he's doing it. I was told the bite from a hellhound causes excruciating and unrelenting pain. In my uncle, its effect seems to be manifesting itself as grumpiness. When I was old enough to understand exactly what happened to him, I asked my mom if there was anything we could do to end his suffering. She told me that Lucifer is the only one who can take his pain away. I knew then that my uncle would more than likely continue to feel his injury until his dying day, because it would take a miracle for Lucifer to ever be so kind.

"I'll meet you at the house," I say to my mom. "I'll just phase my Jeep over to Ella's and then home to save time tonight."

"Well, make sure you go inside and say hello to Tara and Malik," my mom says. "She'll want to see you, too."

"I will." I promise.

"Excuse me for interrupting," I hear an unexpected voice say.

We all turn our attention to a distressed-looking Jered. It's been a while since I saw him last, and he looks like he hasn't slept, or properly groomed himself for that matter, in quite some time. There's at least a week's growth of stubble on his face, and his usually-tranquil eyes look wild with worry.

Jered looks over at Malcolm meaningfully, and it's as if a silent conversation takes place between the two men. I begin to wonder if they share the same psychic connection that my little brother and sister do, but I know that's probably not the case.

"I'll be right back," Uncle Malcolm says to JoJo before he leaves her side to go to Jered. I watch them as they walk off together to a more secluded part of the gallery, presumably to talk in private.

"What's that all about?" Aiden asks no one in particular.

"I have no idea," my dad replies, looking concerned by Jered and

Uncle Malcolm's odd behavior. "I'm sure if it's important, they'll tell us what's going on."

Over the past few years, Uncle Malcolm and Jered have become closer. I vaguely remember a time when my uncle didn't like Jered very much, because he didn't trust him. I think a part of him still doesn't, since Jered used to follow Lucifer. But, like most everyone else I know, even Uncle Malcolm can't question Jered's loyalty to my family, especially since he's one of Caylin's chosen Watchers charged with protecting her descendants.

After Ella and I say goodnight to everyone, we make our way outside and get back into my vehicle. Normally, I like to drive instead of phase. Phasing is nice if you're in a hurry, but you miss so much if you don't drive from point A to point B. My mom taught me that lesson. She doesn't use her phasing ability very much unless it's to visit with us kids.

I phase us to Aunt Tara's house right outside of Denver, which is located on the same mountain as the one my Uncle Malcolm built for my mom years ago. Both my Aunt Tara and my mom have homes here and in Lakewood that they alternate between. Neither of them wanted to live too far away from the other, and they were lucky enough to be able to afford to stay close to each other.

"It looks quiet. A little *too* quiet, if you ask me," Ella says dubiously as she peers at the house, like she expects something to jump out at her.

"Let's go inside," I tell her as I open my door, causing the dome light to come on. "You're imagining the worst when there's probably nothing in there that's frightening."

"You know my mom can go overboard sometimes," Ella reminds me, still sounding hesitant about stepping one foot inside her home.

"Whatever she has waiting for you in there is bound to be interesting at the very least," I try to encourage. "Come on. Let's go see."

As Ella and I walk up the steps to the front porch, we hear the throb of music emanating from inside the house and the high-pitched whir of a blender.

"It sounds like they're having a party in there," I tell Ella as we approach the front door.

Ella opens the door and we step into what can only be described as utter chaos.

We find Aunt Tara exercising in front of the large TV mounted over the fireplace in the living room. The room itself is filled with cardboard boxes of various sizes. Some are small and others are as tall as me, but they all look empty as if they were just unpacked of their contents. An attractive male exercise instructor is on the television screen, encouraging my aunt to sprint in place for only thirty seconds more. I lift a hand to press my fingers over my lips in order to stifle a giggle at what my aunt is wearing. It looks like something straight out of the 1980s, from her hot-pink leggings and black leg warmers to her zebra-print leotard, cropped white t-shirt, and hot-pink headband.

"Can you feel the burn yet, Tara?" Uncle Malik asks as he stands behind the kitchen island, pulse-blending something green and watery as he moves his body in time with the music blaring through the surround-sound speakers in the house.

"I feel it, baby!" Aunt Tara answers, slightly out of breath. "I feel it down to my toes!"

Ella stares at the scene in front of her before making an about-face and heading back towards the front door. I grab her and stop her from leaving, finally allowing myself to laugh at the scene because the shell-shocked expression on her face is priceless.

She looks at me and says in all seriousness. "We need to go *now*. These people have lost their minds, Mae."

I begin to laugh even harder, which causes Ella's parents to finally notice our presence.

Uncle Malik instantly stops blending whatever concoction he's brewing, and Aunt Tara squeals with unabashed delight as she sprints over to where we're standing.

"Mama," Ella says, still looking slightly bewildered by the antics of her parents, "what has gotten into you?"

Aunt Tara continues to jog in place as she says breathlessly, "Baby girl, this is the way your mama rolls when I've been given a challenge."

"Challenge?" Ella asks, still confused. "Are you training for a marathon or something?"

Aunt Tara stops jogging in place and swiftly lifts her arms in the air, causing Ella and me to take a cautious step backwards as she begins to stretch her torso from side to side.

"Didn't you say you were on a diet?" Aunt Tara asks. "If that's the case, you can't diet effectively if you don't exercise, too, baby. Ever since you told me you want to lose weight I've been researching different exercise programs, and your dad has been experimenting with some of his Fae concoctions to see if he can help boost your metabolism a little bit. But, baby, I have to say I think you're perfect just the way you are."

"That's what I told her," I tell my aunt.

"Listen," Ella says with her hands on her hips as she looks between me and her mother, "the two of you can't weigh more than a hundred and twenty pounds soaking wet. I'm not saying I want to be as skinny as you two, but I would like to be able to feel more comfortable inside my own body. A little diet and exercise never hurt anybody as far as I know."

"I'm not trying to talk you out of it," Aunt Tara says. "And your daddy and I will help you any way we can."

"That's right," Uncle Malik says as he walks over to us with a glass full of the green concoction he was making in the blender. He hands it to Ella, who doesn't look very enthusiastic about the prospect of drinking it.

"Do I even want to know what's in this?" Ella asks, scrunching her nose at the contents.

"Try it," Uncle Malik says like a dare as he crosses his arms over his chest and smiles at her. "I'll bet you anything that you'll be asking me to make you one every day you're home."

Ella raises her eyebrows, and looks at her dad like he just may have lost his mind, but she cautiously gives the drink a sniff anyway.

"It smells like pumpkin pie," Ella declares in surprise as she looks at her dad.

"Taste it," he encourages her confidently.

Warily, Ella takes a sip. Her eyes grow wide with wonder. "It even tastes like pumpkin pie!"

In a matter of seconds, Ella drains the glass of its contents and hands the empty container back to her dad.

"More please," she says eagerly.

"I'll give you another glass, but you can only drink two of these a day," he informs her.

"Aww," Ella says disappointedly. "I don't suppose you came up with some other Fae remedies I can drink."

Uncle Malik's smile grows wider. "I sure did! Come on. I'll show you."

"Now just you wait a cotton-picking minute," Aunt Tara says exasperatedly. "I want to show them what we did to Linc's old room before Mae has to leave."

"Linc's room?" Ella asks in confusion. "Did you redecorate it or something?"

"Come on and see," her mother replies excitedly, waving an encouraging hand for us to follow her as she begins to walk towards the hallway where most of the bedrooms are located.

When we reach the door to Linc's room, Aunt Tara opens it and flips on the light switch.

"Tada!" she says with a flourish of her free arm.

What once used to be a bedroom is now a well-equipped exercise room replete with all types of equipment that I don't even know the names of. To me, they look like shiny torture devices.

Ella walks into the room, and slowly turns around in the middle of it as she takes it all in. Finally, she looks at her mom with tears in her eyes.

"You did all of this for me?" she questions in disbelief.

"I would do anything for you, baby," her mom replies, walking over to Ella. "And if you want to get healthier, I'll do whatever I can to help you reach your goal."

Ella wraps her arms around her mom. "Thanks, Mom."

Aunt Tara returns the hug. "You're welcome."

I make my goodbyes to all of them after that, but I know we'll see each other in the morning at my house for breakfast. We'll do that every morning that Ella and I are home from college. It's simply tradition.

As I walk back to my Jeep, I take a deep breath of the crisp cool mountain air of an autumn night and instantly feel the muscles in my body relax. Thanksgiving week is one of my favorite times of the year. During Christmas, almost everyone is in a rush to pick out the perfect gifts for loved ones and wrap them up for the big day, but for my family Thanksgiving is all about spending time with one another and enjoying each other's company before the hectic pace of December sets in.

Just as I reach for the door handle, I feel something sharp being jabbed into the crook of my neck. I don't have time to yell or even phase before total darkness consumes me, rendering me unconscious.

The next thing I'm aware of is being dropped onto a hard surface and hearing the crunch of dead leaves as they break my fall. I feel as though I'm in a dream-like state because every sensation, sound, and thought is covered in a haze my conscious mind can barely break through. When I try to grasp onto a thought, it slips through my fingers like a wisp of smoke. My body betrays me because I can't even open my eyes to see what's happening.

"Cut one of her hands, Jasper," I hear a gruff, hate-filled voice order. "Your brother will be able to track her scent for sure then."

I feel a quick sting as the palm of my left hand is sliced open by something razor-sharp.

"Do you think this will work?" I hear another man ask. I instantly recognize the voice as belonging to Ella's newfound acquaintance, Jay. Apparently, he lied to us about his real name since the other man addressed him as Jasper. "Will this finally break him, Father?"

"If it doesn't I don't know what else will, but you shouldn't feel any guilt about what we're doing. Tristan brought this on himself with his constant meddling in our affairs. I didn't want to go this far because I know Malcolm and the others will try to hunt us down afterwards, but this is the only way I know of to stop him and teach him the lesson of loss once and for all."

"Tristan said he loves us," Jasper replies, sounding as if he wants to believe that his brother's words were true, but uncertain if he should or not.

"He's been hounding us to change our ways for far too long, my son. It's time to put an end to this. We've starved him for over a week now, and his hunger will force him to feed on her. Once he does... once we *force* your brother to kill the person who took him away from us in the first place, he'll finally realize he can't change us or his basic instinct to kill."

I hear the distant howl of an animal. It's a haunting cry, filled with anger but also mixed with a heart-rending sadness.

"There's my hungry boy," I hear the man say, as if he's gratified by the torturous sound. "Since we killed all of the large game in this part of the forest, he'll have nothing else to eat except her. Come stand by my side, Jasper. Let's phase home before he gets here. I wouldn't want him to accidentally attack us instead of his intended target."

"What if she phases away before he finds her?" Jasper asks as I hear the sound of dead leaves and small twigs being crunched under his weight as he walks around me, presumably to go stand by his father's side.

"She won't be able to for quite some time. The drug I gave her diminishes her capacity to concentrate on one place long enough to phase. Tristan will find her well before she's able to metabolize the chemicals in her body. In just a few minutes she'll be dead, and your brother will finally stop trying to save our souls."

I don't hear anything after that except silence. I quickly realize that Tristan's father was right. Try as I might, I simply can't concentrate on a phase point long enough to escape my fate. I hear another forlorn howl fill the air around me and realize Tristan is even closer now. In a matter of seconds he'll find me, and there's absolutely nothing I can do to stop his attack. If what his father said is true, they've starved Tristan and set him free in this forest we're in to force him to devour me.

I hear the pounding of feet running across the forest floor, but I still can't seem to focus my mind long enough to phase myself somewhere safe. All I can do is lie helplessly and wait for Tristan to decide my fate.

I must have passed out again, at least for a few seconds, because when I regain consciousness I feel the warm exhalation of breath washing over my face. Tristan sniffs the air around me and emits a low, almost pained growl. I muster enough strength to open my eyes and look at him. It's been a very long time since I last saw Tristan and, to be honest, I never thought we would meet again while he was in his werewolf form. Drool covers his lower jaw as he pants and whines pitifully. From what I overheard I know he must be starving, and his family has left me as a tasty, unprotected morsel. By some supernatural willpower, Tristan is holding himself back from satisfying his hunger with my flesh. This simple act of control tells me that the bond we shared when I was a little girl must still be present.

I want to reach out and pet him, but my body obstinately refuses to listen to my wishes. The only thing that I'm able to do before I pass out again is whisper three little words.

"Help me, Puppy..."

Chapter 3

Sometimes dreams can bring you closer to your chosen reality. If you allow your mind to drift toward your most heartfelt goals, the thing you thought was out of your reach suddenly materializes in the palm of your hand. It's what you do afterwards to keep your dream alive that matters.

When I open my eyes, I discover I'm lying on a couch in a living room I don't recognize. Built against the wall directly across from me is a gray, stacked-stone hearth that's cold and barren of burning wood to warm its belly. I don't sit up right away because my head is pounding in syncopation with each beat of my heart. I feel as though some villain has used a sledge hammer to crack my skull open. I close my eyes again when the room beings to spin out of control, causing me to become nauseated. My natural curiosity begs me to figure out where I am, but my body simply won't allow that to happen just yet.

The last thing I remember before passing out is Tristan hovering over me in his wolf form. The children of the Watchers who were cursed to live dual lives—human by day and werewolf by night—are not what most people picture when they imagine werewolves. They aren't the cuddly, dog-like creatures you see in almost every horror movie or teen fantasy television show. By design, they're meant to strike fear with their ugliness and cause anyone who has the misfortune of crossing their paths to realize their fate is doomed. Last night was the first time in a long while that I've seen a Watcher child still cursed with the transformation. I'm not sure why Tristan hasn't asked God to remove his curse yet, but I do intend to find out the reason behind such a decision. In order to do that, the first thing I'll need to do is get off of the couch I'm on and search for him.

I tentatively open one eye and then the other to check to see if the room is still spinning out of control. Thankfully, all is well and I feel stable enough to sit up. I really should have thought better of using my hand to help me change positions. It's only when I'm halfway up that I feel the pain of the wound Tristan's brother inflicted on the palm of my left hand. Unfortunately, using it to prop my body up has reopened the gash. I'm grateful that the couch I'm on is a leather one. At least all I have to do is find a wet washcloth to wipe my blood off its surface. I examine my injured palm and discover that the wound is more superficial than life-threatening. Jasper made it just deep enough to bring my blood to the surface so Tristan's enhanced sense of smell could help him find me more easily. I raise my gaze in hopes of finding something to bandage my hand with, when I spy a scene I wasn't quite prepared to discover.

Directly between the plain wood coffee table in front of me and the fireplace is Tristan. He's lying face-down and completely naked, with one arm and leg stretched completely out while their counterparts are slightly bent at the elbow and knee. I know he's still alive because I can see his chest rise and fall with each breath he takes.

After getting over the initial shock of finding him undressed and unconscious on the floor, I quickly look around and grab the soft brown wool blanket from the back of the couch. I stand and walk over to Tristan, intent on covering him with it in order to keep him protected from the chill in the room. I end up hesitating for just a moment, allowing myself a few seconds to take in the beauty of his human form and to check for any injuries. His skin is lightly tanned and unblemished. His blond hair is cut slightly shorter around the sides than the strands on top of his head. With his face turned to the side I'm able to study his profile, and find him just as handsome as I remember. For years now, I've only had a memory of Tristan's face appear in my dreams, but seeing him again in the flesh causes my cheeks to flush with excitement and my heart to yearn to speak with him again.

I quickly drape the blanket over his body from the waist down, to protect my modesty more than his. I begin a great debate with myself about whether or not I should wake him up, but I decide against such an action. I then begin a silent argument with myself on whether or not I should phase directly home and let my parents know that I'm all right. It's something I know I should do, but a part of me also realizes that once I involve them in this situation there's no turning back. They'll probably urge me to stay away from Tristan for my own good. Odds are that's exactly what Tristan will say to me, too. He'll feel guilt-ridden that his family tried to use me to hurt him and that fact, more than anything else, makes my mind up for me.

I look around the house I'm in and discover that it's actually a small, two-story cabin. The bottom floor seems to only have the living room I'm in and a small kitchen and dining area. As I look out the windows towards the front of the cabin, there appears to be a small front porch and a pile of split wood for the fireplace stacked directly underneath the twelve-panel picture window. There's a small staircase built against the wall to the right of me, leading to a second floor. Without actually going up there, I assume it's probably where Tristan's bedroom is located.

I walk over to the small kitchen area and rummage around in the drawers until I find a long enough rag to wrap around my injured hand. Once that's taken care of, I pull open the door of the stainless-steel refrigerator beside the matching stove to see if it contains any food. I remember Tristan's father bragging about the fact that he starved his own son for over a week to make him so hungry that he would devour me whole. Luckily for me, Tristan was able to control his need to feed long enough to bring me here to this cabin. I assume it's where he lives since it looks well-kept, and also because there's a picture of him and his brother smiling with their arms over each other's shoulders propped up on the windowsill above the kitchen sink.

I pull out mayonnaise, mustard, sliced ham, and cheddar cheese from the fridge and place them all on the counter, where a loaf of sliced bread is located. Unfortunately, the women in my family aren't the best cooks. We can make things to eat and survive on, but gourmet meals aren't usually our forte. With that fact in mind I decide to keep things simple, and make a few sandwiches for Tristan to eat after he wakes up. I can't even imagine going without food for as long as he was forced to. Nor can I fathom a father who would torture his own child so cruelly. I have no idea if Tristan ate something when we got back to the cabin, but taking into account his unclothed state and prone position on the floor it seems a fair assessment that he probably fell asleep almost as soon as we arrived. Perhaps the lack of food and the effort it took to carry me here caused him to pass out before he had a chance to eat. I'm not really sure and, honestly, it doesn't matter.

After I prepare five sandwiches for Tristan, I make one for myself because I realize I'm hungry, too. I eat the first one in record time and quickly decide to make another one. This time I add a glass of milk to wash it all down with.

"Mae?" I hear Tristan question uncertainly behind me.

The unexpected sound of his voice makes me practically choke on the bite of sandwich in my mouth. Fortunately, I'm able to wash it down with milk before such a catastrophe can take place. After I drain my glass and set it back on the counter, I turn around to face him.

He's now standing in the same spot I left him in, tying the blanket I laid over his body around his hips like a bulky sarong. Once it's securely in place he lifts his head, and our gazes meet. I immediately smile, and he immediately scowls like I've done something wrong.

"You should have phased home as soon as you woke up," he chastises me. "Why are you still here? Your family is probably worried sick about you."

"I haven't been awake for that long," I inform him as I wonder why he almost looks angry at me for staying. "I was worried about you. I didn't want to leave you here all alone. What if your father and brother came back here to find you again? They've already tortured you once. I wasn't going to let them do it a second time."

"Then you should have phased me home with you or to Jered's

house," he argues a little too logically for my taste. "Besides, it doesn't matter what happens to me. If something had happened to you..."

He doesn't finish his thought. From the pained expression on his face, perhaps just the idea of his family harming me again is unimaginable. I watch as his gaze drops to my towel- wrapped hand.

As he walks over to me, he asks, "How deeply did they cut you?"

I shake my head. "It's not that bad. The only reason I have it wrapped is because I re-opened the wound when I sat up."

Once Tristan is standing in front of me, he holds out his hand and says, "Let me see."

I do as he orders while watching for his reaction as he unwraps the small kitchen towel from around my injured hand. When he sees the laceration his face scrunches up in even more of a scowl, but I know it's not me he's mad at.

"We need to wash it out before it becomes infected," he tells me, never meeting my gaze as he continues to study my wound. Gently, he leads me over to the sink, turns the water on, and positions my hand underneath the stream of water.

"Wow, that's cold!" I say in surprise, briefly yanking my hand back to my side.

"I get my water from a well and it tends to be a bit cold, especially this time of year," he explains. "I'll make it warmer for you."

Tristan leans over to turn the hot water knob. The action causes his body to brush lightly against mine, bringing with it the scent of him. I cough slightly because Tristan smells like he hasn't bathed in days, which is probably the truth. If his father has kept him prisoner for the last week, I'm sure personal hygiene wasn't high on his list of priorities for his son. My reaction to his closeness must make him aware of how ripe his aroma is.

"Sorry," he apologizes with an embarrassed smile as he finally looks me in the eyes. "I haven't been able to take a shower in a long time."

"It's not that bad," I say, but even I can hear the lie in my voice as I try to hold my breath.

Tristan chuckles. "You're not a very good liar, Mae, and you don't need to be with me."

Tristan takes my injured hand again and places it back underneath a more tepid stream of water. Gently, he washes the wound out, being careful not to pull apart what's already begun to scab over. The feel of his thumb as it passes over the palm of my hand sends tiny, pleasant goosebumps dancing across my flesh. He remains quiet as he ministers to my cut, and the look on his face becomes pensive.

"What's wrong?" I ask him, hoping to break his brooding mood.

"You should get your mother to take you to see Rafe when you get home," he tells me, letting go of my hand and shutting the water off. "He should be able to heal it without using much of his power."

"Tristan," I say more forcefully, urging him to look into my eyes, "tell me what's wrong."

He shakes his head as he says, "You'll think it's silly."

"No, I won't," I assure him. "I want to know what you're thinking about right now."

He allows himself to truly look at me, and I watch as his eyes travel the length of my body from head to toe, making me feel a bit self-conscious about my appearance. I'm sure I look a mess. I know my dress is dirty after being tossed onto the ground last night, that's readily visible to me, but my hair and makeup are more than likely disheveled as well.

"I..." he begins, but stops short as he seems to need a moment to collect his thoughts. "For some reason, I forgot that you were all grown up now," he finally confesses. "In my mind, I always visualized you as the little girl I protected."

"Time has a way of making you age," I tell him. "I'm still the girl you saved, just not as little anymore."

"So I've noticed," he replies as his eyes guiltily sweep the length of me again.

"Are you disappointed I'm not like you remember?"

"Oh no," he's quick to affirm with a small uncomfortable shake of his head as he crosses his arms over his chest. He clears his throat nervously before saying, "I mean, it looks like you grew up healthy."

"Uh, thanks, I guess," I reply uncertainly, wondering why Tristan seems to be making a point of keeping his eyes on my face. "Strangely enough, you look almost exactly the same as I remember you."

"I'm still cursed," he says with a shrug of his muscular shoulders. "I age more slowly because of it."

"And why is that?"

Tristan shrugs his shoulders again. "I don't know. You would have to ask God why that was part of His curse."

"No," I say. "Why is it that you're still cursed? Why haven't you asked God to remove it yet?"

"I can't," is his automatic response. "Not yet."

"And why is that?" I prod again, hoping to finally be given a real answer to my query.

Tristan remains silent as he seems to take a moment to decide if he plans to tell me the truth or not. Finally, he makes up his mind.

"I need to save my brother first," he tells me. "I need to get him away from our father's influence before his soul is lost forever."

"When you and the others came back from alternate Earth," I say, "Uncle Malcolm told me that you wouldn't be able to keep your promise to come see me for a long time. He told me that you had some family matters to attend to first, but he never went into much detail. I take it that's what you've been doing since you returned? Have you been trying to convince your brother to leave your father?"

Tristan nods. "Yes."

"I also take it that you haven't had any luck with that."

Tristan sighs heavily. "No. I haven't. It seems like everything I do just pushes him further and further away from me. I don't know if I'll ever be able to save him, but I have to keep trying. I refuse to give up on him."

"You realize that you can't change someone unless they want to change, right?" I ask. "Maybe your brother is happy working for your dad."

"I don't believe that," he replies stubbornly. "Deep down, I believe Jasper wants to change. Of the two of us, he was always the kinder one. He never liked killing for our father."

"You say that as if you *did* like doing what your father told you to do."

"Sometimes I did," Tristan replies, not sounding proud of the fact but not shying away from the truth of what he once was. "I knew it was wrong, but there was a small part of me that liked the thrill of the chase."

"Until you met me," I remind him.

"Yes," he agrees. "Until I met you."

"How did I change you?" I ask, still finding that part of our story unexplained. "What was it about me that made you break your bond to your father?"

"I don't know," Tristan says, appearing helpless for a real answer. "All I know is that I couldn't do anything but keep you protected, and the only way to do that was to leave my family."

"And then you stayed away from me to keep me safe from them," I say. "What's changed? Why did they come after me now, after all these years?"

"I think I was getting to close to turning Jasper against our father. My dad must be desperate to keep him by his side, to attack you. He knows now that Malcolm and the others will be searching for him."

"They'll be searching for Jasper now, too," I remind him.

"Which is probably another reason why he did it. He may think that placing Jasper's life in danger will make me return to him, in order to protect my brother."

"I'm sorry you have a family like that," I tell him. "I can't imagine having a father so twisted in his logic."

"I'm glad you don't. From what I remember, your mom and dad are special people. It's been a while since I saw them last, but I'm sure they haven't changed all that much over the years."

"No, they haven't, and I would never want them to."

An awkward silence develops between us, and it's only then that I remember what I was doing before Tristan woke up. I turn around to face the counter where I left the sandwiches I made for him and pick up the plate.

"I thought you might be hungry after you woke up," I say,

handing him my offering of food. "I know your dad starved you, and I wasn't sure if you ate anything before you fell asleep."

Tristan grins and takes the plate from my hands. "Thank you, Mae. That was sweet of you to do for me. You didn't have to."

"I wanted to," I say, wishing I could have made him something hot to eat instead. "Did you eat before you fell asleep?"

"When we got closer to the cabin, I was able to hunt down some game to curb my appetite while I was still in wolf form."

"How far did you have to walk?"

"It took me a little over four hours to travel back here, so that means it was about twenty-five miles, give or take a few."

"Caylin had an art exhibition of Aiden's work last night," I tell him. "Jered showed up to talk to Uncle Malcolm about something. I'm assuming he's been looking for you since your father abducted you."

"I'm sure he has been," Tristan says, laying the plate of sandwiches I just gave him on the counter by the sink before rushing upstairs without an explanation. I hear him rummage around and slam drawers and doors to cabinets, presumably. A few minutes later he returns wearing a pair of faded jeans that are distressed in spots, and a white tank top.

"Were you looking for something in particular up there, or just something to wear?" I ask.

"I was looking for my satellite phone," he replies, looking worried. "My father probably took it so I couldn't contact anyone when I returned. I need to let Jered know that I'm okay."

And with those words, I know my time alone with Tristan is over. At least for now anyway.

"I can take you to Jered's house, if you want," I offer, even though what I really want to do is stay and talk with him some more.

"I would appreciate that very much," he replies. "You should be getting back home, too, to let your folks know you're safe." His eyes drop to the cut on my hand. "Perhaps not completely sound, but alive."

"After you speak with Jered, would the two of you come to my house and explain everything to my mom and dad? I'm sure you can give them the details they'll want."

"We will," he promises.

"And Tristan," I say, feeling somewhat shy before making my second request. "I think it's time you became a part of my life again. If you really want to protect me, staying away isn't going to work anymore. There's no guarantee your father and brother won't try to use me against you again. I think I'll be safer if you're around."

"That's really up to your parents and you to decide," he replies. "All I can promise right now is that I'll do whatever it takes to keep you safe, Mae. I'll die before I let them hurt you again."

"No one's dying," I state firmly. "Maybe we can figure out a way to deal with them together. As you said, I'm not that little girl you saved anymore. I'm old enough to help you now, if you'll let me."

"Why don't we wait and see what your family says first," Tristan replies, even though his underlying tone seems to indicate that he believes my parents will urge me to stay out of harm's way and let Tristan take care of his own family issues.

I don't strike up an argument with him about it now, but I know in my heart that I'm meant to help Tristan with his problem. I may not have the same effect on his brother that I did on Tristan all those years ago, but a piece of my soul is whispering that I'm on the right track. I can help my one-time savior, but only if he'll let me.

Chapter 4

Before we leave, Tristan gobbles down the sandwiches I made for him in just a couple of minutes. Apparently, whatever he preyed on the night before in the forest didn't quite satisfy his hunger. Once he's through, he comes to stand beside me so I can phase us both to Jered.

"Do you think he'll be at his house?" I ask Tristan, since he knows Jered a lot better than I do.

"It's the best place to start, I think," he replies.

I raise my uninjured hand, intent on touching Tristan to phase him to Jered's house, but I end up hesitating as I look at him uncertainly. I'm not exactly sure where to touch him and not have it become an overtly intimate moment between us. Thankfully, he seems to understand my dilemma and reaches out with his right hand to clasp my raised one. Before either of us has time to think about the fact that we're holding hands, I phase us just inside the front doors of Jered's home in Montana.

I've only been inside Jered's cabin-style mansion a few times with my mom and Uncle Malcolm. My uncle brought me here, so Jered could teach me how to train horses. I was a quick learner because it only took one lesson for me to understand how to make a horse follow my directions. I was only ten at the time, and both Jered and Uncle Malcolm were astounded by my skill. However, my mother didn't seem all that surprised. She told me later that while she and my other brothers and sisters have a natural gift when it comes to dealing with animals, I had been doubly blessed. When I asked my mom what made us special, she told me it was a gift from her father, the archangel Michael. My ability to soothe animals is the major reason I decided to become a veterinarian. Creatures great and small all seem to gravitate towards me for some reason. I've often wondered if that's why Tristan chose me instead of his father that night. I'm not quite sure, but that's one of my working theories. Of course, my other theory is that we're soul mates, but I'm not so sure about that now.

As we stand inside the entryway of Jered's large log-style home, Tristan does something unexpected. Instead of letting go of my hand when we arrive, he tightens his grip on me slightly so the physical contact between us doesn't break as he begins to walk forward. The gesture brings a smile to my face as I willingly follow him towards the back of the house.

"Jered!" he calls up the staircase leading from the foyer to the second floor.

When we don't get a response, he begins to walk deeper into the interior of the house. I've always liked Jered's home. With its walls and ceilings made of exposed wooden logs and mixture of soft furs, natural stones, and leather furnishings, the space gives off a feeling of rustic charm without losing its luxuriousness. We pass the main living room of the house, which has a wall of glass facing a snow-capped mountain range.

"Maybe Jered isn't here," I suggest to Tristan. "He could still be out trying to find you."

Tristan sighs heavily as my words bring a certainty to the situation.

"Can you think of somewhere else he might be?" I ask.

"Didn't you say he spoke with Malcolm last night at the gallery?"

I nod. "Yes."

"Let's go to Malcolm's home, then. Maybe they're there trying to figure out where we both are. I'm sure your family knows by now that you're missing, too."

I immediately phase us to my uncle's house in Lakewood, and I don't even bother with formality by phasing us to the entrance. I take us straight into Uncle Malcolm's library, because that's the most likely place he'll be if he's home. It turns out that I'm exactly right. When we phase into the cozy room filled with books, we find him and Jered studying a large paper map that's spread out across his desk.

As soon as I phase in my uncle lifts his head, and a look of relief washes over his features when he sees me.

"Thank God," he says, grabbing his wolf-head cane from its spot against the side of his desk as he walks over to us.

Jered spins around to discover for himself what my uncle is looking at. His reaction is much the same, as his whole body seems to deflate like a balloon that's just lost all of its air. I let go of Tristan's hand as Jered walks over and pulls him in for a fatherly embrace.

"I thought I'd lost you," Jered says, his voice cracking slightly with relief and joy to have Tristan back safe and sound.

"He never intended to kill me," Tristan replies, hugging Jered back just as fiercely. "He just wanted to punish me."

"Jered," Uncle Malcolm says, gently gripping my right arm as he stands in front of me. "Come to Lilly and Brand's home in Colorado when you're finished here. I'm sure they'll have some questions for you about what happened."

Without any more warning than that, my reunion with Tristan is abruptly cut short and my uncle phases me home. I don't have time to protest, because as soon as we arrive within the home my uncle built for my mom all those years ago I'm swallowed up by family and their multitude of questions.

"Why don't we let Mae have a little air?" Uncle Malcolm suggests when it becomes obvious everyone present wants a hug from me, as if they need to physically prove to themselves that I'm still alive.

When my mother pulls away from me, she notices the cut on my hand. Tenderly, she takes hold of my injured hand, unwraps the towel from around it, and raises it up to scrutinize the laceration more closely.

"How did this happen?" she asks gravely while she examines my injury.

"It's kind of a long story," I say, "but the short version is that Tristan's brother cut my hand."

"I'll be right back," Uncle Malcolm says before phasing. I know by his phase trail that he's gone to find Rafe, because it leads straight into a hospital. His first reaction was similar to what Tristan suggested not that long ago.

"Are you hurt anywhere else?" my father asks, looking both concerned about my welfare and furious that anyone would dare to harm me.

I quickly shake my head to relieve their worries about my wellbeing.

"I'm fine," I reassure them.

"What exactly happened, Mae?" Aiden asks as he and Caylin stand slightly behind my mom and dad, waiting for an answer.

"Where did they take you?" my big brother Will asks, equally concerned.

"I'm not really sure where I was," I tell them truthfully. "All I know is that I was taken to a forest somewhere, and this morning I woke up in Tristan's cabin."

"Then you were in Russia," Aiden says definitively. "Tristan's cabin is located there, in a secluded forest called the Siberian Taiga."

"Why did they take you there, Mae?" my little sister Ariana asks.

As I look between her and Xavier, I suddenly realize that they aren't exactly little anymore. We just celebrated the twins' sixteenth birthday this month. Following family tradition, Uncle Malcolm bought them both brand new vehicles as their presents. Xavier wanted a fancy sports car, but for some reason known only to himself Uncle Malcolm gave him a double cab Ford F-150 instead. Ariana was the one who received the sports car. She asked for a classic red convertible Ford Mustang, just like the one our mother drove when she first met my dad.

Since they were born my parents have known that the twins are special, but it wasn't until they were five years old that we discovered they could send messages to one another through mental telepathy. Sometimes I catch them looking at each other, and I know they're having a silent conversation. It's a little disconcerting to witness but, considering my family, their powers aren't all that strange.

"Would it be all right if we waited for Tristan and Jered to come and explain what happened?" I asked them. "I don't know all the details, and I only have bits and pieces of the story."

Before anyone can answer Uncle Malcolm phases back into the living room with Rafe by his side, giving me the perfect excuse to avoid everyone's questions.

Rafe leaves my uncle's side and makes his way to where I'm standing. Everyone in front of me parts like the Red Sea to provide him a path directly to me.

"Now, you're the one Cole I thought I wouldn't have to use my powers on," he says admonishingly as he flashes his charismatic grin.

"Trust me, it wasn't intentional," I assure him as I return his kind smile with an embarrassed one of my own.

Carefully, Rafe lifts my injured hand and covers the slightly throbbing palm. I watch in fascination as his hands briefly glow blue, mending my wounded flesh and making it tingle as it's being healed. It only takes a few minutes for Rafe to repair what would have taken weeks to completely heal on its own.

Rafe takes his hands away, revealing my restored skin. The palm of my hand doesn't even look like it was ever cut.

"All healed up," Rafe announces with satisfaction. "Now, I expect you to not need my services any further, Ms. Cole."

"I'll do my best," I promise him.

"Thank you for coming so quickly, Rafe," my dad says, holding out his hand to him.

As Rafe shakes my father's hand, he replies, "It was my pleasure. Although, I'm afraid I need to leave just as quickly. I was just about to step into the O.R. when Malcolm found me, but I assume this is just a short goodbye. I'll see you all this evening in Cypress Hollow, right?"

"Yes," my mom answers for us. "We'll be there. Tell Nina we can't wait to see her and the kids again."

"I'll pass along the message," Rafe says, nodding his head respectfully to my mom before turning around to walk back over to Uncle Malcolm's side.

"After I take Rafe back," my uncle tells my mom, "I'll go find Tara, Malik, and Ella and bring them back with me."

"Thank you, Malcolm," my mom replies.

My uncle phases away, but something he said prompts me to ask a question.

"Why does Uncle Malcolm have to find them? Aren't they all at home?"

"They were here with us all night waiting for news on your whereabouts after we discovered you were missing," my mom explains. "Ella was beside herself with worry, though, so her parents took her on a hike to help get her mind off things. She told Malcolm the trail they were planning to take. It won't be difficult for him to find them there."

And it wasn't. My uncle returned with them all within a few short minutes.

"Don't you ever do that to me again," Ella orders as she gives me the tightest hug of my life.

"Ella, I can't breathe," I squeak out.

"I don't care," she declares, finding a way to hug me even tighter, "I'm not letting you go."

Even without being able to take in a decent breath, I find a way to laugh and simply hug my best friend back.

"I'm safe," I whisper close to her ear. "And I found Tristan."

This makes Ella loosen her grip on me a smidge as she leans back to look me in the eyes, utter shock on her face.

"You did not," she says in disbelief.

I nod my head. "I did."

Before we can delve any deeper into a conversation about my reunion with Tristan, Aunt Tara lovingly, yet forcefully, pushes her daughter to the side.

"Quit hogging all the hugs, girl," my aunt says. "I need to hug my niece before anything else bad happens."

"Why don't we remain more optimistic than that," my mother suggests with a roll of her eyes at my aunt's portent of impending doom.

"I can't with this family," my aunt replies, hugging me almost as tightly as her daughter did. "It's been too peaceful for too long, Lilly

Rayne. I knew something was bound to happen eventually. It was only a matter of time."

"At least we're not boring," my Uncle Malcom points out drily. "What's life without a little adventure mixed in every once in a while?"

"I'm all for adventure," my mom tells him with a sigh, "as long as my children don't get hurt in the process. I thought with Mae..." she leaves the rest of her thought unspoken, but I can extrapolate from the pained expression on her face what she was about to say. Apparently, my mom thought things would be different with me, and I wouldn't be propelled into a circumstance where my life would be threatened.

My family's reaction to my abduction makes me wonder if they will be willing to welcome Tristan back into our lives. It's apparent that he brings a great deal of danger with him through his quest to save his brother. I have no idea if he's trying to save his father's soul, too, or if his father is now a lost cause. It's hard for me to imagine that his dad would ever ask for God's forgiveness and mean it. From what little I know about the man, he seems to be a heartless wretch who only thinks of his own needs.

I end up not having a long time to dwell on whether my family will welcome Tristan. Just as my Aunt Tara steps away from me, I see Jered and Tristan phase into the living room. I immediately notice that Tristan has changed clothes during the short time that we've been apart. In fact, it looks like he made a point of taking a quick shower, too, because his hair is still slightly damp. He's now dressed in a pair of black slacks, loafers, and a crisp white shirt. I'm kind of disappointed that he's no longer in his faded denims and tank top, but I suppose he decided to put on more modest clothing in order to make a good impression on my family.

It takes a moment before those present in the room realize Jered and Tristan have joined us. Almost like hive-mind organisms, they all turn at the same time to give the new arrivals their full attention. Tristan looks slightly uncomfortable with all eyes suddenly directed towards him, but he doesn't shy away from their interest. He has to know they all want an explanation about what happened the night before and why my life was placed in jeopardy by his family.

"First of all," he says to everyone present, "I would like to tell you how very sorry I am that my father and brother kidnapped Mae. If I had known what their intentions were, I never would have agreed to the meeting they asked me to attend last week. I thought they wanted to make peace with me, but that was just a lie to make me lower my guard. They asked me to trust them and, honestly, I should have known better. I was so desperate to believe that they wanted to change that I deluded myself by refusing to listen to Jered's advice." Tristan turns his head to look at Jered. "I need to apologize to you as well. I should have listened to your warnings about them and placed my trust in you, not them."

"It's all right," Jered reassures him, placing a comforting hand on Tristan's shoulder. "We all make mistakes from time to time."

"Only, this mistake could have cost Mae her life," Uncle Malcolm points out heatedly. "I can forgive a lot of things, but endangering the life of someone I hold dear is not one of them."

"If I had known they planned to use Mae in such a way, you have to know I never would have gone to them," Tristan replies. His expression is one of desperately seeking understanding from my uncle. "I would rather die than place her in harm's way. I've done my best to protect her all these years by staying away, but I don't believe that tactic will work anymore. My father fears you, Malcolm. For him to willingly use Mae to get to me has to mean he's desperate, and if he's desperate enough to put his own life in danger I believe that means he's doing everything he can to keep Jasper by his side. I know this whole situation has been horrible, but if there's one good thing that can come out of it it's the fact that my brother might be on the verge of leaving my father for good."

"There's no guarantee that your theory is the correct one," Uncle Malcolm says scathingly. "And Mae is a lot more important to me than your wayward brother, Tristan. I've done what I can to help you in this matter during the past few years, but your father and brother have crossed a line with me that can't be uncrossed. I will hunt them down, and I won't show them an ounce of mercy when I find them. If you try to get in my way, I'll take you down with them, too. Is that understood?"

"Malcolm..." Jered says, looking astonished by my uncle's words. "You can't mean that."

"I don't say things I don't mean, Jered," my uncle replies ominously. "You should know that much about me by now, and you should have stopped Tristan from his fool's quest years ago. Like I said, I've done all I can to help, but now they've attacked my family, and I don't have it in me to forgive them for that. Don't either of you realize that they could have killed Mae last night?" By the time my uncle asks this question, he's practically shouting at the two men. "If anything worse than a cut on the hand had happened to Mae you wouldn't be alive right now, Tristan. I would have held completely responsible and killed you myself. As it is I'm only after your father and brother now, unless you're dead set on being added to my list."

"I would never let you harm him," Jered growls protectively. "That would be *you* crossing *my* line, Malcolm, and you don't want to do that."

"Is that a threat?" Uncle Malcolm asks incredulously, narrowing his already-angry eyes at Jered.

"Stop!" I yell, causing those around me to jump slightly after hearing my angry outburst. "Just stop it!"

All eyes turn to me, and I know this is my moment to bring an end to what is quickly escalating into a dangerous and volatile situation between my uncle and Jered.

"Stop threatening each other," I beg them. "I refuse to be the reason the two of you end your friendship."

"I wouldn't exactly call us *friends*," my uncle grumbles.

"You're not enemies either," I remind him, "but you're talking to one another like you are, and I refuse to be the reason behind that. Don't use me as an excuse to hurt each other, and Uncle Malcolm, if you hurt Tristan I will never be able to forgive you."

My uncle doesn't look pleased by my last statement, but I know he truly loves me and would never do anything that would intentionally cause me pain.

"What happened last night wasn't Tristan's fault," I remind everyone. "He's as much a victim in this as I am."

"How so?" my father asks me.

I look to Tristan. "I only know a small part of the story. Can you tell us the rest of it?"

Tristan nods his head, determined to clear up the situation as quickly as possible. As he looks at me, his expression is one of gratefulness that I diffused the building tension between Jered and Uncle Malcolm before it had a chance to spiral out of control. I know my uncle still doesn't quite trust Jered, because he used to work for Lucifer, but I thought after all these years and everything they went through together on alternate Earth that he had pushed their past differences behind them. Now, I'm not so sure. It makes me wonder if my uncle knows a secret about Jered that I don't. Has he done something recently that's made my uncle question his loyalty to my family? I find that hard to believe since Jered is one of Caylin's chosen. He's one of the Watchers whose job it is to watch over the princes of Hell until the birth of a descendant from her and Aiden's line. Only she will able to finally take care of them. As far as I know, Jered has always tried to do whatever we ask of him. It became quite clear to me at an early age that he feels unworthy to help us or be included as a part of our extended family. Yet, it seems like something has happened to cause my uncle to not trust him as much as he used to. I'm just not sure what's caused him to lose some of his faith in Jered.

"Last week," Tristan begins, "my father contacted me and asked if I would come over to his house to have supper with him and Jasper. As most of you know, I've been trying to find a way to show my brother that he doesn't have to stay with my father. I know it's a bond that can be almost impossible to break, but I've held onto my hope that Jasper is strong enough to do it. He's always hated the things our father made us do in the past, and I'm counting on his natural decency to help him finally leave and come live with me."

"Even if Jasper finds the strength to break his bond with Rolph like you did," my dad says, "what makes you think your father will let either of you live? Once he loses both of his sons, he may end up coming after you and your brother and killing the two of you for betraying him."

"He hasn't killed me yet," Tristan points out. "And I still believe there's some good left in him."

"I reserve the right to argue against that point," Uncle Malcolm says. "Why don't you tell us why they kidnapped Mae. Then maybe we can decide for ourselves whether or not your father can be saved."

Tristan looks uncomfortable with my uncle's challenge. He has to know that after he tells everyone the truth behind why his father kidnapped me, no one in this room, except for maybe Jered, will have any sympathy regarding his plight to save his family from their own deeds.

Tristan shifts back and forth on his feet, as if bracing himself before he speaks.

"As I said, my father invited me over for supper last week. He promised me that we could talk and that he would try to listen to what I had to say with open ears. I've been so desperate to find a way to reach him that I accepted his offer." Tristan pauses, as if he doesn't want to continue. I see him swallow hard before he resumes his tale. "At supper, he must have laced the drink he gave me with a sedative because all I remember after drinking it is falling to the living room floor and waking up in a basement of a strange house. I've been his prisoner since then. During the past week, he left me in that dark room without any visitors and with nothing to eat. Last night, he took me to the forest and let me run free to find food. He's always hated Mae because she's the reason I broke my bond with him. I think his twisted sense of logic led him to believe that if I killed her it would bring me back to his side."

"And what part did your brother play in all of this?" my mother wants to know.

"Jasper talked to me and Ella while we were all at Caylin's gallery last night," I tell her.

"He did?" Ella asks, a confused look on her face. It takes her a few seconds, but she finally catches on to who I'm talking about. "You don't mean that cute boy, do you? Jay?"

I nod. "Yeah. That was Tristan's brother."

"Oh, my goodness," Ella says, covering her mouth with one hand as her eyes grow wide with realization. "Mae, I'm so sorry. I should have known something was up when he asked me what I would be doing after the art show. I just blurted out that you would be taking me home. He knew exactly where you would be because of me."

"It's not your fault," I tell her sternly. "You didn't know who he was, or what he and his father were planning to do to me. Don't you dare blame yourself for this."

"I'm the only one who should feel any blame right now," Tristan tells Ella. "It's my meddling in their lives these past few years that's caused my family to lash out like this. Mae's in danger because of me, and I accept full responsibility for that."

"But you're not the only one responsible," I point out. "I was the one who took you away from them in the first place, remember? I phased you to my house and decided to keep you like my own personal pet and playmate. You shouldn't feel like you need to shoulder all the blame, Tristan. I played a part in you losing your family, too."

"I may have lost my brother and my father," Tristan says to me, "but I regained control over my soul because of what you did for me, Mae. I had been living in my father's dark shadow for so long, I forgot what it felt like to think for myself again until you helped me."

"Why is it that you haven't asked God to remove your curse yet?" my dad asks.

Again Tristan shuffles his stance slightly, as if he's uncomfortable with my father's question.

"It's not the right time," he replies. "I can't do that until Jasper can go in front of God with me and ask for the same thing. He's my little brother. I can't go off and live a happy life, knowing the things that my father is making him do. I'm stronger the way I am. You of all people should know what it's like to be made human and lose all of your powers."

"It's not as bad as you might think," Aiden is quick to say since he, too, is now physically human.

"I want to be human," Tristan clarifies, "but I can't until I know I've done everything within my power to save my brother."

"And after last night," Uncle Malcolm says, "do you still hold out hope that you can save your father as well?"

"Honestly, I'm not sure anymore," Tristan admits. "If he's desperate enough to throw caution to the wind and attack a member of your family, then he may be beyond saving. He knows that you'll be coming after him, Malcolm, and I can promise you he won't be easy to find. They've probably both gone so far underground that I'm not even sure I could find them now."

"Oh, don't worry. I'll find them," Uncle Malcolm says confidently.

"If you do," Tristan begins as he takes a step towards my uncle, "I'm begging you to at least spare my brother's life. Give him one more chance. I know he can change. I just know it!"

My uncle remains mute on the subject. He's never been one to make a promise he never intends to keep, and I'm not sure the anger he's feeling right now will allow him to agree to Tristan's plea for mercy on his brother's behalf.

The room grows eerily quiet afterwards as Uncle Malcolm continues to just stare at Tristan, either unable or unwilling to give an inch.

"Well now," Aunt Tara says to break the tension, even though it's so thick a knife and not words alone may be called for in this circumstance, "I don't know about the rest of you, but I'm starving. Why don't Brand and I make us all something to eat?"

"Thank you for the kind offer," Jered tells my aunt, "but I believe Tristan and I should be going now."

"Are you coming to the hayride in Cypress Hollow tonight?" I ask Tristan before Jered has a chance to phase them back to his house.

"I don't think so," Tristan answers.

"You should come," I encourage, hoping he takes the hint that I want to see him again without forcing me to spell it out for him in embarrassing detail in front of my family. "Jess and Mason's community goes all out every year. Everyone decorates their homes and yards with luminaria. We talk and sing songs while we ride around and look at everything. Then, we go to the corn maze that their local fire department organizes every year. I would really like it if you came tonight. You've never been able to come before. Now you don't have any reason to stay away."

"I don't think my little sister is going to accept a no from you, so you might as well give in," Will tells Tristan with an easy-going grin. "I'll come pick you up. Will you be at Jered's house at around six o'clock this evening?"

Tristan appears uncertain. In a way he looks like he wants to join us, and in a way he looks like a trapped animal who isn't really being given much of a choice.

"Yes, he'll be at my house then," Jered answers for him. "Come over anytime, Will. You're always welcome in my home."

"I guess I'll see you both then," my big brother tells them.

Jered places his hand on Tristan's shoulder and phases them back to his house in Montana.

"Mom," I whisper to her, "I'll be right back. I just need to speak with Uncle Malcolm in private for a moment."

My mother nods her head in understanding before I walk over to my uncle and loop an arm around one of his.

"Do you feel up to a walk outside while Aunt Tara and my dad cook?" I ask him.

"If that's what you want to do," he replies, but I can already see him building a wall behind his eyes in order to shore up his resolve about Tristan's family. My uncle isn't stupid. He knows exactly why I want to speak with him in private.

We walk arm in arm out of the house and make our way down to the lake in front of my family's home. I don't say anything right away. I know I need to be careful with what I say, because the last thing I want to do is set my uncle's plans into stone for him. The harder I push for what I want, the harder he'll push back.

Once we reach the shoreline of the lake, we stop and stare out across it towards the mountains. I turn towards my uncle and wrap my arms around his waist while laying my head against his chest. This simple action has just the effect I was hoping for. My Uncle Malcolm sighs deeply, and the tension in his body slowly dissipates. I feel him place his free arm around me and pat my back.

"I'm sorry if I upset you back there," he tells me, "but you're like a daughter to me, Mae. I refuse to just stand by and let you get hurt again."

"That's not exactly a promise that you can keep," I tell him. "You can't guard me every second of every day."

"I know," he begrudgingly admits, "but it would be my preference."

I tighten my arms around my uncle one more time before letting him go so I can take a step back.

"Uncle Malcolm, you're not really going to kill Tristan's father and brother, are you?"

"Do you believe they deserve mercy after what they did to you?" he scowls. "I don't. I believe they've sealed their fate by kidnapping you and placing your life in danger. They intended to make Tristan kill you last night, Mae! I cannot let that go unanswered."

"Whatever happened to 'thou shall not kill'?" I ask. "I don't think God would want you to kill them."

Uncle Malcolm narrows his eyes as he studies me. It's an expression he normally reserves for others, not me.

"What would you have me do then?" he asks in a low voice. One that's on the verge of sounding extremely angry. "Should I just ignore what they did to you? Is that what you want?"

I don't really have an answer to his question. No, I don't believe they should go unpunished, but I definitely don't want my uncle to kill them either.

"Can't you punish them another way?" I plead. "Tristan needs his family, just like I need mine. If you kill his brother and father it will kill a part of him, too."

Uncle Malcolm looks away from me and peers out across the lake.

His pensive mood and silence are good indicators that he's seriously contemplating my suggestion. All I can do is hope that he realizes it's the right thing to do.

"They fear you, Uncle Malcolm," I say. "They're probably hiding right now, hoping you don't find them. I would much rather you let that be their punishment. It's like they've placed themselves in voluntary exile."

"Strangling them would be much more gratifying," my uncle replies, so matter-of-fact that I know he's telling the truth.

"I don't think we have to worry about them anymore. I truly don't."

Uncle Malcolm sighs and turns to look back at me.

"I'll try not to kill them, Mae," he says. "But if they threaten you or any member of this family again, they've sealed their fates. Can we at least agree to that much?"

I nod. "Yes. If they try to hurt anyone else, then I won't attempt to talk you out of killing them. I won't have them endangering the lives of the people I love."

Uncle Malcolm nods. "All right, then. We have an agreement. Now, let's go back inside before your mother decides to try to help Brand and Tara make breakfast for everyone."

I laugh as I loop my arm around my uncle's. "Do you remember that time she decided she would try to make Thanksgiving dinner for everyone?"

"Ahh yes, the Turducken Incident of 2035," he says knowingly, nodding his head as he recalls the tragic event. "How could any of us forget that? I thought I was going to have to rebuild this house from scratch. Thank goodness my father showed up before anything besides the kitchen was destroyed."

"Why do you think God came down Himself to put out the fire?"

"I think he knew how much work I put into it and didn't want to see it destroyed," he replies. "He also probably figured that if your mother burned it down, it would sadden her. She loves this house. She told me once that this is where she wants to be when she dies."

I tighten my arm around his, because the thought of my mother no longer existing in this world is simply a concept I would rather not consider. I know Uncle Malcolm feels the same way.

"That won't happen for a long time yet," I reassure him, since I see the thought of life without my mother has suddenly made him sad. "She's more active than a couple of lazy teenagers I know who live with her."

My uncle laughs because he knows I'm right.

"That's exactly why I bought Xavier the truck," he tells me.

"I don't understand," I say in confusion. "How will the truck drag him away from his video games and YouTube?"

"This coming summer I plan to give him a project," my uncle reveals. "I bought some land that needs a fence built around it. The truck will help him carry supplies to do that."

"Have you told my little brother that you have his summer all planned out for him?"

"No. But I did tell Lilly and Brand before I bought the truck, to make sure I had their approval."

"I'm sure that wasn't hard to get," I laugh.

"Not at all. They were grateful that I had a plan. The boy needs to disconnect from the electronic world every once in a while. Look at Ariana. She's always helping JoJo in her design studios. JoJo told me that your sister has the talent to become a world-famous designer herself one day."

"Really?" I ask, pleased to hear such high praise for my sister. "I don't doubt it one bit. She's always drawing out her ideas for new outfits. She's done that since she was seven years old."

"Ariana couldn't ask for a better mentor than JoJo."

"Uncle Malcolm, have you ever considered marrying JoJo?"

My uncle comes to a complete stop, forcing me to stop, too, and look at him. The expression of shock on his face at my suggestion is almost comical.

"I love JoJo, but not in that way," he states emphatically. "So don't start thinking about playing matchmaker between the two of us, because it will fail miserably."

"Why?" I ask. "The two of you are already like a married couple. Why not make it official?"

"Like I said, I don't love her in that way. She's one of my best friends. I'm with her and Gabriel a lot because I like being around them, and because I promised Gabe I would always look after them. When I make an oath, I keep it. That's what an honorable man does, Mae."

"I'm sorry I suggested it," I tell him, seeing the error of my assumptions concerning his feelings for JoJo. "I just want to see you happy, Uncle Malcolm, and it doesn't seem like any of the women you go out with bring you any sort of joy. Surely, there has to be someone in the world you can give your heart to."

"I'm a lost cause, Mae," he replies. "Besides, who wants to put up with a crusty old curmudgeon like me?"

"You don't even remotely resemble a grumpy old man," I protest, even though I realize the description isn't that far off the mark regarding his attitude lately.

"I may not look as ancient as I am, but you can't deny that I'm ill-tempered."

"Not with me," I remind him. "Grumpy old men don't build little girls playhouses that look like castles with rainbow-colored slides."

Uncle Malcolm holds out his arm for me to loop mine through once again as we continue to make our way back up to the house.

"Maybe one day your daughter will be able to play on it," he suggests.

"Maybe," I admit as visions of a blond-haired little angel flit through my mind as she flies down the rainbow slide of my childhood into the arms of her father. I shake my head slightly when I realize the man I just envisioned filling that role is Tristan.

W hen we walk back inside the house, I brace myself for a deluge of questions from my family. Surprisingly the only one I'm asked is by my father, who wants to know if I would like waffles or pancakes for breakfast. I hate to tell him that I'm not hungry since I already ate two sandwiches at Tristan's house, so I opt for a couple of his buttery pancakes.

The conversation in the room soon turns to tonight's main event: the hayride with Jess' family in Cypress Hollow.

"Are Kate and Luke still not speaking to one another?" my mom asks Caylin as the females of the group sit around the kitchen table. The men are relegated to the stools around the kitchen island.

"Unfortunately, yes," Caylin replies exasperatedly. "My stubborn daughter..."

"*Our* stubborn daughter," Aiden interjects as a quick reminder to my sister that he's at least half responsible for my niece's obstinate streak.

"*Our* stubborn daughter," Caylin amends with a smile to her husband, "refuses to admit that what she did was wrong and apologize for her behavior."

"Sorry for what exactly?" Ella asks with a look of confusion. "What did Kate do?"

"Yeah," I say. "What is it that she should be sorry for? I haven't heard this story yet."

"That's because it only happened last night during the party all the kids went to," Caylin tells me. "You know how resistant Kate has become to the whole 'soul mates' thing between her and Luke. She feels like her life has already been planned out for her, since destiny has determined that they should be together for the rest of their lives."

I nod my head, letting my sister know I understand exactly what she's talking about. For the past few months, Kate has been agitated by the notion that Luke is the only boy she'll ever have feelings for, and that the path of her life was decided for her eons ago when her soul was matched to Luke's.

"Unfortunately, last night she decided to take the next step in her rebellion. A cute boy named Troy was at the party and all of Kate's friends have a crush on him. In all her teenage wisdom, Kate decided to put her connection with Luke to the test. She walked up to Troy and kissed him right on the lips in front of everyone, including Luke."

"Holy cow," Ella says in surprise, inching up in her seat towards the table, excitedly. "What happened after the kiss?"

"Apparently, Luke and Gabriel left the party. Kate came home crying and saying that she had made the biggest mistake of her life by kissing Troy, because she knows how much she hurt Luke since she can feel his pain."

"Has she tried to talk to Luke about it?" I ask.

"He won't talk to her," Caylin sighs. "I called Jess to see if she could make him speak with Kate, but she said he just needed some time alone. He isn't ready to talk to her yet, and I can't say I blame him. My daughter should have known how much it would hurt Luke to see her kiss another boy, and now she's paying the price for her childish behavior."

"She's young," my mom says, defending her granddaughter. "Did she happen to say whether or not she enjoyed kissing Troy?"

"She said it was like kissing a wet toad," Caylin replies with a small laugh and shake of her head. "She knows now that Luke is her prince charming. She's just praying that she hasn't ruined things between them with her selfishness."

"He'll forgive her," my dad says as he places the last of the pancakes on a plate filled to overflowing on the counter by the stove. "He loves her too much not to forgive what she did."

"We're confident he will," Aiden says from his stool at the kitchen island. "We're just not sure how long it will take for it to happen. I asked Mason to have a talk with him so he knows how badly Kate feels, but I'm sure Luke knows she's hurting, too. I just hope he doesn't make her suffer too much longer. I don't know if I can take seeing her so heartbroken."

"Mason will straighten Luke out," Uncle Malcolm says to Aiden reassuringly. "And if he doesn't, I'll have a talk with the boy."

"In a way, I hope he doesn't for a few days," Caylin says surprisingly. "I don't like seeing my baby upset, but I think this is an important lesson for her. She needs to understand that you shouldn't play around with other people's emotions for selfish reasons, or take their love for granted."

"Did you ever feel like Kate?" I ask Caylin. "You were pretty young when you found out Aiden was your soul mate. Did that bother you?"

"Never," Caylin answers readily. "But Kate has been with Luke since he was born. They practically grew up together, knowing that they would eventually marry and join our family with Jess and Mason's. I can't imagine growing up knowing that your life has basically been planned out for you already. She'll more than likely never date anyone besides Luke."

"You didn't really date anyone either," my mother reminds her. "The only other person you went out with was Joshua, and that was only one date."

"You used to date Leah's husband?" Ella asks in surprise. "How come I don't remember that?"

"Probably because you had just been born, and he and I only went out once," Caylin tells her. "It was Valentine's Day and we went to one of Chandler's concerts. That was the night I first saw Aiden, and after that there was no one else in the world I wanted to be with."

"How did you know Aiden was the one?" I ask my sister, keenly interested in hearing her explanation. "What did it feel like when you first saw him?"

"It's hard to explain," Caylin replies as her eyes grow distant, and a smile graces her face while she remembers the moment she first saw her soul mate. "It was like the earth gave way underneath my feet and the planet came to a grinding halt. The connection between us was so strong that I knew he would be the only man I would ever love."

I look over at my mother. "Is that how you felt when you first met Dad?"

"Very similar," she replies as she turns her head to look over at my father.

He gives her one of his special smiles, the one he reserves only for her.

I grew up knowing that my parents would always love and respect one another. I never worried that they would divorce, because I knew their love was everlasting.

I sit back in my chair at the table, feeling slightly dejected.

I didn't feel like the earth beneath my feet gave way when I first saw Tristan. I don't even feel a certainty that he's the only man I'll ever love. Does that mean my fantasy that Tristan and I are soul mates is just that, a fantasy? And if we're not soul mates, does that mean I'm supposed to wait until mine comes along sometime in the future? What if he never shows up and I waste years of my life waiting for him to find me? My mother said that being united with your soul mate is rare. Most people never even meet theirs during their lifetime. But what if I marry someone and then run into my soul mate years later? What would happen then?

"Are you all right, sweetie?" my mom asks, sensing that my mood has taken a contemplative turn.

I do my best to smile at her to erase her worry. "I'm fine. I think I'm just tired. Tristan's dad drugged me with something to knock me out. It could just be that the drugs are still in my system."

"Why don't you go up to your room and take a nap?" my mom suggests. "You've been through so much. I think you need to get some rest while you can."

With the mention of sleep I involuntarily yawn, which causes practically everyone else in the room to follow suit.

I say so long to everyone before I make my way up to my

bedroom, but I don't make the walk alone. Ella joins me upstairs, and I know exactly what she wants to talk about before she even asks her first question.

"So, what happened while you and Tristan were *alone* in his cabin?" she asks, wiggling her eyebrows suggestively as she takes a seat on the side of my bed and watches as I close the door to my room.

"I made him some sandwiches," I tell her truthfully as I lean my back against the door with my arms crossed at the wrists behind me.

"Sandwiches?" she asks, looking confused. "Is that code for something I don't know about? Like Jess and Mason always saying they need to get matches, when we all know what they're really going to get?"

I laugh, because I know exactly what she's talking about. I feel sure that Jess and Mason both know we're all in on their little joke by now, but they still use it. I think they've simply used the code for so long that it's become a part of their legacy.

"No codes," I sigh disappointedly, pushing myself away from the door to go sit beside my best friend. "I literally made him sandwiches. We talked a little bit, but that was about all."

"Considering the questions you were asking downstairs, I have to ask," she says, watching my reaction to her query closely. "Is Tristan your soul mate?"

Instead of giving her my answer right away, I fall back on my bed and simply stare up at the white ceiling. Ella lays down on her side next to me and props her head on a bent arm. She doesn't prod me to speak. We've been best friends long enough for her to know I need a moment to collect my thoughts.

"I don't think we are," I tell her honestly. "I didn't feel like the earth beneath my feet gave way, or have some other grand revelation that he's my soul mate." I turn my head to look at Ella as she remains quiet on the subject. "I was so positive that he would be, Ella. How could I have gotten it so wrong?"

"Did you feel anything for him?" she asks. "Or was it like being reunited with an old friend?"

"I did feel something," I say, feeling my face flush with embarrassment as an image of Tristan lying on the floor completely naked lingers in my mind.

"Mae Cole," Ella says, obviously noticing my reaction. "Tell me what happened!"

I shake my head, closing my eyes briefly. "I can't. It's too embarrassing."

"Girl, you know you can tell me anything. Now, spill! I want all the juicy details."

I remain silent for a moment, biting my lower lip as I consider whether to tell Ella what happened. Finally, I realize the answer is a forgone conclusion. I don't keep secrets from my best friend. I never have, and I firmly believe that I never will.

"I saw him naked," I blurt out.

"You did *what*?" she exclaims, sitting up on the bed like a jack-in-the-box. "How? Why? And in what room?"

"He fell asleep in his living room after he transformed back into his human form last night. Oh no!" I say, quickly sitting up as something about Tristan's condition occurs to me. "I completely forgot that he has to transform every night. Maybe that's why he was hesitant about going on the hayride. I'm such an idiot."

"I don't think that was it," Ella says. "If it was a problem, Uncle Malcolm or Jered would have said something."

"Maybe he just doesn't want to be around me," I say, deeming this a real possibility. "I don't want to force him to be. Do you think that's what I'm doing?"

"I don't think so," Ella says reassuringly. "But, then again, I don't really know Tristan all that well. Neither do you, for that matter."

"Even though I'm certain that he isn't my soul mate, I still feel drawn to him," I confess. "Is that crazy?"

"Uh, now that I've seen Tristan with my own two eyes, I'm feeling a little drawn to him myself," Ella jokes. "He's hot! Go for it! And, to be honest with you, I think the only reason he hesitated about tonight is because he doesn't know what his father and brother's next move will be. Sure, they could go somewhere to hide from Uncle

Malcolm and the other Watchers but, then again, they could try to attack you a second time. I'm firmly in Uncle Malcolm's corner in this argument, Mae. He needs to hunt them down and stop them from hurting anyone else, especially you."

"I know they need to be punished, but I asked him to not kill them. I don't think Tristan could handle that. He would live with the guilt of their deaths for the rest of his life."

"I suggest you let Uncle Malcolm do what he thinks needs to be done," Ella advises. "He'll make the right decision. He always does."

"He does when he's thinking straight. You know how much he loves us. He'll do whatever he needs to do to protect me. I just don't want him to let his anger take control and lead him do something he'll regret later."

"I tell you what. Why don't you lie down and get a little cat nap in before tonight? I love you, girl, but those bags under your eyes are just getting puffier the longer you try to make yourself stay awake."

"Bags?" I ask, suddenly remembering my disheveled appearance. "You're probably right. I should take a shower first before I climb into bed, though. Just promise me one thing, Ella."

"You know I'll do anything for you."

"Don't let me oversleep. My parents will if they believe I need the rest, but I need to count on at least one person in this family to make my romantic interest a priority."

"You have my word that you won't miss the hayride this evening." Ella leans over and gives me a quick kiss on the cheek before standing. "Now, go hop in the shower and get some rest afterwards. I promise I'll wake you later if I have to."

After Ella walks out of my room, I immediately go to my bathroom and shower. When I snuggle underneath my covers, I close my eyes and try to go to sleep. It takes me a while but I finally doze off, wondering what the night will bring.

I do indeed wake up all on my own. I send Ella a text just to let her know that I'm awake. In fact, I end up having plenty of time to style my hair, dab on a little makeup, and find something casual, but nice, to wear to the hayride. Just as I'm grabbing a blue denim jacket from my closet, I hear someone knock on the bedroom door.

"Come in!" I call.

"Are you ready for the hayride?" I hear my little sister Ariana ask me as she enters the room.

I exit the walk-in closet with the jacket over my arm and smile at her. "About as ready as I'm going to get."

Ariana briefly considers what I'm wearing before nodding her head approvingly.

"Yep," she says, "that'll do it."

"Uh, do what exactly?" I ask, looking down at my slightly distressed jeans, tennis shoes, and slouchy beige sweater.

"Get a certain someone's attention, of course," she replies with a conspiratorial wink. "You look way better than you did when you came home this morning."

"Uh," I say, feeling somewhat offended by the remark. "Thanks, I guess."

"Tristan will definitely be keeping his eyes on you tonight," she assures me with teenage certainty.

"I didn't exactly dress to impress him, Ariana. This is what I would have worn anyway."

"Oh, come on," my sister says exasperatedly. "I know I'm only sixteen, but even I could feel the chemistry between the two of you earlier. Is he your soul mate?" she asks eagerly. "Is that why you kept asking Caylin and Mom about how they felt when they met theirs?"

I automatically shake my head, realizing all too well that I know in my heart Tristan isn't my soul mate. The realization is disappointing, but not as heartbreaking as I would have imagined. Ariana is right. There *is* a natural attraction between me and Tristan that I can't deny exists. I just don't know what it all means yet.

"We're not soul mates," I tell her. "But I am attracted to him. I guess that was obvious, though."

"Just a little," she replies with a smile. "But who can blame you? He's smoking hot."

"And on that note," I say, feeling slightly awkward to have my sister say such a thing as I walk over to her, "why don't we go down-stairs? I'm sure Mom and Dad are ready to leave."

"Yeah," she replies as she willingly follows me out of my bedroom. "They sent me up here to see if you were ready to go."

"Then we shouldn't make them wait any longer."

Ariana and I make our way downstairs, where my parents and Xavier are waiting.

"You look like you got some much-needed rest," my mom says, smiling with pride as she watches us descend the stairs to the foyer and walk over to where they're standing.

"I slept like a baby," I tell her. "Where are Caylin and Aiden?"

"They said they would meet us there," my dad answers. "Apparently, Kate wanted to get over there early to see if Luke would talk to her about what happened last night."

"Does that mean she's ready to apologize?" I ask.

"That, I couldn't tell you," my father replies with a grin. "I would never presume to know what's going through a woman's mind, especially not one from this family."

"That's very wise of you, sweetie," my mother replies, looping an arm around one of my father's and patting it with her free hand. "It's one of the many reasons I love you so much."

"Can we go now?" Ariana whines. "I want to see JoJo and tell her about my new idea for a dress in her spring collection."

"How did I raise you to be so impatient?" my mother asks jokingly as she holds out one of her hands to us kids. We can all phase ourselves to Cypress Hollow, but my mom prefers it when we all arrive at the same location together.

I place my hand on top of my mother's first, followed by my younger siblings. Within a split-second we find ourselves standing on Jess and Mason's newly-built back patio where a large group of our friends and family are already gathered. Mason and Uncle Malcolm are manning the charcoal grills as they cook the obligatory hot dogs, hamburgers, and roasted corn for the supper. I do a double take when I see my Uncle Malcolm, because he's standing in front of his grill only wearing a pair of faded jeans and tennis shoes. He has a blue and green plaid flannel shirt tied around his hips. I'm used to seeing him wearing his shirts unbuttoned in the front, but it's rare to see him without a top on at all unless we're swimming.

I instantly spy Kallie and Chandler sitting side-by-side on the semi-circular stone bench around a matching rock-wall firepit. I excuse myself from my family to walk over to them and speak with Kallie about my internship at her veterinary clinic during Christmas break. Just before I reach them, my attention is captured by the sound of my niece's pleading voice. When I look past where Kallie and Chandler are sitting, I spy Kate chasing after Luke by the edge of the woods, begging him to stop.

"Please talk to me, Luke," she beseeches him as tears stream down her beautiful, distraught face. "How many different ways can I say that I'm sorry?"

Luke spins around to face Kate, an angry scowl marring his otherwise-handsome features. Even though Luke is a little over a year younger than Kate, he doesn't look it. In fact, if I didn't know that Jess' youngest son was only a few months away from turning thirteen, I would have pegged him as being at least fifteen, if not older. Not only is Kate's soul mate one of the handsomest young men I've ever seen, but he's also extremely smart from what I understand. He was able to skip an entire grade level to be in the same class as Kate. I was also told that he could have gone even further than that academically if he wanted to, but he decided staying with Kate was more important. I wonder if he's regretting that decision now, considering my niece's selfish behavior the night before.

"I don't need you to tell me you're sorry, Kate. I need you to stop fighting something that can never be changed! I'm sorry if you feel like being my soul mate is a curse, but there's nothing either one of us can do about that. It is what it is, and you need to either accept it or let me go."

"Luke..." Kate's voice cracks with anguish after hearing his ultimatum. "I love you. Please, you have to forgive me. My heart can't take you being so angry with me."

The wrath on Luke's face softens a bit, and I can tell he's finally allowing himself to realize just how upset Kate is about the whole affair. I watch as he takes a few deep, calming breaths before he walks over and pulls her into his arms. Kate continues her heart- wrenching cries against the comfort of his shoulder, but it's obvious to those of us watching that their quarrel has run its course. I faintly hear Luke whisper something to my niece. I don't know what he said exactly, but I do see Kate nod her head and follow him wordlessly to a spot behind a large oak tree to shield them from prying eyes.

"Young love," Chandler says with a shake of his head as he softly strums the strings of his guitar. "I should probably write a song about the two of them one day."

"I can't imagine finding the person you're supposed to spend the rest of your life with at such a young age. I can understand why Kate rebelled," Kallie tells her husband, sympathizing with my niece's plight.

"It doesn't look like rebelling has done her much good, though," I say as I walk over to them. "All it did was cause them both pain."

"Feeling pain isn't always a bad thing," Chandler tells me as he lightly sweeps his fingers across the strings of his guitar again to fill the air with music. "Sometimes, it forces you to realize what you have before you lose it. I think Kate has learned an important lesson from kissing that other boy."

"And what lesson would that be?" Kallie asks, looking intrigued to hear her husband's words of wisdom.

"That you can't fight fate no matter how hard you try," he replies. "Some things are just meant to be. Lord knows I tried to fight my feelings for you in the beginning."

"Yeah. I noticed that," Kallie says as she crosses her arms defensively, and gives her husband a reproachful look. "Why exactly did you do that?"

"Sometimes when you find the one thing that you want in life, you realize just how many shortcomings you have. I wasn't sure I was good enough for you, and risking rejection wasn't something I was used to doing. If I remember correctly, you weren't exactly impressed with all my charms when we first met."

"That's because you were hiding behind your obnoxious rock star persona," Kallie reminds him. "If it wasn't for Jess, I wouldn't have given you a second chance."

"I guess I owe her for finding you for me in the first place, and for convincing you that I was more than just a pretty face," Chandler jests.

"You bet you do," I hear Jess say with conviction from somewhere behind me.

I feel her hand rest on my back right before I turn slightly to meet her gaze.

"And how is one of my favorite people in the world doing this evening?" she asks me, rubbing her hand gently along the contour of my spine in a soothing up and down motion.

"I'm fine," I tell her automatically, only realizing when I try to smile reassuringly that I'm not being completely honest.

From the look of doubt on Jess's face, I can tell that she isn't buying it.

"It'll take a little time to recover from what happened to you last night," she tells me. "But I think I might have part of the remedy, if you're interested."

"And what would that be?" I ask, curious to discover what Jess considers a cure for my trauma.

"Come on and I'll show you," she says, looping her arm around mine.

As I start to follow Jess' lead, I assume she'll be taking me inside the house. Instead, we end up walking off her patio and head towards the front of her home.

"Where are we going?" I ask, wondering if she plans to drive me somewhere since we're rounding the corner of her garage.

"There's someone on my front porch who's been hiding out from the crowd," Jess whispers to me. "I think he's probably just been waiting for you to arrive before he makes some lame excuse to leave early."

I turn my attention to Jess's porch and find my brother Will sitting on the top step with Tristan. When the pair spot our approach, they cease their conversation and immediately stand to walk down the steps and meet us.

"You look a lot better," Will says to me, a relieved smile on his face as Jess lets go of my arm so my big brother can give me a welcoming hug.

"So I've been told," I say, wondering just how badly I appeared earlier in the day when I arrived home.

When Will steps away, I look over at Tristan and see him grinning uncertainly at me. I sense he's a little nervous about seeing me again, but I don't understand why.

"You should probably go get Amanda and your kids," Jess tells Will. "The food will be ready soon."

Will nods in agreement. "I was just waiting for Mae to show up before I left. I'll be back in a minute with the family."

Will phases back to his home in Biloxi, where he lives with his wife and two kids. After Will graduated from Southeastern College with his MBA, Uncle Malcolm gave him a job at his casino on the Mississippi Gulf Coast. Now, Will runs that casino and also the one my uncle acquired in Las Vegas a couple of years ago.

"I'd better go inside and make sure we don't need anything else for the cookout," Jess tells us. Her reason for leaving is obviously an excuse, but I'm grateful that she's giving me a few moments alone with Tristan before our time is completely swallowed up by the evening's planned activities.

Jess walks around us to her front porch, and enters her house.

I stare at the closed door she just went through, realizing too late that a horde of butterflies have suddenly invaded the pit of my stomach. Cautiously, I look over at Tristan and see that he's staring at the door as well. When he turns his head in my direction, the look of uncertainty I noticed on his face earlier reappears.

"Have you heard any news about your father and brother's whereabouts?" I ask, since it's the only question that readily comes to my mind.

Tristan shakes his head. "As far as I know, no one has found them yet. Jered is still out searching for them, as are some of the other Watchers Malcolm sent out."

"I had a talk with my uncle," I tell him. "I asked him to give Rolph and Jasper a second chance. He seemed to indicate that he would be willing to do that."

"And how exactly did you work that miracle?" Tristan asks.

"As long as your father and brother remain hidden he won't kill them, but if they try to hurt any of us again they're fair game. It was the best I could do."

"If he doesn't plan to kill them, then why does he have people out searching for them?" Tristan asks, not sounding the least bit convinced my uncle doesn't still plan to kill what remains of his family once he locates them.

"It could be that he wants to make sure they understand that what they did to me comes with dire consequences. He probably hopes to keep them on the run for now before he lets up on the search. Once that happens, odds are they'll stay hidden."

Tristan sighs deeply, looking dejected by such a notion. "Then that's going to make it a lot harder for me to find them again."

"Why are you still trying to convince them to change their ways?" I ask, confounded by his persistence. "From what I've been told, you've been attempting to do that ever since you came back from alternate Earth. How long are you going to waste your life on what might be a lost cause?"

"They're my family, Mae. I can't just give up on them. You of all people should know how important family is. Look how close you are to your own. I may never be able to save my father, but I still believe in my heart that Jasper can be convinced to leave him."

"How much longer do you plan to try to save him?" I ask.

"However long it takes," he answers.

"What if it takes a thousand years?"

Tristan hesitates before answering. "Then that's how long I'll have to wait. I refuse to give up on him, Mae. I don't have it in me to consider him a lost cause."

I feel the excited butterflies in my stomach get squashed by the dropping of my heart. If what Tristan just said is how he truly feels, the only way I'll ever know if we're meant to be together is if he finds his family again. We may not be soul mates, but there is definitely a connection between us that can't be denied. From the torn expression on his face I can tell his emotions are in turmoil over the whole dilemma, and I know there's only one thing that I can do to help him and myself.

"Then we'll find them," I pledge. Tristan looks at me in confusion. "You understand how your family thinks better than anyone else. I'm sure you know about places they might go to hide from my uncle and the others. I can take you to those places faster than you can get to them on your own."

"Have you lost your mind?" Tristan asks, looking slightly flabbergasted by my offer. "If your uncle ever found out..."

"He won't find out," I assure him. "No one will. This will be our secret."

"I can just have Jered phase me to the places I suspect they're hiding," Tristan says unconvincingly.

"Yet you haven't done that, and I'm assuming the reason is because you're not certain what Jered would do if the two of you found them. You know that protecting your life would be his first reaction to whatever your father might do in retaliation."

"And what about you?" Tristan asks. "I know what your mother and Caylin are capable of doing. Are you able to kill angels with a single touch like them? Can you honestly tell me that you won't use your powers on my family?"

"Do you need me to promise you that I won't before you'll trust me?" I ask, willing to do whatever it takes to help Tristan.

"You would do that for me?"

"I'm willing to promise not to use my power on them unless our lives are in danger. I understand you need to do everything you can to save your brother. I even love that about you, but I won't die for your cause."

"I would never ask you to," Tristan says, slightly aghast. "I'm not even sure I should accept your offer of help, considering how dangerous it will be."

"Now that I know what your family is capable of, I'll be extra cautious around them. Let me help you with this, Tristan." I reach out a hand and gently take hold of his arm. "You need to figure out whether you're wasting your life on a lost cause or not. If you are, then you need to find the strength to move on and find another reason to live."

"I'll only agree to this if your family knows what you're going to be doing," Tristan tells me. "I don't want you to go behind their backs to help me."

"I'll tell my mom and dad," I compromise. "I won't tell Uncle Malcolm, though, because I know what his response would be. He's overprotective to a fault when it comes to the safety of my family. The less he knows about this the better."

"He'll be angry if he finds out on his own," Tristan points out.

"And he'll get over it with time."

Tristan tilts his head as he considers me. "Why are you offering to help me like this, Mae? All my family has done is place you in danger ever since you were a child. You don't owe them anything, much less mercy and compassion."

I let my hand drop away from Tristan as I consider just how truthful I should be with him concerning my true agenda. Then I decide I'm either all in with him or not, and realize that decision was made for me a long time ago.

"I want you to be free to live your life the way you want to," I say. "I have a hard time believing spending more years trying to convince them that they need to change their ways is how you want to live. Don't you want more for yourself? Wouldn't you like to start a family of your own one day?"

"And what do you want out of life, Mae?" Tristan asks in a quiet voice. From the expectant look on his face, I can tell that he already knows what my answer will be. He simply wants to hear it from me.

"A lot," I answer truthfully. "Which is exactly what everyone should want since we only have one life to live on this earth. I want a family I can be proud of, and I want to be as good a veterinarian as Kallie one day. Right now, I want you to tell me that you'll accept my offer of help."

"Why is helping me so important to you?"

"Can I give you that answer later?" I ask, feeling suddenly shy because I don't feel like it's the right time to answer his question. "All you need to know right now is that I want to help you, and I'm willing to do whatever it takes to accomplish that."

Tristan takes a moment to consider my words before saying, "Then I accept your generous offer. When should we start?"

"Tomorrow morning would probably be the best time. Once you transform back into a human, call me. Are you planning to stay here in the States or go back to your cabin in Russia?"

"I'll be staying with Jered for the time being. Since there's an eight-hour time difference between here and Russia, I decided it would be better if I stayed with him while the search is still ongoing."

"When do you need to go back to his house to transform?" I ask, knowing the children of the Watchers must revert to their werewolf form every night.

"Not for quite a while," he reassures me. "I've been able to delay my need to be in wolf form until the early morning hours."

"Good to know," I reply with a smile. "I was worried you might not be able to stay the whole evening. I would hate for you to miss the combined talents of Aiden and Faison trying to sing in harmony during the hayride."

"I know Aiden can't sing in tune," Tristan says amused, "but I had no idea Jess' sister was tone deaf, too."

"Oh yeah," I assure him. "Neither of them can sing, but that doesn't stop them from trying. The funny thing is that Faison doesn't seem to realize she can't sing."

"Why hasn't anyone told her?"

"It would break her heart," I reply simply, "and none of us is cruel enough to do that to her. Sometimes when you love someone, you have to support them even if it hurts you."

Tristan chuckles. "I'll remember that."

"We should probably go around back before all the hamburgers get claimed."

Tristan matches his stride with mine as I turn around and begin to walk back towards the patio where everyone is gathered.

"Thank you," he tells me as he gives me a sidelong glance. "Knowing that you want to help my family means a lot to me, Mae."

"You're welcome," I reply.

I want to be completely honest with him that I'm helping myself as much as I am him, but I stay mute about that point. First and foremost, I want us to become friends. I want Tristan to know he can trust me with something as important as helping his family find their way back to God's light. Secretly, I hope what I feel for Tristan is mutual, but I'm not comfortable enough to presume such a thing. If we're meant to be together, we will be. Right now, all I want is for Tristan to feel as though he's done all he can to save his family, and not live with any regrets or misgivings. Even if he isn't meant to be with me, I want him to feel free to live a life filled with the love of a family of his very own.

W hen we reach the back patio, Tristan is instantly whisked away by Chandler, Joshua, and Zack, who apparently came over with Faison while Tristan and I were talking. I don't mind him being dragged off by the men, because it gives me a chance to speak to Kallie about my internship with her. At least, that was what I wanted to talk about, but apparently the rumor mill about my connection with Tristan has reached her ears and piqued her curiosity.

"You know," she says as I sit down next to her, "I always wondered why you shied away from forming a lasting relationship with some-one. Is Tristan the reason?"

"Yes," I answer honestly. "I thought I knew what he was to me, but now I'm not so sure."

Kallie looks puzzled by my statement. "I don't understand. What did you think he was to you?"

"My soul mate," I tell her, only then realizing Kallie may not understand what I'm referring to. "Do you know what that is?"

"Chandler told me about it once," she replies. "So you thought Tristan was your soul mate, but now you know he isn't?"

I nod. "Yeah. I don't feel that connection to him, at least not in the way my mom and Caylin described it to me."

"But you feel something for him, right?"

Again, I nod. "I do. I'm just not sure what it is exactly."

"Maybe it's just good old-fashioned human attraction," Kallie suggests. "From what Chandler told me about soul mates most people don't find theirs, yet people manage to fall in love with one another all the time. Chandler and I are prime examples of that. I never would have thought I'd end up with the most famous rock star on the planet, but I did. Chandler and our kids are my world now, and I wouldn't want it to be any other way. If I know you as well as I think I do you seem a little disappointed that Tristan isn't your soul mate, but have you stopped to consider that it might actually be a good thing?"

Now it's my turn to look at Kallie with a perplexed expression. "Why would that be a good thing?"

"You get to choose who you fall in love with now. You're not restricted by all this soul mate business anymore. I guess the only question you need to answer for yourself is if Tristan is someone you can see yourself spending time with and getting to know better."

"Honestly, that's exactly what I want. We barely know one another. The last time we were together was when I was a toddler."

"Considering how long you've waited to see him again, I think you owe it to yourself to figure out whether or not he's the man for you."

"That's my plan," I tell her.

"What's your plan?" I hear my big sister question.

Caylin and Leah walk over to us, each of them carrying a white paper plate in their hands loaded with a dressed hamburger and a pile of chips. They sit down on the other side of me to join in on the conversation.

"I plan to get to know Tristan better," I tell them. "I thought he was my soul mate, but he isn't."

"Really?" Caylin says, finding my revelation odd. "I could have sworn he would be, since he broke his bond with his father for you."

"I thought that was the reason, too," I admit.

"Have you asked him about that yet?" Leah asks. "Has he told you why he did it?"

"No. We haven't spent that much time together. I haven't had a chance to discuss it with him."

"If I were you, I would ask," Caylin advises. "When it first happened, he was so confused about things that he couldn't give us an answer about why he did it. Now that some time has passed, maybe he has a clearer perspective about why he decided that saving you was more important than staying with his family."

"Do you think he regrets that decision now?" I ask.

Caylin shakes her head. "I don't think so. At least he's never said that to anyone, as far as I know. From what I've been told, he loves his life the way it is now. All he needs to do is get over his guilt about leaving his brother with his father."

"He'll need to find them again before he can do that," I say. "Caylin, I need to tell you something, but you have to promise me you won't tell anyone else, especially Uncle Malcolm."

"Okay," my sister says uncertainly.

I go on to tell the others about my plan to help Tristan find his family so he can talk to them. All three women begin to argue against my plan.

"Keep your voices down," I whisper to them. "I don't want Uncle Malcolm to hear about it. If he does, he'll find a way to keep me from helping Tristan."

"For good reason!" Leah says.

"Shh," I tell her, cautiously looking over to the grill where Uncle Malcolm was earlier, but finding that he isn't there anymore.

"Uncle Malcolm went to New York to bring JoJo and Gabriel here," Caylin tells me after seeing where my gaze traveled. "He's not the only one you'll have to worry about, though. Mom and Dad will never let you traipse around the world looking for the people who just tried to kill you, because it's a really bad idea, Mae."

"I'm old enough to make my own decisions," I reply stubbornly. "If you were in my position and this was Aiden we were talking about, what would you do? I think some of you have forgotten that I'm an adult now. I don't need anyone's permission to do what I believe is right."

"That's true, Mae," Caylin begrudgingly agrees, "but I never pegged you as the type of daughter who would go behind her parents' backs to do something you know they won't approve of."

"I don't plan to do that. I promised Tristan I would tell them what we're going to do."

"They'll try to talk you out of it," Kallie says with certainty. "And whether you know it or not, you're not the type of person who will go against her parents' wishes. Bearing in mind that fact," Kallie pauses for a moment to think over the situation, "we have to come up with an alternative plan to ease their worry over your safety. I assume your offer to help Tristan has a two-fold purpose. I know you're the kind person who would do anything for your friends, but I also sense you view this opportunity as a way for the two of you to get to know one another better. Am I right?"

"You're not wrong," I admit.

"Then there has to be a way for you to help him and still remain safe."

"Safe from what?" I hear Jess ask as she walks over to join us.

I quickly and quietly tell her how I plan to help Tristan find his family.

"Have you lost your mind?" Jess explodes.

"Shh," Caylin, Kallie, Leah, and I say in unison.

Cautiously, I look towards the back of the house where my parents are talking with Rafe and his wife, Nina. My mom looks over at us, and I smile reassuringly at her. She smiles and returns her attention to Nina.

"I'm doing it no matter what anyone else says," I tell Jess in a low voice. "We're just trying to think of a way I can do it as safely as possible."

Jess narrows her eyes at me disapprovingly, but it soon becomes apparent that she understands my mind is made up.

"Let me think about this for a minute," she tells me as she considers the facts. It takes a few seconds, but Jess' eyes light up as she thinks of a way to solve my dilemma. "I'm not sure if I have a complete solution to your problem, but if you do what I suggest your folks might not put up as much of a fight when you tell them."

Jess tells us her plan, and we all agree that it's the best way to ease my parents' worry.

"When exactly do you plan to help him start searching for his family?" Jess asks me.

"In the morning."

"Okay. I'll have Mason bring me over to your house in the morning before you set out on your search with Tristan."

I stand up and give Jess a hug. "Thank you. And thank you for not trying to convince me not to help him."

"I know you Cole women well enough by now to understand your stubborn streaks," Jess jokes as she hugs me back. "Just promise me that at the first sign of danger you phase straight to the Watcher Agency headquarters. If anything happens, that's the safest place for you to go. Can you promise me that?"

"I promise I'll go straight there if we're in any danger," I tell her.

"Good. Now go get a hamburger before your only choice is a hot dog."

Kallie and I make our way to the inside of Jess' home to reach the kitchen where all the food is. I was told Jess lived in this house before she married Mason. I know for a fact that the two of them prefer to live in Cypress Hollow than anywhere else in the world. Mason still has mansions scattered around the globe, but the home they spend the majority of their family time in is this one. Their home in Colorado houses what remains of the Watcher Agency in the concealed lower level, and the house in the Bahamas is where we all gather for family get- togethers during the summer months.

"Hey," I say to my little brother Xavier, who is filling his plate up with chips, "have you seen Ella and her folks yet?"

"Uncle Malcolm said something about them coming later," he tells me as he continues to shovel chips onto his already overly-burdened plate. "Ella didn't want to be here while we were eating. I guess she thought it might derail her diet."

"Ahh. That makes sense," I reply as I grab a paper plate and quickly assemble my own dressed hamburger. I'm thankful Jess suggested I come in when I did, since there are only a few patties left in the serving dish.

"I'm told having a hamburger at this party is a requirement," Tristan says behind me.

Startled by his unexpected closeness, I involuntarily drop my plate. With quicker reflexes than my own, Tristan saves my supper by catching my plate with one hand before it has a chance to hit the floor.

"Dude," Xavier says in utter amazement as he stares at Tristan in awe. "I can't believe you just did that!"

"Quick reflexes," Tristan says with a slight shrug, as if the fact embarrasses him.

As he hands me back my plate I say a quiet 'thank you,' which is all I'm able to say before my little brother grabs Tristan by the arm and starts tugging him towards the patio.

"I call dibs on you for our team," Xavier declares. "Come on. We need to tell my dad you'll be playing with us."

"Uh," Tristan says, looking confused, "playing what exactly?"

"Our annual football game," Xavier explains. "My dad and Uncle Malcolm each put together a team to play against one another every Thanksgiving. I'm claiming you for our side."

Tristan looks over at me with a helpless expression as he allows my little brother to drag him outside to talk with my dad.

"Just accept your fate!" I call after him, unable to prevent myself from chuckling at his expense.

"See," Kallie tells me. "He's already fitting into your family."

"Mommy," we both hear as Kallie and Chandler's young daughter walks up between us.

Kallie kneels so that she's eye level with four-year-old Rachel Megan Cane.

"What do you need, sweetie?" Kallie asks as she tucks a wayward lock of blonde hair behind Rachel's left ear.

"Can I have a hot dog?" Rachel asks sweetly. "Brian wouldn't make me one. He told me to come ask you."

"Oh, did he now?" Kallie replies, not sounding at all pleased with her ten-year-old son's response to his sister's request. "Don't worry, sweetie. I'll have a talk with him later about his responsibilities.

Right now, why don't we make you a hot dog with all the trimmings?"

Rachel vigorously nods her head in agreement, as if she's starving to death.

Once Kallie, Rachel, and I have our plates filled with food, we sit down together at the kitchen table to eat. I make sure to position myself so I can look out onto the patio. I spy Tristan speaking with my father, and pray that he doesn't inadvertently say anything about my plan to help him find his family. He has to know that I haven't had time to speak with my parents yet, but sometimes people say things before thinking them through clearly. I breathe a sigh of relief when I see Leah's husband, Joshua, and my big brother Will join their conversation. I can tell they're having a strategy session about the football game that's been a family tradition for years now. The coaching rivalry between my dad and Uncle Malcolm is a friendly one, but that doesn't mean they take the game lightly. Each of them likes to win, and they recruit whoever they believe will help them achieve victory. The only restriction on the game is that the players can't be Watchers. I don't believe a rule was ever made that a Watcher child who still went through the transformation couldn't play, which might very well help lead my father's team to victory this year.

After everyone has eaten, I volunteer to go get Ella and her family. When I arrive at her house, they're just finishing up their supper of grilled chicken salad.

"Did I miss anything?" Ella asks me as she wiggles her eyebrows up and down, indicating she wants to know if she missed anything that might have happened between me and Tristan.

"I'll tell you later," I whisper to her as Aunt Tara and Uncle Malik are retrieving light jackets from the hallway closet. "Do I need to go get Linc and his family?" I ask them.

"They won't be able to make it this year," Aunt Tara informs me. "Linc's wife decided she wanted to take the family on a cruise since the kids have the whole week off from school."

"Does Uncle Malcolm know?" I ask. "He always uses Linc as his running back during the football game."

"He knows," Uncle Malik tells me. "He's not happy about it, but he knows."

"Tristan will be playing on my dad's team," I tell them.

Aunt Tara starts to laugh. "That's definitely going to make this year's game interesting. I'm surprised Malcolm is letting that happen."

"He doesn't know yet," I tell her.

Aunt Tara smiles. "I hope I'm there when he finds out then. I always love seeing that man argue with your dad."

"Why?" I ask, amused by her obvious eagerness over the prospect.

"Those two have been arguing about things since the moment I met them. I just find it funny when they bash heads."

"Uh, that's a little on the sadistic side, Mom," Ella says, looking at her mother as if she's seeing a totally different side of her.

Aunt Tara shrugs her slim shoulders. "I'm not going to make any excuses for myself. I just hope I have a front row seat to the argument."

After I phase myself, Ella, and her family back to Jess' house, Aunt Tara gets exactly what she wished for. Uncle Malcolm is arguing with my dad that Tristan should be disqualified from playing in the game since he has enhanced powers, and my dad is arguing the fact that the rules they set into place years ago doesn't preclude a Watcher child from playing. After a few minutes, my mother steps in and ends the argument by siding with my father.

"But Dearest..." Uncle Malcolm begins, but is cut off by my mother holding up a hand to stop his next words.

"The rules are the rules, Malcolm," she tells him. "Tristan is eligible to play and there's nothing you can do to change that. We've had Linc and Malik play on the teams, and they're Fae. There's no reason Tristan shouldn't be able to play, too."

"Lilly is right, *mon ami*," JoJo chimes in. "Now, let's stop this silly arguing and enjoy the rest of the evening together. I swear the two of you act like a friendly family game of American football is the Super Bowl."

"It's a game of skill and strategy," Uncle Malcolm states. "And my strategy just went out the window because I didn't factor Tristan into it."

"You are one of the smartest men I know," JoJo tells him. "I am sure you will figure something out. Besides, what's the worst thing that can happen? You lose to Brand. It's no big deal."

"No big deal?" Uncle Malcolm says, as if JoJo has just spoken blasphemy. "And let him have bragging rights for the next year? I'd rather not."

"Oh, good grief," JoJo says with a shake of her head, "sometimes you are just too much. Come on. Help me into one of the wagons for the hayride so we can leave this silliness behind us for now."

JoJo tugs on the sleeve of Uncle Malcolm's plaid shirt, urging him to follow her to the front of the house.

"If I'd known agreeing to play in the game was going to cause such a fuss, I would have declined," I hear Tristan say from behind me, causing my heart to leap into my chest yet again by his unexpected closeness.

I turn around to face him.

"You've got to stop doing that," I declare as I place a steadying hand over my heart to calm its rapid beating.

"Doing what exactly?" he asks, looking perplexed by my request.

"Coming up behind me and speaking," I tell him. "You've startled me twice now by doing that."

"I'm sorry," he says sincerely. "I didn't mean to."

"Oh, don't worry about it," Ella tells him with a wave of her hand, like his behavior is no big deal. "Mae could use the excitement. All she ever does is study. A little startling is good for her heart."

Tristan smiles as he turns his attention from Ella back to me. "Does that mean I make your heart race?"

I end up laughing nervously because that's the only thing I can think to do to buy myself some time.

"Why don't we go find a seat in one of the wagons before they're all taken?" I suggest, hoping both Ella and Tristan will take the hint and drop the subject. Thankfully they do, and we make our way to the street in front of Jess' house where the five horse-drawn wagons are waiting for us.

Over the years, as the families have grown in number, more and more wagons have been added to the procession that travels around Jess' neighborhood and ends at a corn maze set up by the local fire department as part of their charity fundraiser.

Thankfully, Kallie thought ahead and saved the three of us seats in her and Chandler's wagon, keeping us from having to sit with the kids in their wagon. However, I do glance in the children's wagon to check on Kate and Luke. I'm happy to see them sitting side by side, whispering to each other as they hold hands. I feel a sense of relief to see them back together because I know it will ultimately be their union that will eventually produce the descendant who will end the threat the princes of Hell present. I'm not sure how she'll do it, but if God says she can handle them I have no doubt whatsoever that she will.

Tristan chooses to sit directly across from me in the wagon, while Ella sits beside me.

"Everybody ready?" Beau, the proprietor of the local convenience store in Cypress Hollow, maker of the best cinnamon rolls in existence, and designated driver, asks from his perch on the spring seat at the front of the wagon.

We all say that we're ready, causing Beau to gently use his reins to signal the horses pulling us to move forward.

Twilight has settled over Cypress Hollow, allowing for the luminaria everyone lit in Jess' neighborhood to sparkle brightly in their yards. This yearly tradition always reminds me that Christmas is just around the corner. As I breathe in the sweet smell of autumn and freshly baled hay we're sitting on, I feel a sense of peace and comfort permeate my core because I'm surrounded by those I love most in the world. I realize how blessed I am to have so many people in my life that I can count on for love and support. The thought causes me to look over at Tristan because I know how isolated his life has been the past few years. The only person he's consistently had in his life since he left his family has been Jered. It's surprising to me that he doesn't seem more uncomfortable being around such a large group of people, but perhaps he's ready to leave his quiet life of solitude behind and finally rejoin society.

Chandler draws my attention when I hear him strum the strings of his guitar and begin to sing. The song he composed for the hayride is soothing as it weaves a tale about a man who thought he had everything he could possibly want in life, but discovered he actually had nothing until he met the woman of his dreams. It's not hard to tell that the song is about him and Kallie.

During the time I've interned with Kallie at her clinic, Chandler often stops by when he isn't working on new music just so he can steal a kiss from his wife. She shoos him away and tells him she's too busy for the likes of some rock star, but you could tell she loved the fact her husband still felt the need to woo her. The pair will soon be celebrating their twelfth wedding anniversary, but each of them acts like they're still newlyweds. Quite a few teenage hearts were broken the day Kallie married Chandler, but anyone who knows them personally can clearly see they were made for one another.

After Chandler plucks the last note of his song, everyone cheers and claps for his performance. It doesn't take long before people from the other wagons ask him to sing another one of his songs. This time he plays a popular one that everyone knows the words to and sings along with him. As soon as Faison adds her voice to the sing-a-long, I see Tristan sit straight up in his seat and look around as if we're under attack by some nefarious force. I can't help but laugh at his reaction, which causes him to look over at me.

"Who is that?" he whispers, leaning forward in his seat.

"That's Faison," I tell him, identifying the voice that sounds like the braying of a donkey in distress.

"I thought you were joking earlier," he tells me, "but I can hear for myself that you weren't exaggerating about her voice."

"Oh, just you wait until Chandler plays a song that Aiden knows," I warn him. "Then you'll get the full effect."

Tristan laughs, causing my heart to warm just from the sound of his voice.

On the next song Aiden does indeed join his voice with the rest of us, but his discordant tones end up being drowned out in our wagon when Tristan begins to sing. I find his voice surprisingly strong, with a rich warm tone that has a natural rasp, causing it to break in just the right spots. I find myself singing just barely over a whisper just to make sure I can hear Tristan's singing clearly.

"Boy, you can sing!" Ella praises Tristan after the song ends. "Who taught you how to sing like that?"

"No one," Tristan shrugs, looking slightly embarrassed by her praise. "I guess after living for so long I just got better at it over the years."

"I know some singers who would kill for a voice like yours, man," Chandler tells him. "If you ever want to lay down some tracks, just let me know and I'll let you use my studio. We could make some wicked cool music together."

"Thanks. I appreciate the offer," Tristan says.

I have a feeling Tristan won't ever accept Chandler's proposal. He doesn't seem like the type of person who would want to be in the limelight like our resident rock god.

"Do you work?" I ask Tristan, wondering what he does with his time during the day. Since I know he lives in an isolated part of Russia, I can't imagine he has a lot of job opportunities available out there.

"Jered helps me travel around the world to manage various Habitat for Humanity projects that he funds," Tristan says. "I've always liked working outside with my hands, and construction has always been easy for me."

"Aww," Ella says as she looks at Tristan all doe-eyed. "That's so sweet of you to do."

Tristan shrugs like it's no big deal. "I like to keep busy during the day, and there are a lot of families in the world who need homes."

"Did you build the cabin you live in?" I ask.

"Jered, Mason, and Aiden helped me build most of it. Malcolm even helped some when he had the time."

"Do you like living out there all by yourself?" I ask. Since the cabin is out in the middle of nowhere, I'm curious to know if Tristan will want to remain isolated from the world even after he asks God to lift his curse.

"I wouldn't necessarily say that I like being so far away from civilization," he admits, "but it does have its advantages for me at night. I can remain uncaged without having to worry about unintentionally harming anyone."

"And what do you plan to do once the curse is removed?" Ella asks, never the shy one when it comes to something that she wants to know.

Tristan looks at me before he answers. "I plan to move back to the States and settle down. Where is it that you plan to live, Mae?"

I clear my throat nervously, because I wasn't expecting to be asked the question.

"I can't say that I've decided yet," I reply.

Tristan nods his head like he understands my dilemma. "Whenever you figure it out, let me know."

And that's all he says. He doesn't give me an explanation about why I should let him know, just that I should.

As Tristan strikes up a conversation with Chandler about the type of guitar he's playing, I look over at Ella and see that her mouth is in the shape of a perfect 'O' and her eyes are lit up with excitement. I quickly shake my head at her as I signal that she needs to stop looking so shocked by Tristan's words to me.

Thankfully, we arrive at the corn maze set up by Jess' local fire department a few minutes later. The men and women who volunteer at the station use the money raised from the event to help buy Christmas presents for lower-income families. Not only do they have the maze, but they also have a pumpkin patch with a jack-o-lantern station, a large jumping pillow for the kids, and stalls that sell hot cocoa and kits to make s'mores around the large bonfire. They also set up a miniature pig race that's always good for a laugh or two because everyone picks a favorite to cheer for.

"Wow, I wasn't expecting it to be this large," Tristan says as he hops out of the back of the wagon and onto the ground. He automatically turns around to first help Ella out of the wagon and then me.

"It's their biggest fundraising event," I tell him as the three of us walk over to the entrance of the corn maze.

"Come on, JoJo," I hear Uncle Malcolm say excitedly. I turn my head to see him help her down from their wagon. "We need to go scout out the pigs and pick our winner."

"You act like such a child sometimes," she tells him. The smile on her face tells me that her words are meant as a compliment and not an expression of disapproval. "We better hurry before Brand and Lilly claim the best one."

When we reach the entrance to the maze, Tristan begins to pull out his wallet from the back pocket of the jeans he's wearing, but the volunteer fireman taking the money tells us to go right in because Mason has already donated money to cover all the activities for the members of our party. We thank him and walk into the maze cut within the tall standing of dried corn stalks.

"Why don't you two go that way," Ella says, nodding her head to the left, "and I'll go the other way. If I win, the two of you have to jump on that humongous pillow out there with me."

"And what if we win?" I ask. I know exactly what Ella is doing. She's giving Tristan and me some alone time. I doubt her unsubtle ploy is lost on Tristan either, but he isn't complaining, so I take that as a good sign.

"Then I'll jump on the humongous pillow with the two of you," Ella says with a smile. "It's a win-win situation all the way around if you think about it."

I laugh at her and wish her good luck as she walks in the opposite direction from us.

"I get the feeling she wanted us to spend some time alone together," Tristan says, voicing my exact thoughts and sounding slightly amused by my best friend's role as matchmaker.

"Yeah, she's an expert when it comes to being subtle," I joke.

Tristan laughs while he holds out his right hand for me to take. It's a simple gesture, but it's one that tells me he views us as more than just friends. Earlier in the day when we held hands, I wasn't sure if it meant much to him. I'm not completely sure that it does now either, but from the expectant way he's looking at me I have a feeling this might be the start of something more than merely friendship.

I rest my hand in his and smile when I feel his fingers intertwine with mine intimately.

"How has your life been so far, Mae?" he asks. "I assume it's been good, but I'm really just viewing things from an outsider's perspective."

"I've had a wonderful life," I tell him. "I'm blessed with a family who loves me and friends who would do anything for me."

"Not many people can say that," he replies.

"I know," I say, realizing Tristan is including himself in that group of people without putting it into so many words. "I have a confession to make."

"Really?" he says, looking intrigued to learn my secret. "What's that?"

"While I was growing up, I wanted you to keep your promise and come back to see me, but now that we've met again I'm kind of glad that you didn't."

"Why?" he says in surprise as he looks over to study my face, making me wonder if he hopes to decipher the answer with just a glance.

I hesitate to answer his question because I'm not sure how he'll react, but the decision ends up being taken out of my control.

As Tristan and I make a right turn in the maze, we come face to face with God.

"Hello, Mae and Tristan," He says with a welcoming smile that instantly puts me at ease. "I believe it's time the three of us had a little talk."

During my childhood, I've talked with God on the few occasions He came to visit my mother. To this day, I'm not sure what they talked about, but His visits always seemed to coincide with my mother's bouts of depression. They didn't happen very often, and for some reason I always associated them with something that had to do with Uncle Malcolm. I tried to ask my mom about it once, but she simply brushed my concerns aside and told me that it wasn't anything that I needed to worry about. I never pushed the issue with her because I didn't want to make my mom's melancholy even worse than it was.

As I look at God, I realize this is the first time He's ever sought me out. The mere fact that He's here and wants to speak with both me and Tristan indicates that something important is about to take place and that we'll be in the middle of it. The prospect of having a mission from God of my very own, just like my mother and sister before me, makes me slightly giddy with eagerness.

"Before you get too excited," God says as He meets my gaze, having sensed my keen mood, "I should warn you both that the request I have to make won't be an easy one for either of you, and it will more than likely take the rest of your lives to complete."

"Whatever you need us to do for you can't be any worse than going to alternate Earth," Tristan says, as if his adventures in that strange parallel world were the pinnacle of horrible experiences. "Or can it?"

"I'm afraid the answer to that question isn't up to me," God replies with a great deal of regret. "The only promise I can make is that neither of you will have to leave this reality to accomplish the task I'm about to give you."

"What is it that you want us to do?" I ask.

"I want you to help some of my children find their way back into the light," He states simply. God looks over at Tristan before saying, "When you broke your bond to your father, you proved some of the other Watcher children that such a miracle can take place. There are those who wish to come before Me to ask for forgiveness, but they're afraid to do it on their own. They lack the courage and conviction you were able to muster to follow your heart and not bow down to your father's wishes when he wanted to harm Mae."

"That moment still confuses me," Tristan admits, unknowingly answering a question I had about the incident.

"Do you know why he was able to break his bond to his father?" I ask God. If anyone would know the answer to that mystery, surely it would be the Almighty Himself.

God turns His gaze on Tristan. "Can you tell me what it was you felt when you held Mae in that moment?"

Tristan sighs heavily, and he tightens his grip on my hand as he thinks about his answer.

"I felt like the whole world suddenly opened up," Tristan says as his eyes become slightly unfocused. It's almost as if he's remembering the night we first met in great detail. "When I held her for the first time, my mind became clearer than it had been in centuries, and all of the horrible things my father had asked me to do for him over the years suddenly came crashing down on top of me like a wall of guilt that had been growing all that time. But, when I looked into Mae's eyes, I felt like I had returned home after a long and difficult journey. She was my

pinpoint of light in a world that had been made up of nothing but darkness up until that time. When she said that we were going home, I felt a peace settle over my heart that I had never experienced before. All I knew back then was that I wanted to always feel the way she made me feel in that moment."

After hearing Tristan's explanation of that night from his point of view, I suddenly know what it is that I was born to do.

When I was a child, Caylin would often mention how holding me brought her comfort. I never gave it much thought until this very moment.

"Is that my gift?" I ask God. "Do I bring comfort to those who need it the most?"

"That's part of it," God reveals. "Not only do you bring comfort, but you're also a natural leader, Mae. One of your most unique qualities is that you are able to convey a sense of strength to those who need it, while also allowing them to feel the pure intentions of your heart. It's one reason animals trust you so much. They sense those special qualities about you and instinctively know that you would never hurt them, only guide them to where they need to be."

"Is it because I was in werewolf form that I was able to sense that about Mae?" Tristan asks.

"Yes."

"The other Watcher children who were with us that night," Tristan says, "why didn't they have the same reaction to her that I did?"

"Since you were the one holding her at the time, you were the only one who came into direct contact with the powers she possesses. Also, your heart was ready to accept what she was offering you. That's a key component that can't be coerced in someone, and it will be one of the obstacles that you face when dealing with the others."

"If I touch other Watcher children, will they react the same way Tristan did?"

"More than likely, yes, but like I said, they have to want to change who they are and be open to what you have to offer them," God replies. "Tristan had been contemplating leaving his father's side even before he met you."

I look over at Tristan in surprise. "Is that true?"

Tristan nods. "I had been thinking about it, but actually doing it seemed so crazy to me at the time."

"Yet, you found the strength to leave him," God reminds him. "I believe that if the two of you work together, you will be able to help others who are now in the same position Tristan was back then."

"I'm confused. If it's as easy as me just touching them," I say, "then why did You say that it might take the rest of our lives to accomplish our mission?"

"I also said that the people you're trying to convince to leave their fathers will have to want to do such a thing. That part will take time. Right now, there are only a handful who are ready to accept the guidance you're able to offer them. It's those few I would like for you to go to first. I feel sure that after you guide them back to Me, the others will eventually follow after they have some time to mull over their own fates. As Tristan said, when he contemplated leaving his father on his own, he considered it an insane notion. That's the same exact emotional and mental state these few are in now. They simply need you to lead them, Mae. They don't know it yet, but all they need is for you to nudge them in the right direction."

"It seems like Mae is the one who needs to do all the work," Tristan says. "What's my part in all of this?"

"For one, you know the world the others live in. You understand what it is they're fighting against, and you're the first example they have of what will become of them if they choose to leave their fathers. They'll need your guidance and support, both emotional and financial, just as much as they'll need Mae's leadership. Also, I believe she would benefit greatly from your counsel and encouragement."

After spending so many years assuming Tristan was my soul mate, I have to say that I'm slightly disappointed to have it confirmed that he isn't. If he was, God would have mentioned it just now.

"Tristan, would you mind if I spoke to Mae privately for a moment?" God asks. It's a politely-put request, but we all know that it was more of an order for Tristan to leave us alone for a while.

"Of course not," Tristan say, letting go of my hand and meeting my gaze. "I'll make my way through the rest of the maze and see you on the other side of it when you're finished."

"All right," I agree. "I'll phase out once we're through here."

Tristan begins to leave, and I watch him walk away from us until he turns the next corner and is out of my sight.

I turn my full attention to God and wait for Him to speak.

"I take it you're upset that Tristan isn't your soul mate," He says to me.

"Not necessarily upset," I correct, trying to find the right words to describe how I actually feel, "but I am a little disappointed."

"Why is that?"

God's question catches me slightly off guard. It's a good question. Why does it upset me so much that Tristan isn't my soul mate?

"I'm not sure exactly," I admit. "I suppose I thought that if we were soul mates, it would help explain why he left his father and why we've always had a special connection."

"I do understand the attraction of being able to find your soul mate," God says, "but isn't it also just as magical to be able to choose who you will love? Making a conscious decision to love someone so much that you're willing to spend the rest of your life with him seems just as special to me. When soul mates are meant to be romantically linked, they don't really have a say in the matter. It's simply decided for them by a power neither of them can control. But to be able to choose your lifelong companion is a gift beyond measure."

"I guess I never thought about it like that," I confide. "Since my mom and Caylin were able to marry their soul mates, I just assumed I would end up marrying mine, too."

"Lilly and Caylin's cases were special because each of them needed to meet their soul mates in order to carry out one of their purposes in the universe. You, on the other hand, were given the gift of choice. You can choose to see if Tristan is the man for you, or the two of you can just remain friends, if that is your preference."

"I don't think that decision is strictly left up to me, though," I say, already knowing what I desire. "He has to decide what he wants, too."

"I believe he made his mind up the moment he found you in the woods bleeding," God tells me. "He simply needs to separate the woman you've become from the child version of you that he's lived with in his mind for all these years."

"I guess I didn't think about it like that," I admit. "It must be strange for him to see me all grown up."

"Strange and wonderful," God adds. "Intellectually, he knew you would have aged after all these years, but seeing the result of so much time passing has thrown him for a bit of a loop. I don't believe he expected to be as attracted to you as he is now."

"Really?" I ask, feeling my cheeks grow warm as my lips stretch into a pleased smile that I just can't stop. "You think he's attracted to me?"

God smiles indulgently. "I would have to say that observation is a painfully obvious one, and not something that he's necessarily trying to keep hidden."

I mull over what God has said and can only see one thing that might derail the relationship I hope to develop with Tristan.

"You mentioned that there are a few Watcher children who are ready to leave their fathers," I say. "Can you tell me if Jasper is included in that small group?"

"In time, you will meet those who are ready to accept your help," God answers. "I'm afraid that's all I can tell you right now, Mae."

"It sounds like you're counting on me to work a small miracle with these people." I begin to feel the first tingles of doubt that I won't be able to live up to the high standards God has set for me, but I keep in mind that He never gives people more than they can handle.

"Can you answer one other question for me?"

"Perhaps," He replies, as if He's teasing me. I know from overhearing my parents and Uncle Malcolm talk about their conversations with God that He can be rather mysterious and frustrating with His responses. He doesn't often give people a straight answer to their questions. With this information in mind, I temper my expectations.

"My gift," I begin, "does it come from my mother's father? All of his descendants are able to control the Watcher children to an extent."

"Partially," God tells me. "However, your ability is different from everyone else's. I made a special request to the Guardian of the Guf who molded your soul, and asked her to imbue it with the light of peace to warm the hearts of those around you."

"Thank You for that," I tell Him. "I'm grateful You considered me worthy of such a gift."

"I know you will use it wisely," He encourages. "Now, why don't you join the others? I believe I've monopolized enough of your time this evening."

"Am I allowed to tell my parents about this meeting?" I ask Him before He phases away.

"Of course you are. And if I may be so bold, I would also encourage you to tell them about your plans to help Tristan find his family. Your journey with him is crucial to the work I would like for you to start. By doing that, it will bring you into contact with the people who are ready to follow your lead and accept your help."

"I've never seen myself as a leader," I confess. It's not a protest made because I'm modest about myself. It's simply not a role I ever saw myself being thrust into.

"In time, I believe you'll understand just how strong you are, Mae. There are loved ones around you now who see it, and as those numbers grow you'll finally realize you were destined to lead those who need a strong voice to follow. Always believe in yourself, especially when darker forces would have you doubt your abilities and try to weaken you with uncertainty. I know you will succeed in your mission. Now, it's time for you to believe it, too."

With those parting words, God phases back to Heaven, leaving me alone inside a maze carved out of cornstalks. I stand completely still for a few seconds, allowing myself time to absorb what just happened.

In essence, God just gave me the job of saving the souls of the few Watcher children who remain here on Earth. It's a hefty burden to lay on the shoulders of anyone, but when you factor in the added strengths He imbued my soul with, I don't believe it's an unachievable goal. My parents have always encouraged us kids to believe in ourselves and never doubt that we can accomplish whatever we set our minds to do. I can't say I've ever second-guessed myself, and I'm not about to start now.

When I hear the far-off ring of Ella's laughter, I'm reminded that I told Tristan I would phase to the exit of the corn maze to rejoin him.

I phase to a point near the exit and walk out to find him and Ella laughing at something that was undoubtedly said between them.

"What's so funny?" I ask them both.

They look over at me with welcoming smiles that could warm even the coldest of hearts.

"I was just telling Tristan about the family sleepover we have the night before Thanksgiving at your mom's house. I invited him to join us and just warned him about what my mom might be wearing to it."

I'm a little taken aback that Ella would invite Tristan to what is traditionally an immediate-family-only event, but I can't say that I'm upset with her for doing it. Perhaps she thought that if the invitation came from her instead of me, there wouldn't be any way for Tristan to feel obligated to come.

"Ella says she dressed up in a manatee onesie last year," Tristan says, sounding amused by the mental imagery.

"I think she's just trying to figure out what my Fae form is," Ella says with a shake of her head at her mother's antics. "Apparently, I'm a late bloomer among my kind. I still haven't transformed into an animal yet."

"It'll come," I reassure Ella as I place a comforting arm across her shoulders and give her a small hug. "Sometimes you just can't rush perfection."

"See," Ella says to Tristan as she hugs me back, "this is why I love Mae so much. She always sees the bright side of things."

I kiss Ella on the cheek right before letting her go.

When I look over at Tristan, he has a thoughtful look on his face. I'm not sure what he's thinking, but I do know it's nothing bad. His expression is warm and there's a yearning quality to his mien that tells me he could use a hug too. Although I wouldn't mind giving him one, it doesn't seem like the right time for such an intimate act between the two of us. We haven't even spent a whole twenty-four hours together yet, and there's still plenty of fun left for all of us to have together.

"Come on, you two," Ella says, grabbing one of my hands and pulling me behind her as she begins to walk towards the large air-filled pillow that all the young children present are jumping on. "Let's go bounce on that thing. The little kids shouldn't be the only ones to have all the fun."

I can't help but laugh at her enthusiasm to look ridiculous participating in a kid's activity, but neither Tristan nor I make a protest. Just like every year, jumping on the oversized pillow is only step one of Ella's plans for the evening.

When the horn blows to signal the start of the pig race, we all walk over to the small ring that the baby pigs will run around. Each of them is wearing a different color kerchief around their necks to identify them. As soon as they're released from their starting pins, everyone begins to cheer for their favorite. Uncle Malcolm is the most vocal of us as he and JoJo urge the pig wearing pink to outrun its fellow competitors. The couple who picked the winning pig ends up being Jess and Mason, who promptly kiss when their chosen pig crosses the finish line. JoJo consoles my uncle over their loss with a pat on the back, and is able to cheer him up with the promise of a cup of hot chocolate.

Our next stop is the pumpkin patch, which is quickly followed by spending half an hour carving the picked pumpkins into something to commemorate the Thanksgiving season. Both Ella and I cut out a simple 'Happy Thanksgiving' in our pumpkins, while Tristan carves the head of a howling wolf.

"That looks a lot like the logo we use for our pizza company, love," I hear my eldest sister, Abby, tell Tristan as she stands behind us while we're still seated at the pumpkin-carving station.

I immediately stand from my chair and give her a hug, since we haven't had a chance to talk yet.

"Where's Sebastian?" I ask, knowing that her husband, who is Uncle Malcolm's son, wouldn't miss the yearly gathering. Although their children, endearingly called 'the pack' by my uncle, don't usually come to this event anymore, my big sister and Sebastian always make time to join us.

"He's talking with his father about the football game," she tells me with a small exasperated shake of her head. "You know how seriously they take it." Abby looks back at Tristan. "I heard you'll be participating in the game this year, Tristan. I hope you know what you've signed up for."

Tristan grins. "I'm starting to believe I should have declined the offer when Brand and Xavier made it, but," Tristan glances in my direction, "I think I made a better impression on them by accepting."

"If you help them win, they'll love you forever," Abby declares with one of her signature giggles. "I just came over here to see if the three of you are ready for the S'mores More part of the evening."

"S'mores More?" Tristan questions, looking confused by the term. "What in the world is that?"

"Basically, we just sit around the bonfire, eat s'mores, and tell each other what we want more of from the next year," Ella explains.

"I'm up for some chocolate and marshmallows," he replies as he stands from his seat.

"Come on, love," Abby says to Tristan as she loops an arm around one of his, "let's go get the s'mores kits." Abby looks over at me and says, "We'll meet you over by the fire in a bit, sweetie."

I watch as Abby basically absconds with Tristan towards the s'more station. I instantly miss his presence by my side, and hope that my sister doesn't intend to keep him away for very long.

"He'll be back," Ella reassures me, having apparently read my expression with her usual accuracy. "Come on. Let's go grab our spots by the fire so we don't have to stand."

I let Ella lead me away, but I take one last look back towards Tristan. When I do I see that he's looking back at me as well, which gives me a reason to smile.

Ella and I sit down on one of the logs around the fire, leaving room in between us for Tristan to sit when he joins us. Directly across from where we're sitting I spy Will, his wife Amanda, and their two children. I wave at my sister-in-law and immediately receive a wave back.

"Is this my seat?" I hear Tristan ask a few moments later as he walks up behind us.

"It is if you brought us some s'mores kits," Ella declares.

Tristan hands her one, but it doesn't stay in her grasp for very long.

"Oh no, you don't," I hear Aunt Tara say with her usual sassiness as she snatches the ziplocked kit out of her daughter's hands.

"Mom," Ella whines in disappointment as she watches her dream of a gooey s'more be taken away. "One won't hurt me."

"That might be true," Aunt Tara agrees. "But one step off the diet train will just lead you down a trail of 'oh, one won't hurt'. Before you know it you'll be off your diet, and all the hard work you've put in so far will have been for nothing. So, no, sweet child of mine. I won't just stand here and let you fall off the wagon for a few minutes of sugary bliss."

"She's right, Ella," I say, handing Aunt Tara my own bag of s'mores supplies. "And since you're not going to eat any, I won't either."

"Then I guess you'd better just take mine, too," Tristan says in solidarity of our support of Ella.

"I knew I liked you for a reason," Aunt Tara says as she looks at Tristan with approval. "Now, the three of you should use this time to put your thinking caps on. You don't want to be struggling for an answer when it's your turn to tell us what you want more of next year."

"I already know what I'm going to say," Tristan tells her.

"Well, look at you overachieving," my aunt teases him. "I swear, you're just as cute as I remember you, Tristan. It's like you haven't aged a day."

Tristan looks slightly uncomfortable with the reminder. The children of the Watchers do age, but at a very slow rate. Tristan may look like he's in his early 20s, but he's actually much older.

"Can I have everyone's attention please?" we hear my mother say, breaking the sudden tension that developed after Aunt Tara's statement. "While everyone toasts their marshmallows and eats their s'mores, I think we should start our tradition of saying what we each want more of in the coming year. I'll start it off and then we'll go clockwise around the fire, so everyone has a turn. What I would love to have more of this coming year is grandchildren."

My mother eyes Caylin and Amanda in particular as she makes her statement, causing both women to blush profusely.

"I'm getting a little old, Mom," Caylin protests.

"Nonsense. I had Ariana and Xavier when I was around your age," my mother reminds her.

"I'm always up for the challenge," Aiden declares, realizing a little too late that his words could be taken a different way from what he intended, especially in this crowd.

"You might be 'up' for it," Caylin says as she smiles at her husband's sudden embarrassment, "but I don't know if my body is. We'll see."

"That isn't a definite no," my mom points out as she smiles at my sister. "I'll take it."

My mother turns her gaze on Amanda, waiting for her response.

Amanda is a shy creature when it comes to speaking to a crowd, and being singled out by my mother probably isn't helping matters.

"Well," Amanda says, looking over at Will, "we were going to wait until Thanksgiving Day to tell you, but I suppose now is as good a time as any. You'll be getting your wish for another grandchild next June."

When I hear a squeal, I assume it's my mother, but when I look over I see it actually came from my Aunt Tara. My parents and Aunt Tara walk over to Will and Amanda to congratulate them on the latest addition to the ever-growing Cole family.

As more and more people take their turns saying what they want more of this year, I try to decide what I should say when it's my time to speak. It doesn't seem to take very long before I hear Ella make her declaration.

"I want to lose more weight," she says, looking to Tristan as a silent signal that he's next.

"I want to spend more time with the people I care about the most," he declares as he looks over at me. In this situation, I'm not sure if he's including me in his wish or if he's simply signaling that it's my turn to speak.

"I want..." I begin, but falter because I'm not sure if now is the right time to reveal my mission from God to the others. I quickly decide that it isn't because it would simply disrupt things. "I want to be able to help all creatures great and small more."

It was true, and included my desire to see God's plan for me through without saying it in so many words.

JoJo follows me, but I feel the stares of my parents even before I look over at them. I can instantly tell that they know something is up with me. My hesitation in saying what I wanted more of was a tell-tale sign to them that I was holding back something important. I know as soon as everyone has finished saying what they want more of, my parents will come over to find out what's wrong. I feel nervous and excited all at the same time. I know they'll view my mission as dangerous, but I see it as a way to continue a family tradition of serving God and following through with His plan for us all. Not many people have the chance to meet the Creator of the universe and carry out a personal request that He makes. I feel privileged that He views me as an important part of His overall plan.

Just as I thought, my parents stand from their seats as soon as everyone has said what they want more of during the coming new year and walk over to me.

"Can we speak to you alone for a moment?" my mom asks me.

"I think it might be better if Tristan was included in this discussion," I tell them. "He's a part of it, too."

My mother nods her understanding.

"What's going on, Mae?" Ella asks, confused by the sudden serious turn of the evening.

"I'll explain it to you later," I promise her before following my parents and Tristan to a more secluded spot over by the wagons we rode in on.

"What's happened?" my father asks once we're all gathered together.

I take the lead and tell them exactly what God told Tristan and me in the corn maze. As I suspected, my parents look worried about the mission God has given us.

"I had hoped you would be spared from all this," my mother says, unable to hide her distress over the quest I've been given by God. "I thought perhaps you had served your purpose when you helped Tristan break his bond with his father."

"Apparently, God thinks I can help the other Watcher children break their bonds as well. It could be that, by helping them, the other Watchers who are still working with Lucifer will see the light and ask God for forgiveness, too. I think they just need to be reminded of who they once were and who they can be again."

"Still," my father says, not looking the least bit pleased by my new mission, "it's dangerous, Mae. Did my Father happen to say whether or not He gave you a guardian angel like He has Caylin's descendants?"

I know that my brother's namesake and my mother's childhood friend, Will Kilpatrick, was made Caylin's guardian angel. I clearly remember my big sister's story about him bringing her back to life after a run-in with one of the princes of Hell. According to him, he will be the guardian angel of every first-born female child of their family line. Kate holds that dubious distinction now, and will until she and Luke have their first child, which is destined to be a girl who will carry on the line of descendants.

"He didn't mention one," I tell my father. "But He did hint that my mission would take a long time to accomplish, so that must mean He expects me to live for quite a while. I don't know if that makes you feel any better, but to be honest, I'm not worried about my safety. The two of you know that He never gives us more than we can handle, and I know that I was born to do this. I can help these people find their way back to Him. I don't have any doubt that I can, and neither should you."

"It still won't make us worry any less," my mother says with a sigh of resignation. "And, of course, we know you're right, but we're also your parents, Mae. We'll worry about your safety regardless."

"I'll be by Mae's side to help protect her," Tristan pledges. "I doubt that will make you worry any less, but I hope it eases your minds at least a little bit."

"It helps," my dad says, "but you're right. We'll still worry."

My parents silently consider Tristan for a moment.

"Would you mind giving us a minute alone with Mae?" my mother asks him.

"Of course," Tristan says. "I'm sure you have a lot to discuss."

Tristan bows slightly at the waist, out of respect for my parents, and turns to leave. Once he's out of hearing range, I return my attention to my folks and wait for them to say what's on their minds.

"Mae," my dad begins, "we've been wondering about your relationship with Tristan."

"No," I tell them, already knowing what their real question is, "he isn't my soul mate."

"Really?" my mother asks, looking stunned by my revelation. "You're certain about that?"

I nod. "Yes. I already knew that he wasn't, but God confirmed it for me when He spoke with us earlier. He said He gave me the gift of choice concerning who I decide to spend the rest of my life with."

"That's interesting," my dad says, looking as confused as my mother about the situation. "I guess we all just assumed he would be, since he broke his bond to his father for you. But then again, with this new information you just gave us, I suppose the other Watcher children couldn't also be your soul mate."

"How do you feel about that?" my mother asks with a concerned look. "Are you upset that the two of you don't share that type of connection?"

I pause for a moment to collect my thoughts and to put my emotions into perspective.

"Honestly, I was disappointed at first," I admit. "But after I talked with God about it, I realized that it doesn't matter whether or not he's my soul mate. Plus, it gives us a chance to get to know one another better. I feel like I'm okay with it now."

My parents don't look convinced. I suppose since they're soul mates, the concept of not instantly falling in love with someone is a strange concept to them.

"Then I assume we should start getting used to seeing Tristan around more," my dad says. "Even if God didn't pair you up to help the other Watcher children, he would probably be a permanent fixture in our family regardless."

"I guess we'll see," I say. "I can't really speak for Tristan, only myself."

"And what is it that you hope happens between the two of you?" my mother asks.

"Whatever is meant to," is the best answer I can give her.

"Then I suppose you should get back to him, so you can figure out what that is sooner rather than later," she suggests with an encouraging smile.

"I probably should," I agree. "I'll see you both later back at the house."

"Do you know what time you'll be home?" my dad asks. Even though I'm of an age where I don't need my parents' permission to stay out late, I will always respect them enough to ease their worries over my welfare.

"I won't be late getting home, but I'll probably take Tristan back to Jered's house once we're through here."

"Have fun, then. We'll be waiting for you back home," my father says, satisfied with my answer.

I turn away from my parents to walk over to Tristan, who is sitting back on the log beside Ella, having a conversation. I hate the fact that my mission will cause my parents worry, but they're no strangers to following God's plan. In fact, it was because of His plan for them that they found one another, and everyone who matters knows how well that turned out.

Chapter 8

By the time the festivities come to an end, I realize Tristan and I haven't had much time to spend alone. I was hoping we could find a moment or two to get to know one another better, but since our trip through the corn maze was interrupted we haven't had another opportunity to speak privately. As everyone else is climbing back into the wagons, I make a unilateral decision.

"I'm going to phase Tristan back to Jered's house," I tell Ella as Tristan helps her back into the cart.

"You're not coming back to Jess' house to have hot chocolate?" Ella asks in surprise. She knows how much I love Mason's homemade hot chocolate, and my willingness to pass up the once-a-year treat should be a testament to her that I'm desperate to find an excuse to be alone with Tristan.

"Maybe you can tell my mom to take some home for me," I suggest.

"I'll do that. Have fun, you two," Ella says with an understanding smile.

Before she has a chance to say anything that might make things even more awkward, I take hold of Tristan's left arm and phase him to the living room in Jered's Montana home. Once we're there, I'm not quite sure what to do next. Thankfully, he does.

"I may not be able to duplicate what Mason makes," he tells me, "but Jered usually keeps some powered Abuelita in his kitchen."

"Abuelita?" I ask. "I'm not sure I know what that is."

"Then, come on," Tristan says with an eager smile as he takes hold of one of my hands. "Let me make you one and you can tell me if it's as good as what Mason serves."

As I follow Tristan to the kitchen he continues to hold my hand until we reach it, and only then does he let it go so he can start heating up some milk on the stove. I sit down at the bar built into the kitchen island where the stove is, and watch him stir the cold milk in a copper pot over a gas burner.

"You seem to know your way around this kitchen pretty well," I comment. "Do you spend a lot of time here?"

"I have during the past few years," he says as he continues to stir the contents of the pot with a wooden spoon. "Jered's been forcing me to be more social. He said I was becoming a hermit, living out in my cabin alone for so long."

"Didn't you get lonely out there all by yourself?"

Tristan shrugs. "After a while, you get used to it. There's a certain harmony to being on your own for a long time. It's almost like time stands still. I found it calming, but Jered just thought I was trying to hide because I was failing so miserably with my family."

"I would imagine God's quest for us has given you some newfound hope where they're concerned."

Tristan meets my gaze. "It has. I hope my brother is one of the Watcher children He was talking about."

"I asked Him about that," I admit. When Tristan looks at me with hope in his eyes, it makes me immediately regret having mentioned my question to God. "He wouldn't tell me if Jasper is one of the ones He was talking about. I'm sorry. I can see that I just got your hopes up that I had an answer to your question."

"Don't be sorry," he tells me. "I should have known God wouldn't give you an outright answer. He almost never does."

"That doesn't mean that Jasper isn't ready, though," I point out. "We just have to wait and see what happens."

"Do you mind me asking what else God told you after I left?"

"He didn't really say much more than what He told the two of us," I say, leaving out the whole conversation I had with God about Tristan and me not being soul mates.

As Tristan continues to stir the milk in the pot, I ask him to tell me about his work with Habitat for Humanity. Not only do I learn that Tristan is a master builder, but I also learn he can speak several languages fluently. I suppose having lived for as long as he has, he picked up certain skills during that time. I find his enthusiasm for helping others intoxicating, which leads me to tell him about my work with animals and all the time I've spent with Kallie at her veterinary clinic.

"Isn't Kallie's clinic close to where Jess lives?" Tristan asks as he pours the steaming hot milk into two blue stoneware mugs painted with white snowflakes.

"Yes. That's how Jess met her. She was taking care of Faison's dog while she and Zack went on vacation, and he ate some chocolate that Brynlee had left out."

"Did the dog survive?"

"Yeah. He was fine after all that chocolate passed through his system. Jess decided it had to be divine intervention, though, because the next day she took Chandler over there to meet Kallie."

"How did she know Kallie was the one for Chandler?"

I shrug. "I don't have a clue. She just did. I guess she had enough of a sixth sense to play matchmaker between the two of them. Jess told me that Chandler needed someone who would ground him and not look at him as a 'rock star'. Kallie is definitely that sort of person. She isn't someone who is easily impressed by how famous or rich someone is."

"It certainly seems to have worked out for them. How long have they been married?"

"Going on twelve years now, if memory serves me correctly."

I watch as Tristan uses a spoon to mix the dried chocolate packet he already placed in the mugs with the milk. Once he's satisfied, he places the spoon in the sink and begins rummaging through the cabinets in the kitchen.

"Are you looking for something in particular?" I ask him, curious to find out what it is he's searching for.

"Yes, I am," he answers, but doesn't give me any more information than that.

After another minute of searching, I hear him say, "Aha!"

I strain my neck to try to see what it is he's found, but he closes the door before I can sneak a peek.

"Would you mind taking the mugs back into the living room?" he asks me sweetly.

"Sure," I reply, drawing the word out because I'm suddenly suspicious of the request. "Will you be joining me in there any time soon?"

He nods his head. "I'll be there. Just give me a couple of minutes to put something together."

"Okay," I say, more curious now than I was before about the reason behind his request.

I pick the two mugs up by their handles and make my way to the living room. A couple of minutes later, Tristan joins me with a large platter in his hands. I begin to laugh when I see what's neatly arranged on its surface.

"I guess I wasn't the only one who was disappointed that we didn't get to make s'mores," I say, seeing that Tristan has brought all the makings for the delectable treats in for us. "All we need now is a fire."

"Coming right up!" Tristan declares as he sets the tray onto the large coffee table in the room and immediately makes his way over towards the fireplace.

"Would you like some help?"

"Sure. Can you wad up some of those newspapers for me?" he says, nodding his head toward a small pile of papers next to the stack of wood.

In no time at all, we have a roaring fire just begging us to let its flames toast our marshmallows for us.

As we sit on the raised hearth of the fireplace, toasting our first marshmallows, I ask Tristan, "Have you ever made s'mores before?"

He tilts his head slightly as he considers the question. "You know, come to think of it, this will be the first time I've had one."

I can't help but smile because I'm happy we're able to share this experience together. Sure, making s'mores isn't an earth-shattering event, but it does tell me that even though Tristan has lived a very long time, there are still things we can do together that will be firsts for him.

"What else haven't you done in your life?" I ask him.

"I'm sure there're lots of things," he says with a shrug. "What about you? Is there something you've never done but always wanted to?"

Fall in love is the answer that immediately comes to my mind, but I keep that particular 'first' to myself, at least for now.

"I've never climbed Mt. Everest," I say.

"Been there done that. It's cold," Tristan laughs.

"Duly-noted," I reply, unable to stop myself from giggling.

"Uh, Mae," he says, looking into the fire. "I think your marshmallow is ready."

I was so wrapped up in talking with Tristan that I completely forgot about my marshmallow. When I turn to look at it, I see that it's now a ball of fire at the end of my stick.

"And the family curse strikes again," I comment disappointedly, unsure what I should do with it now since the thing is struggling to stay on my wooden skewer. It turns out gravity has the answer, as the molten blob of burnt sugar falls onto the top log of the stack. Tristan quickly lays his skewer on his plate and opens the flue to give the resulting smoke of my gourmet disaster a larger escape route.

"Sorry about that," I say, cringing with embarrassment on the inside. "Can I blame my mother for that one? It's her genes that transformed us all into inept cooks."

Tristan laughs. "I heard about the Turducken Incident of 2035. What in the world made her decide to try to cook that?"

"To this day, I have no idea," I admit. "But it's a Thanksgiving that we'll all remember for the rest of our lives."

I watch my poor marshmallow as it continues to bubble up and be charred by the heat of the flames.

Tristan sits back down and grabs his mug of hot chocolate to take a sip.

"Jess would probably disown me for burning my marshmallow."

Suddenly, I hear Tristan make a choking noise right before he spits the hot chocolate in his mouth into the fire.

He begins to chuckle as he wipes his wet lips with the back of his hand.

"Wait," I say, realizing something by his reaction. "Do you know what that code word means? Ella and I finally figured out what 'matches' meant when we were sixteen, but we still haven't deciphered what marshmallow refers to."

Tristan immediately begins to shake his head. "I can't go there with you, Mae. You're going to have to ask someone else to explain it."

"Oh, come on!" I whine. "It can't be that bad. Just tell me."

Tristan shakes his head even more vigorously. "Seriously, I just can't. Trust me when I tell you that you're better off asking Jess or Kallie. Don't ask your mom. She probably wouldn't tell you either."

I huff slightly in disappointment, but I don't push the issue. Tristan already looks uncomfortable enough about the subject, and we're supposed to be using this time to get to know one another better.

Tristan quickly assembles a s'more from his perfectly-toasted marshmallow and hands it to me.

"I can make one for myself," I tell him. "I swear it."

"Take this one," he urges, continuing to hold it out for me. "I want you to have the first one."

I accept the kindness of his gesture, but immediately break it in half and hand him part of it.

"Let's eat it together. That way we can share your first s'more at the same time."

Tristan accepts my offering and takes his first bite. When I see his eyes light up, I know we've found a new treat that he'll enjoy from this day forward.

As we sit and eat s'mores while drinking our hot chocolate, Tristan ends up asking me a ton of questions about my life so far. Normally, when people begin asking me questions I clam up, because my life is not a book that can be opened to many people. Since Tristan is a part of the unique world I live in, I feel a freedom in speaking with him that I don't usually get with members of the opposite sex who aren't directly related to me in one fashion or another. The majority of people in my life aren't linked to me by blood. Most are people my parents have chosen to surround me with, such as my Uncle Malcolm and Aunt Tara. I find it impossible to fathom a life without either one of them in it. They've influenced who I've become just as much as my parents and siblings have. I feel fortunate to have such a large extended family to call my own, and I wouldn't want it any other way.

"Do you see yourself having a big family one day?" Tristan asks me unexpectedly.

"I haven't really thought about it too much," I admit. "I want children, but I don't believe in putting a number on such things. I think there are advantages to having one child, as well as a whole pack of children like Abby and Sebastian. I'm sure when the time comes I'll know what's right for me. How about you? Do you want a lot of kids?"

"I guess I haven't allowed myself to think that far ahead," Tristan admits. "I've been concentrating on fixing my family for so long, I haven't let myself consider the possibility of starting one of my own. I want to, but I need to know that I've done everything I can to help my brother first."

"And your father?" I ask, curious to know if saving his dad is something he's willing to spend even more years of his life endeavoring to do.

Tristan lowers his gaze from mine. "I guess it's my brother I'm more concerned about. I know there's still good in him, Mae. I just need to find a way to tap into it. Does that sound crazy? Am I just deluding myself by holding out hope that I can help him?"

"I don't think you're crazy. I think you just love your brother. If I were in your shoes, I can't imagine abandoning any of my brothers or sisters either. What you're trying to do is noble, but I also believe you've earned the right to have a life of your own. For some reason I get the feeling you don't think you deserve happiness."

"It's not so much that," he says. Tristan pauses as he collects his thoughts before continuing. "I feel like I've done everything God has wanted me to do, and with this new mission that He gave us I know now that He believes I've earned my forgiveness."

"You don't have to earn forgiveness, Tristan. You just have to ask for it."

"I realize that, but you also need to understand that I used to be someone who killed people for the sport of it. I don't just feel a deep-set need to earn God's forgiveness, but also the forgiveness of those I killed because my father told me to do it. Now, I feel like I can face those people in Heaven one day, knowing I did everything I could to earn a place at their side. Does that make sense to you?"

I nod. "Yes. I can understand that."

"I want my brother to have the same peace of mind, but he has to want to be forgiven first. Sometimes, when I'm with him, I feel like he's right on the edge of breaking his bond to our father. Considering what God said about you, I'm hoping you can help sway his heart just enough to do that."

"From what God said, it sounds like the Watcher children need to be in their werewolf form for my gift to fully work on them. I'm not sure how we're going to do that. Do you have any ideas? Are any of them kept somewhere that we can get to easily?"

"I can think of one way, but I don't know how to get the information we need to make it work."

I sit up straighter, feeling hopeful that our mission might not be a fool's errand.

"What kind of information do we need?" I ask eagerly.

"There's a game that the Watchers like to play. It's called Bait."

"I've heard of it," I say, nodding my head. "My Aunt Tara was wounded in a game like that. She still has the scar on her neck to prove it. Is it something that happens at specified times during the year?"

"See, that's the problem," Tristan says with a resigned sigh. "It's random now. They used to meet on specific days, but that's when there were a lot of Watchers who allowed their children to play. Now, there're only a few and they get together whenever the mood strikes them."

"Uncle Malcolm may be able to help us," I say, which earns me an immediate shake of Tristan's head.

"I'm not so sure he will, Mae. Like you said earlier, he's extremely overprotective."

"Yeah, but that was before we were given direct orders from God to help these people. Even Uncle Malcolm won't argue against a mission sanctioned by his Father."

"I'll let you handle that since you know him a lot better than I do."

"I'm sure my mom has already told him about the mission God gave us, when they returned to Jess and Mason's house. She doesn't keep many secrets from him, especially not about something this important. If anyone can convince him to help us with our mission, it's her. She's basically the only person he listens to."

"Well, hello, Mae," we hear Jered say as he walks into the room. "Kind of late for you to be here, isn't it?"

"What time is it?" I ask him.

"Almost two o'clock in the morning," he tells me.

I immediately stand up. "I had no idea it was that late. I need to go home."

"And you," Jered says to Tristan, "need to go downstairs and allow the transformation to take place. I'm surprised you didn't realize how late it was getting."

"I did," Tristan admits, looking only slightly ashamed. "But I didn't want Mae to have to leave so soon. It's been a long time since I was able to talk to someone without having to watch what I said."

I feel my heart flutter with joy when I hear Tristan's words. I realize he and I are very much alike in a lot of ways. We both have our own secrets to hide away from the world, but with each other we're able to eliminate those barriers and just be ourselves. It's an addictive feeling, and I know it's something I'll want to feel more than once.

"I really should be going," I say to Tristan, unable to conceal my regret over having to leave. "If I know my parents, they're probably waiting for me to get home."

"I'm surprised your mom didn't come here herself to check up on you," Tristan says.

"They wouldn't invade my privacy like that unless there was an emergency back home," I tell him. "My parents do worry, but they also trust me."

"What time would you like to get together tomorrow?" Tristan asks me.

I notice that he doesn't say that we'll be searching for his family tomorrow morning in front of Jered, so I don't mention it either.

"We usually have our family breakfast around eight o'clock. Would it be all right if I came over around nine o'clock?"

"Sounds good," he says.

There's an awkward silence between the two of us. I'm not exactly sure if I should hug him, shake his hand, or do nothing at all before I go. If Jered wasn't watching us, the dilemma would most likely include a kiss of some sort, but since he's staring straight at us that option is definitely out the window.

"I'll see you in the morning," I say to Tristan. "I hope you sleep well."

"You, too, Mae. See you in the morning."

I look over at Jered, and notice him darting his eyes between me and Tristan with a look of amusement on his face.

"See you later, Jered."

Jered smiles. "See you later, Mae."

I phase to the living room in my mother's Colorado home. Just as I suspected, my parents are there waiting for me, but it looks like they both fell asleep doing so. I debate whether I should wake them up to let them know I'm home, but they look so comfortable snuggled up together underneath the quilt on the couch that I just don't have the heart to do it. Instead, I find a piece of paper and a pencil in the kitchen and write them a short note letting them know that I made it home, and that I'm in my room sleeping. I leave the letter on the coffee table in front of the couch and make my way upstairs to my bedroom.

As soon as I lie down on my bed, my mind begins to race with thoughts of Tristan and the night we just spent together. In my heart, I know he's the one for me. We've known each other almost all my life, even if we weren't together during the short time I've been on Earth. Each of us has had the knowledge of the other for several years, and now that we're finally back together again I can't imagine ever letting him go. Keeping in mind God's plan for us, I have hope that He knows we belong together, just like I do.

Even though I'm physically exhausted, I find it impossible to go to sleep. I can't seem to stop thinking about Tristan, and I know there's only one way to calm my mind enough for me to finally find rest. I quickly sit up in bed and put my tennis shoes back on. When I stand, I phase myself to the living room in Jered's house.

"Hello, Mae," Jered says to me from his spot on the couch, startling me by his unexpected presence. Although, this is his house. I suppose it's me who's the unexpected one here. He looks puzzled by my late visit, as well he should, and immediately asks, "Is something wrong? Is there trouble back at your house?"

"No," I say, wishing I had thought my plan through a little bit better instead of acting on impulse. "I couldn't sleep, so I thought I would come back to see if Tristan was still awake."

It's then that I hear the first howl. The plaintive cry tears a piece of my heart out because I know who's making it.

"He's down in his room right now," Jered tells me, also looking distraught by the sound Tristan just made. "You know he has to change form once a day or he'll die."

"Yes, I know that," I answer, wondering if it's too late to just phase back home and pretend that I didn't come here at all.

Before I have a chance to act on my impulse, and just as another one of Tristan's howls fills the air, Jered stands to his feet.

"That was Tristan, right?" I ask. After receiving a nod from Jered I have to ask, "Why does he sound like he's in pain?"

"He doesn't like being locked up like an animal," he explains, just as we hear another one of Tristan's plaintive cries. "Follow me. I'll take you to where he's staying."

"Are you sure?" I ask.

"I think that's probably a question I should be asking you," he says kindly. "Are you sure you want to see him in his werewolf form?"

"It's how I dream about him most of the time," I confess. "It doesn't bother me. Do you think it will bother him if I see him like that?"

"I guess there's only one way to find out," Jered replies, turning to walk out of the room.

It seems impolite not to follow him, so I do.

Jered walks me through his home, towards the back. Surprisingly, we walk out the back door and onto the porch.

"Where exactly is his room?" I ask him, finding it unlikely that Jered would stick Tristan outside.

"It's in the basement, but the only way to access his room is from the exterior," Jered explains. "I didn't want to run the risk of someone accidentally stumbling across the room while he was in his werewolf form."

I follow Jered down a set of spiral stone steps leading from his back porch to the basement level, all the while having to listen to Tristan's pained howls. A bronze, lantern-style wall sconce is mounted by a thick iron door, and is the only source of light illuminating the small area. The door itself has no knob. The only marking on the smooth grey surface is a single keyhole in its center. Jered pulls a key from his pants pocket and slides it into the hole.

"Wouldn't it have been easier to just phase me inside the room?" I ask him.

"It would have," he agrees, "but I wanted to give you time to rethink going in there. Are you sure you still want to see him, Mae?"

I don't even hesitate with my answer. "Yes, I'm sure."

Jered unlocks the door and pushes it open, making one simple request.

"If he does anything that seems the least bit off to you, promise me you'll phase out immediately."

"I will," I assure him, "but you don't have to worry, Jered. Tristan would never harm me no matter what form he's in."

From the look of doubt on Jered's face I can tell he isn't as sure as I am. However, he's willing to give me the benefit of the doubt in this matter considering my track record with Tristan.

After I step inside the dark room, Jered shuts and locks the door behind me. As I peer into the darkness, straining against the pitch-black to locate Tristan, I hear a deep guttural growl echo off the metal walls of the room. It takes a minute for my eyes to adjust to the scant light available; I soon realize that there are a multitude of miniature pinpoint lights embedded in the ceiling that are arranged like the constellations in the night sky above us. I feel something swipe at my leg, causing me to lose my balance and fall to the floor.

Tristan, now in full wolf form, pounces on me, pressing my shoulders down to the cold metal floor with his front paws. His hot breath washes over my face as we stare at one another.

"Tristan," I say to him, doing my best not to lose my nerve and phase out of the room, "it's me...Mae."

Tristan growls at me but moves his paws to a point on the floor right above my shoulders, releasing his hold. I can see the glistening of his eyes as he looks at me, like he's confused by my presence in the room.

Cautiously, so as not to frighten him, I lift my right hand and slowly place it palm- down on the center of his forehead.

"You know me," I say to him in a soothing voice. "Do you remember when I did this to you when I was a little girl?"

Tristan doesn't move or even make a sound as I begin to stroke the length of his snout. He remains stock-still above me, and I take it as a good sign that he's allowing me to caress him.

"I remember doing something else that first night we met," I tell him. "I sang you a song. Do you remember that?"

Tristan snorts, as if that's his answer to my question.

I begin to sing "Over the Rainbow" to him just like I did that first night I brought him home with me. I feel the tension in Tristan's body lessen and eventually he lifts his paws from my shoulders, so I can sit up. I feel the presence of a wall behind me and scoot closer to it until I'm able to use it to rest my back against.

As I continue to sing to him, he inches closer until he's able to curl up beside me and lay his head in my lap. I begin to stroke the side of his wolf-like face and continue to sing until his breathing becomes even as he falls sound asleep. Once I'm confident he's no longer awake, I look around the small room we're in and feel my heart go out to Tristan for having to stay down here while he's in wolf form. I understand now why he chooses to live in the forest in Russia. At least there he's able to run freely through the woods without having to worry about harming a human. He can hunt deer and other animals in the forest to satisfy his animalistic urges without having to face any repercussions or judgment from others.

I continue to stroke his face and pray to God that we can find a way to turn Tristan's brother against his father. I fear that will be the only way Tristan will give up this half-life and finally realize that he deserves a better existence, one we can share together.

I close my eyes and rest my head against the iron wall at my back. Right before I allow myself to drift off to sleep, I feel Tristan's body snuggle in even closer to mine as if he's attempting to keep me warm. I smile right before I doze off to find my own land of dreams.

When I wake up the next morning, I feel someone lightly stroking the side of my face. As the fog of sleep lifts, I don't even have to open my eyes to know who's tenderly caressing my exposed cheek. I soon become aware that I'm no longer sitting up with my back against the wall. During the night, I somehow found my way to the floor, but that's not the only thing that's changed. I'm also lying against a very warm and naked body.

My eyes fly open as this revelation sinks into my sleep-clouded brain and my gaze immediately locks with Tristan's.

"Good morning," he whispers in the still-dark room. A sliver of light coming from beneath the door illuminates the space, giving us just enough light to see each other by.

"Good morning," I reply as I remain motionless. I fear any movement on my part might inadvertently cause me to touch a protruding part of Tristan that wouldn't be appropriate.

"Why did you come down here last night, Mae?" he asks, sounding dumbfounded that I would want to be with him while he was in his werewolf form.

I could lie and tell him that it was an experiment to see if my touch still had the same effect on him when he was transformed, or I could fess up and simply tell him the truth.

"I wanted to be with you," I say, opting for the whole truth instead of a half one.

He stares into my eyes as he mulls over what I just said.

"I'm glad you came back. I don't like being in this room," he replies, revealing a vulnerable part of himself to me that he could have kept hidden. "I prefer roaming free in the woods by my cabin, but having you here during the night calmed me. I didn't feel like a creature that had to be hidden away and forgotten about."

"I'm glad I could help," I tell him as the coldness of the metal floor we're lying on seeps even deeper into my bones, causing me to shiver slightly against its chill. "I don't like it down here very much either."

"You should probably go back home, Mae," he says, even though I feel him wrap his arms even tighter around me to provide me what warmth he can from his own body.

Leaving him is the last thing I want to do, but I know he's right. Hopefully, my parents haven't tried to check on me yet. I can only imagine the worry they'll feel if they find my bedroom empty and my bed unslept in this morning.

"Let me phase you out of here before I go," I tell him.

Tristan helps me to my feet in the semi-dark, and brings me in close to him by placing his hands on both my elbows. I resist his effort at first because it doesn't seem proper to be right up against him while he's still naked.

"You should probably stay close. Once we're back in the light, you might see more of me than you want to if you're too far away," he tells me, sounding amused by our predicament.

"Good thinking," I tell him right before I phase us into Jered's living room.

Thankfully, Jered is nowhere to be seen. If he had been in the room, it would have made this moment even more awkward for me.

Tristan continues to lightly hold my elbows to keep me positioned in the right spot to preserve my modesty.

"Are we still on for 9 o'clock this morning, or do you need more time?" he asks me.

"Do you know what time it is now?" I ask as I look out the wall of windows in the room. The sun hasn't even risen yet here in Montana, but its light is beginning to peek over the horizon.

"Close to 8 o'clock back in Colorado," Tristan informs me.

"I didn't realize it was so late!" I say in a panic. I'm sure my parents have gone to my room by now, only to find it empty. "I forgot about the time difference between here and there."

"Then go make sure your parents know you're all right," he urges. "I'll be ready whenever you come back."

Tristan starts to lean his head down towards mine, and I immediately begin to panic that he intends to kiss me. It's not that I don't want him to kiss me, but I'm acutely aware of my morning breath.

Instead of kissing me on the lips, Tristan turns his head at the last second and kisses me on the apple of my right cheek.

I feel a sense of relief from the intimate, yet proper, action. Hopefully, when the time is right for us to share our first kiss, it'll be a magical moment neither one of us will forget.

"I'll be back soon," I promise him as he pulls away from me slightly.

"And I'll be fully clothed when you do," he promises, a look of amusement in his eyes.

As soon as Tristan drops his hands to his sides, I phase back to my bedroom. The door to my room is open, telling me that someone, most likely my mom or dad, did indeed come into my room to find me. I quickly phase downstairs to the kitchen and discover my family gathered around the table, having breakfast. Not only are my parents, Xavier, and Ariana there, but also my Aunt Tara, Uncle Malik, Ella and, surprisingly, Jered.

Jered and my mom notice my sudden appearance first.

"There you are," my mom says, not looking the least bit concerned over my tardiness. "We were worried you would miss breakfast. You didn't bring Tristan along with you?"

"No," I say uncertainly, because I'm not quite sure why everyone is acting like things are normal. "He needed some time to get ready for the day."

"I'll bring him over when he's ready," Jered volunteers as he stands from his seat at the table with his empty plate. His gesture seems to serve a dual purpose: to indeed go back home to retrieve Tristan, and to provide me a seat at the table in order for me to eat my breakfast.

I watch Jered walk over to the sink and set his empty plate down in it. When he turns around to face me again, he sheds some light on why he's there in the first place.

"I came over to let your parents know you were with Tristan in his cell last night," he tells me. The revelation is surprising, but I can see the wisdom of his action. It was better that my parents know exactly where I was instead of simply finding me missing from my room this morning.

"Thank you for coming here, Jered," my dad says from his seat at the table beside my mother. "You saved us a lot of worry."

"It was the least I could do to thank Mae."

"Thank me?" I ask, finding Jered's statement odd. "Thank me for what exactly?"

"Tristan doesn't like the room he has to stay in at my house. Usually, he ends up howling for most of the night until he becomes so exhausted that he eventually falls asleep. After you joined him last night he stopped, so thank you for that. He needed you there more than he'll probably admit to you."

"I'm glad I could help," I reply. Knowing how much I was able to help Tristan fills my heart with a warm joy and a sense of accomplishment. I have no doubt now that ministering to the other Watcher children is part of my destiny, and will only enrich my life with more meaning.

"I'll bring Tristan over when he's ready," Jered says. "And I'll make sure he dresses appropriately, Tara."

"You do that," my Aunt Tara says. "I don't need him going to church in a tank top and shorts. God might be forgiving, but the ladies of my church certainly aren't. All I need is for them to have even more to gossip about."

"Church?" I ask, just then noticing how nicely everyone is dressed.

"It's the Sunday before Thanksgiving," Aunt Tara says, as if I should have already assumed we would be going. "And we're having a potluck lunch after the services this year to welcome the new pastor."

"New pastor?" Ella questions. "When did that happen?"

"Like a month ago, you heathen. If you went to church with us like you should, you would know that he started preaching to us a couple Sundays ago."

"I had tests and projects to finish," Ella says lamely, as her only line of defense.

My Aunt Tara simply looks up at Heaven and prays, "Lord, help my wayward child before she forgets her roots."

"Like you would ever let that happen," Ella says under her breath, but not low enough not to be overheard.

"Girl, I know you didn't just sass me," Aunt Tara replies, looking at Ella as if she's crossed a line that may lead to a slap on the back of the head for her insubordination.

"Trust me, Ella," Ariana says to break the sudden tension, "you are going to *want* to meet the new pastor."

"Really?" Ella asks my little sister. "Why is that?"

"If I didn't know any better, I would think he was a movie star instead of a preacher," Ariana replies. "*And*...he's not married."

"*Really?*" Ella says, sounding even more intrigued to meet the new pastor of our family church. "How old is he?"

"He's young," my aunt tells her, deciding to forget about her daughter's insubordination and move on to a juicier subject. "But he confided to me that he's looking for a nice girl to settle down with."

"Oh, well, that kinda leaves me out of the running," Ella mumbles. "I might be too *sassy* for him."

Aunt Tara acts like she didn't even hear Ella. "You know, come to think of it, the two of you might just hit it off. He's into body-building, and you're wanting to exercise more..."

"Body-building?" Ella says, perking up at this revelation. "Just how built is he?"

"He's not quite as big as Malcolm, but that would probably be a little too much man for you anyway. He's nicely toned, though."

"I didn't realize you had been looking so closely at Pastor David," Uncle Malik says, raising his eyebrows at his wife. "Should I be concerned?"

"Why would I be interested in a boy when I have a man to warm my bed?" Aunt Tara says as she hugs Uncle Malik's arm.

"Eww," Ella says loudly, looking at her parents as if they both just grew extra heads. "We're trying to eat here, Mom!"

"Oh, *pfft*," Aunt Tara says to her daughter. "How do you think you were made, Ella?"

Ella promptly places her hands over her ears and looks up at me. "Tell me when she stops talking," she begs.

All I can do is laugh at her predicament as I realize just how blessed my life is because of the crazy people in it.

After I eat a quick breakfast, I make my way back up to my room to get ready for church. I had completely lost track of the days, not realizing it was Sunday until Aunt Tara pointed it out to me. I'm not sure why she invited Tristan to go with us, but I'm grateful. If she hadn't I would have had to wait until after lunch to see him again, and that would have been like torture.

I don't spend a lot of time styling my hair. I simply blow it out straight and pull it back into a high ponytail. I keep my wardrobe simple, too, only wearing a nice beige sweater dress with a matching infinity scarf, leggings, and knee-high boots.

While I'm putting my shoes on, there's a knock at my door.

"Come in!" I call, assuming it's probably Ella. To my surprise it turns out to be Jess, carrying a small black duffle bag in her hands.

"I came to bring you one of my suits," she tells me as she walks into my bedroom and closes the door behind her. "I didn't want to leave it with your folks because I wasn't sure if you'd had time to tell them about your plan to help Tristan yet. I assumed that you hadn't when they told me, Mason, and Malcolm about the mission God has given you. They didn't mention anything about you searching for Tristan's family during our talk."

"No, I haven't told them that part of the plan yet," I say, slightly chagrined as I take the bag from Jess. "Thank you for letting me borrow this. I'll give it back as soon as I can."

"No worries, kiddo. JoJo made me a backup suit that I can wear."

"So how does it work exactly?" I ask, unzipping the bag to peer at the white leather outfit inside.

"Basically, just think about being invisible and you will be. It's pretty much dummy- proof."

"Simple works for me," I tell her as I walk into my closet to hide the bag. I'll need to tell my parents about helping Tristan before I tell them that Jess is lending me one of her leather outfits.

Jess leans in and gives me a hug. "Promise me you'll keep safe today," she says.

"I promise," I tell her as she pulls away. "Would you and Mason like to go to church with us?"

"Thanks for the offer, but Mama Lynn is expecting us at our church this morning. I'll see you later, though. If not tomorrow, then Tuesday at the football game for sure."

After Jess leaves my room, I go back into my closet to find a coat to wear before heading back downstairs. By the time I make it there, Tristan and Jered have returned. My father and Xavier have Tristan cornered as they talk about the upcoming football game, but when he catches a glimpse of me I feel like I'm the only person in the room. His eyes never leave me as I make my way to him.

"You look beautiful, Mae," Tristan says as I join the group of men.

"She always does," my father agrees as he leans over to give me a small kiss on the cheek in greeting.

"Are y'all ready?" I hear Aunt Tara say as she walks into the room. "We need to get going."

Since we attend a church where none of the members know about our true nature, we make a pretense of arriving there like normal people. What we actually do is hop inside our cars, phase them a mile away from the church, and then drive into the parking lot just like everybody else in the congregation does.

The church we attend is the same small one that my parents got married in all those years ago. It was my namesake's place of worship, which became my family's after her passing. From what I know of Utha Mae she was a force to be reckoned with, and I wish she was still with us. My mother has offered to go to Heaven with me to introduce me to her, but I've resisted doing such a thing. For some reason, phasing to Heaven while I'm still alive just seems wrong. From what Caylin and my mother have told me they never feel comfortable when they go there, which makes their trips few and far between. Until I have a good enough reason to traverse the veil between the living and the dead, I plan to keep my feet firmly planted in the world of the living.

When we enter the sanctuary, we all find our seats in our regular pews. Tristan takes the spot on my left while Ella sits in her normal place to my right. The church's choir walk out from the back of the church first to take their places on the benches behind the pulpit.

Then it happens.

Pastor David walks out, and I feel Ella grab hold of my right hand so hard I fear she's going to pulverize its bones with the force of her squeeze.

"That's him," she whispers to me, never taking her eyes off David for one second. When I look over at her, her expression is one of utter shock.

"Him who, Ella?" I whisper back.

Still, never taking her eyes off the new pastor, Ella tells me, "That's the man I'm going to marry."

Never have I heard these words pass Ella's lips before. She's had numerous boyfriends in the past, but that's really all they were, friends. She never talked about them as if they were potential life partners. Now, this man, someone she hasn't even spoken a brief 'hello' to yet, is someone she declares as her future husband. Pondering this, I take another look at Pastor David to better understand why my best friend is so sure this stranger is the man she's fated to marry one day.

David is handsome, well-groomed, and has a kind face. He has a nicely tanned complexion and dark brown hair. Just from looking at him, you can tell he's someone who can be trusted with your deepest secrets. Yet, I don't sense anything special enough about him that would make Ella so sure that he's her future husband.

"Is everything all right?" Tristan asks me as he glances down at the death grip Ella still has on my hand.

"Ella thinks she's going to marry him one day," I answer, tilting my head in David's direction as the choir rises to their feet to sing the first hymn.

"Really?" Tristan questions, looking back at David just like I did to size the man up. When he looks back at me, he asks, "How does she know?"

I shrug my shoulders, because the answer to that is still a mystery to me; to be honest, I believe it's a mystery to Ella also. When the choir director asks us to all stand to sing a hymn, Ella finally lets go of my hand to grab the hymn book from the back of the pew in front of us. I shake my hand to help return blood to my deprived extremity while Tristan shares his hymnal with me.

I keep my voice low, so I can enjoy the sound of Tristan's singing. At one point, he uses a falsetto voice that completely takes me by surprise. When the song is over, and we sit back down, I lean over to whisper to him.

"You really do have a gorgeous voice," I praise.

"Thanks," he replies, looking somewhat embarrassed by my compliment. His modesty is endearing, but I get the feeling Tristan doesn't believe he sounds as good as I keep saying he does. I definitely need to find a way to prove to him just how wonderful his voice is.

During the service, Ella seems to hang on every word David speaks like they're priceless gems. At one point he seems to notice her in the crowd of parishioners, and falters in his sermon. It takes him a few seconds to recover from his initial reaction of seeing her, and he seems to wrap up his sermon earlier than he expected. I instantly find it curious that he should have the same reaction to her as she did to him. Could it be a mutual 'love at first sight' scenario? Or could it be something even more meaningful, like two human soul mates meeting for the first time?

A pang of unwanted jealousy pierces my heart at the thought. Logically, I know I should be over the moon with happiness for my best friend. If she has indeed found her soul mate here on earth, it's a moment that should be cherished and celebrated. Yet, after living for so many years assuming Tristan was my soul mate, I can't help but feel somewhat cheated out of having a once in a lifetime experience that very few people get to enjoy. I know I'm being selfish, but I'm also only human. Sometimes we have feelings that we don't agree with but that we can't hide from, even if that's exactly what we want to do.

After the final prayer is spoken and the service officially comes to an end, Pastor David makes a beeline directly to our pew. When I look between him and Ella finally standing face to face, the jealousy I feel becomes overshadowed by joy. How can I possibly envy something so pure between the two of them that it practically lights up the room?

"Hello," David says as he stares at Ella like she's an angel sent straight from Heaven. I'm glad he sees her that way because it's how I've always seen her.

"Hello," Ella replies breathlessly. The look on my best friend's face is filled with a happiness I've never seen her express before.

"That was a wonderful sermon, Pastor David," Aunt Tara says, shaking David's hand vigorously.

"Why thank you, Sister Tara," he says politely. "I'm glad you enjoyed it."

"This is my daughter, Ella," Aunt Tara says, making an introduction that almost seems unnecessary.

"Miss Ella," David says, "may I have the honor of escorting you to the picnic? I hear there's going to be quite a feast laid out for us this afternoon."

Tristan and I step out into the aisle, so Ella can join David.

"I would love that," Ella says, still smiling brightly and looking up at David as if her world has finally been made complete.

As I watch them walk down the aisle and out of the church together, I absently say, "I believe we'll be having another wedding here soon."

"Another one?" Tristan asks, seeming to find my words curious.

"My mom, Caylin, and Aunt Tara were married here," I tell him. "It's sort of become a tradition with the females of our family."

Tristan looks around the well-kept church and nods his head. "It does have great architecture. You can almost feel the history here embedded in each piece of wood. I can see getting married in this church."

I look over at Tristan, because I wonder if he's hinting at something. The only answer I receive from him is a shy smile before we're interrupted.

I feel Aunt Tara grab my arm and urgently ask, "What the heck is going on with Ella and David?"

"I would have thought seeing it happen multiple times yourself, you would recognize it by now," I say.

Aunt Tara looks confused for a moment, but then the truth of the matter seems to dawn on her.

"They're soul mates?" she practically screams, drawing quite a few unwanted glances our way. "Are you kidding me?"

"I don't know for sure, but that's what I'm assuming. The attraction between them seemed pretty destined to me."

"Who are soul mates?" my mom asks as she and my dad come to stand with us.

"My baby and Pastor David," Aunt Tara tells her as she begins to cry. "I'm going to lose my baby, Lilly."

My mother gives Aunt Tara a hug and whispers, "She'll always be your baby, Tara. Falling in love, and even marriage doesn't change that fact. Besides, I think we're jumping the gun here a little bit. They literally just met."

Aunt Tara pulls away from my mother's embrace to wipe the tears from the corners of her eyes.

"You're right," she sniffs. "My Ella wouldn't just jump into a marriage that fast."

"She'd better not," Uncle Malik says definitively while crossing his arms over his chest and setting a stern expression on his face. "That man has a lot of proving to do before I consent to him marrying my little girl."

I have no doubt David will pass any test either Aunt Tara or Uncle Malik place in his path, but I can't say it won't be interesting to watch Pastor David jump through their hoops to gain their approval.

"How did he end up at this church anyway?" I ask, finding it remarkable that Ella's soul mate just happened to become the pastor of our family church.

"You know," Aunt Tara says as she considers my question, "it was Malcolm who suggested him to the search committee. I just assumed they'd crossed paths at some point, but now that I think about it David has never mentioned Malcolm to me. I'm not even sure they know each other."

That's definitely strange, and something I'll have to ask my Uncle Malcolm about later.

As we all make our way outside to the picnic tables that have been set up behind the church, Tristan keeps close to my side but doesn't make a move to take hold of my hand. Since I woke up in his arms while he was completely naked this morning, I would have thought holding hands would simply be a natural thing for us to do now. As I continue to consider his odd behavior, I quickly figure out why he's keeping his distance.

We're surrounded by my family. Odds are he doesn't exactly feel comfortable showing physical affection for me in front of them. It's just one more reason we need to find a way to leave the potluck lunch earlier rather than later.

After we fix our plates, my family takes over one of the picnic tables. When David sits down with us, I see my Aunt Tara put her plastic fork down and twine the fingers of her hands together in front of her as if she's preparing for battle. I've often heard about my aunt's interrogations of would-be suitors, but I've never actually witnessed one for myself. Seeing as how David is showing interest in her only baby girl, I put down my fork as well and wait for the show to begin.

"Now, Pastor David," my Aunt Tara begins, "where is your family from exactly? I don't think you've ever mentioned your parents."

"No, ma'am, I haven't," David says. "I was one of the last people who ever came through the Tear."

"You came through the Tear?" Ella asks in surprise. "How old were you?"

"I was six at the time," he tells her.

"But the only people who came through the Tear were people who wanted to leave their own planets," my dad says, stating a fact that isn't exactly public knowledge. "Why would a six-year-old want to leave his own world?"

"I came from an alternate Earth; my parents were not what you would call nice people," he says, looking uncomfortable talking about his past. "I may have been young, but I had already experienced the world in a way no child should ever have to. All I remember is praying that I would be lucky enough to be chosen to go through the Tear, but I never dreamed God would actually answer my prayers. The night I was able to leave the Earth I lived on, I promised God that I would serve His needs for the rest of my life, and I've kept my promise to Him ever since."

"What happened when you got here?" Ella asks.

"I was placed in a foster home by the Watcher Agency in Memphis," he tells us. "I drifted from foster home to foster home until I turned eighteen and found a way to go to seminary school to keep my promise to the Lord."

"And you've been on your own ever since then?" I ask, finding David's life tragic in many ways, but also a miracle. It was like his whole life had been leading him to this point, just so he could find the one person in the universe he was meant to be with. Ella.

"I have friends," David says as he smiles at me. "I'm not a complete shut-in."

"I guess that means you've probably also dated other girls," my Aunt Tara says knowingly.

"Yes, ma'am," David says with a nod. "I've dated women in the past."

"Have you been tested?" she blurts out.

"Oh, dear Lord, woman," Uncle Malik says, hanging his head in shame. "It's like that's the only question you know how to ask people."

"You can't deny that it's important!" Aunt Tara defends. "If you don't have your health, you don't have anything. Do you want your daughter kissing someone who might be infested with diseases?"

I hear Tristan snicker next to me and quickly shake my head at him to be quiet.

"Well, don't laugh too hard," Aunt Tara warns him, looking over at Tristan like he's going to be her next target. "Trust me. You'll be getting your own interrogation soon enough."

The look of amusement on Tristan's face is quickly wiped away by her words, which seems to satisfy my aunt for the moment.

"I can assure you that I am not infected with any type of diseases," David tells my aunt, looking amused by her worry.

"How can you be so sure unless you've been tested?"

David looks uncomfortable, and I begin to wonder if he intends to get up and walk away from the table to end my aunt's questions. However, he stays, and seems to decide that answering her honestly is the better course of action in this case.

"I don't need to be tested because I've never been with a woman in a way that would require it."

Silence reigns supreme, not only at our table but at every table behind the church. The only sound to be heard is the chirping of the birds in the trees around us and the whisper of an autumn breeze through the leaves.

Finally, my aunt breaks the silence by asking in disbelief, "Are you serious?"

"I would never lie to you, ma'am," David says. "I try to make it a point not to lie to anyone, unless it's to spare their feelings about something nonconsequential. I believe God can forgive small white lies if they're told in the spirit of showing love to another person. As far as not having been with a woman in the biblical sense yet, I decided a long time ago that if I was going to preach abstinence until marriage that I should walk the walk and not just tell other people to do something I wasn't willing to do myself."

In that moment I know David is the perfect man for Ella, and that no matter what my aunt might ask him next he'll answer her questions honestly and without shame.

I lean over and whisper into Ella's ear, "He's a keeper."

She smiles at me and nods her head before looking back at her man.

I can't believe how Ella's life has changed in less than thirty minutes. What's happened to her just goes to prove the age-old proverb that God works in mysterious ways. I push my own feelings of envy behind me and pray that Ella and David have a beautiful life together, filled with more joy and love than they can ever ask for or dream of for themselves. In my heart, I have no doubt that my prayer will be answered.

Chapter 10

After lunch, Ella and David find a quiet spot away from the rest of us to talk and get to know one another better. I decide to pull my parents aside and tell them about my plan to help Tristan find his family, including the use of Jess' white leather outfit. They react better than I thought they would, but I can tell they're still worried about my safety.

"At the first sign of trouble," my dad says, "you do what Jess said and phase to the Watcher Agency headquarters right away."

"I will," I promise them.

"I don't trust Tristan's brother or his father," my mom says, "but I trust Rolph even less than Jasper. For the sake of my sanity, I need you to also promise that if you come across Tristan's father you'll phase home immediately, whether there's trouble or not. He's a Watcher, Mae. He's physically stronger than you are."

"Caylin fought against Watchers," I remind her.

"Yes, but Caylin also has your father's strength," she in turn reminds me. "You and Will don't. I need you to promise me that you'll leave if you come across him."

"What if Tristan doesn't want to leave with me? I can't just abandon him."

"Tristan can handle himself," my father says, "and we'll send him back-up to help. Your safety is what we're most concerned about here, Mae. I don't believe we're making unreasonable requests."

I know they're not, but what they want me to agree to still makes me feel like I'm a little girl who needs to be looked after.

"I'll do what you ask," I relent.

The only reason I acquiescence to their request is because I love and respect them. In my mind I believe they're being overprotective, but I also know from years of living with them that that fact will never change. They're still protective of Caylin and Will, even though they're both married with kids of their own. It's just the way good parents are with their children. But good parents also know when to loosen the reins, and that's exactly what mine are doing now. I know I'll always be their baby girl, but there comes a time when parents have to trust that they've raised their children well enough to make their own decisions. That doesn't mean that they'll ever stop giving me their advice, though, and I'm smart enough to take it from mine.

When I step away from my folks, Tristan ends his conversation with Xavier and walks over to me.

"How did they take the news?" he asks me.

"A lot better than I thought they would," I tell him. "Let's go before they change their minds."

"We probably won't even find my dad and Jasper," Tristan tells me. "This might be a colossal waste of time, Mae. If they don't want to be found, they'll hide somewhere no one would think to look for them."

"Or maybe they're hiding somewhere that only you know about," I point out. "We won't know until we try. Where do you think we should start first?"

"France," Tristan tells me. "I already called Mason and got his permission for us to use one of the vehicles he has at his villa. I assume you have a phase point there."

I nod. "Yes. I've gone there quite a bit. I just need to go home and change into Jess' outfit. Then we can phase to France."

While we were making s'mores and talking the night before at Jered's house, I told Tristan about my plan to use one of Jess' leather suits to remain invisible during our search for his family. He agreed that it was the safest course of action, and looked relieved that Jess had thought of using it to help with our quest.

It doesn't take me long to change clothing. When I go back downstairs, the smile that appears on Tristan's face when he sees me indicates that he likes the way I look in the tight-fitting outfit. I can't say his reaction is much of a surprise to me. He's a man, after all.

"I think you might need to ask JoJo to make you one of those just to wear all the time," he suggests as his stare turns appreciative.

"I just might do that," I tell him, unashamed of the way I look.

Tristan holds his hand out to me to indicate that he's prepared for whatever the rest of our day may bring. After I grab hold of his hand, I phase us to the living room of Jess and Mason's villa. Tristan keeps hold of my hand as he leads me through the house and down to the garage.

"You must come here a lot to know the layout so well," I comment as he types a code into the electronic keypad of a metal box on the wall of the garage. When he swings the front panel open, I see two rows of key fobs hanging from hooks. Tristan grabs one and shuts the box.

"Jess and Mason always invite me over a few times a year," Tristan tells me as we walk past all the cars and head for the only truck in the garage. "I guess it's their way of making sure I leave my cabin and socialize every once in a while."

"Or maybe they just want to spend time with you," I suggest. "It's not like you're awful to be around."

Tristan laughs. "I'm glad you think that way."

Tristan opens the passenger door of a rather large, jacked-up truck. After he helps me climb inside, I have to ask, "Where exactly are we going in this monster?"

"Somewhere that probably doesn't have a clear road to get to it," he tells me. "To be honest, we'll probably end up having to travel part of the way on foot, but this is the best vehicle to get us the furthest before we have to resort to walking."

After we leave the villa, Tristan begins driving us to the first location he wants to check.

"How long will it take us to get to where we're going?" I ask him.

"About an hour, I think," he says, not sounding confident in his time assessment. "Like I mentioned, there isn't a road that leads straight to it. We'll have to drive through the woods a good way to reach it."

"And what is 'it' exactly? A house?"

Tristan nods. "It's a small cabin my father built ages ago for him and my mother."

This is the first time Tristan has mentioned his mother. I know from the stories I was told that the women the Watchers had children with ended up going into a coma-like state right after they became pregnant. When it was time for a child to emerge from his mother's womb he would claw his way out of the woman's body in wolf form, killing his mother in the process.

"Why do you think they would be there?" I ask.

"My father has kept the cabin up all these years. It's fully stocked with supplies, so if he wanted to hide out for a few months it would be the most logical place to stay. I'm the only other person who even knows it exists."

"I promised my parents that if we found your father, I would phase home immediately and they would send backup for you," I tell him.

"That's probably a good idea," he says. "But if that happens, all I would ask is that you give me five minutes alone with my dad before sending in the cavalry."

"I can do that," I tell him.

About thirty minutes into the drive, Tristan turns off the main road and into the woods. The ride is bumpy, but there's a natural path that we're able to follow for a good distance. When we come to a dense standing of trees, Tristan parks the truck and tells me that we'll have to walk from here.

"You should probably use the suit now," he advises me. "On the off chance that we do run into them, I would rather they didn't see you. It would just cause more problems."

I do what Jess instructed and mentally say that I want to be invisible. Since I can still see myself, I'm not sure it worked.

"Can you see me?" I ask Tristan.

He shakes his head. "No. I can't. It's working. Just follow behind me while we walk deeper into the woods."

As we make our way through the forest, I'm struck by how quiet it is. I don't even hear the chirping of birds, which is a sound that is normally prevalent among so many trees.

"Is it just me or does it seem a little too quiet here?" I whisper to Tristan.

"Jasper is close by," he whispers back.

"How can you tell?"

"I can sense him."

As if he heard Tristan say his name, Jasper steps out from behind a large oak tree twenty yards ahead of us.

"I figured you would try to find us," Jasper says disdainfully. "Why can't you just leave us alone, Tristan? It's because of you that we're on the run from the others."

"Don't blame me for what you did to Mae," Tristan tells his brother tersely. "That's all on you, brother. What did you think would happen if you attacked someone under Malcolm's protection?"

"We knew the fall-out would be bad, but we also hoped it would bring you to your senses," Jasper sneers. "I can see that it hasn't. Father might be right about you being a hopeless cause that we should forget about."

"After all these years, you're still blindly believing whatever our father says and doing whatever he orders. When will you start thinking for yourself, Jasper? Don't you want a better life? What you have now isn't a life at all, it's only existing."

"Are you telling me your life is so much better than mine?" Jasper scoffs. "Living up in that cabin, isolated from the world, doesn't sound like a better way to live if you ask me, Tristan."

"I only live that way because I'm still holding out hope that I can make you see reason." Tristan takes a step forward. "I want us both to go before God and ask for His forgiveness one day, Jasper. I don't want to do it if you're not by my side."

"I won't abandon our father like you did!" Jasper's rage causes his face to turn beet-red. "You might be able to turn your back on him, but I can't! I don't know why I should be surprised by your selfishness. You've always been like that, even before I was born."

Tristan remains silent as he continues to stare at his brother. I may not be able to see the expression on his face, but I did notice how his body tensed after Jasper's last heated words.

"What do you mean by that?" Tristan finally asks, confused by Jasper's accusation. "How could you possibly know how I was before you were born? What did Father tell you?"

"He didn't have to tell me anything," Jasper replies scathingly. "The simple fact that I exist tells me all I need to know about you."

"You're not making any sense," Tristan says, still sounding confused by what his brother is trying to accuse him of. "What is it that you think I did?"

"You let my mother die!" Jasper says, pointing an accusatory finger at Tristan. "You might as well have murdered her yourself!"

"How was I supposed to stop that? Both our mothers died. It was just a part of the process."

"You knew what would happen to my mother!" Jasper growls. "You knew the moment our father chose her to have me that she was doomed to die, yet you didn't do anything to stop it. You just let it happen. Why is that, Tristan?"

Tristan remains silent before saying in a quiet voice, "There wasn't anything I could have done to help her."

"You could have warned her! You could have told her to run as far away from our father as possible, but you didn't. Why, Tristan? Why did you let him kill my mother?"

Tristan begins to shake his head. "You don't know what he was like back then. He was even worse than he is now, but when he was with your mother it was like having a real family. She was so loving and kind. I had never been around someone like her before, and she made our dad laugh. I thought she was magical at the time. I was only a child, Jasper. I couldn't imagine anything bad happening to someone so full of life. I thought she was indestructible, and that our father loved her enough to forget about his plan of having another child with a human woman."

"Then you're more of a fool than I thought you were," Jasper spits out. "You should have protected her. You never should have let her get pregnant."

"If she hadn't become pregnant, then you wouldn't exist," Tristan points out.

"That would have been a better fate than living like this. I blame what I am on you, Tristan! So, stop trying to convince me that I should abandon our father for selfish reasons. I'm not like you. I don't leave the people I love because it would make me feel better. I may be a monster, but at least I'm a loyal one and not some traitor like you turned out to be!"

Jasper turns, and runs back into the forest so fast I quickly lose sight of him.

Tristan doesn't turn around to face me. I continue to silently stand behind him as he takes a few deep breaths.

I assume all I need to do to become visible again is tell the suit that's what I want. After doing so, I walk around Tristan until I'm standing in front of him. He keeps his gaze directed toward the forest floor even though he knows I'm waiting for him to speak to me.

"Tristan," I say, "look at me."

Reluctantly, he lifts his gaze to meet mine.

"He's just angry with you, and he knew exactly what buttons to push to make you feel guilt over something you had no control over."

"Maybe, but he's also not wrong in what he said."

"You didn't kill his mother," I point out. "Your father did when he impregnated her."

"I could have warned her what would happen, Mae. I could have done exactly what Jasper said and told her to run as far away as possible from my dad, but I didn't."

"About what age were you back then?" I ask. "I know you age at a slower rate than humans, but what would have been the human equivalent?"

"I was about five years old when my father met Jeannie," he tells me. "She was like a ray of sunshine when she entered our world. I instantly loved her, and wanted her to be my mom."

"Had your father told you what happened to your own mother by then?" I ask. "Did you know she died giving birth to you?"

Tristan nods, and I can see the burden of guilt transform his face into an impenetrable mask.

"I knew what would happen to her if she became pregnant, but I also thought my father loved her enough to not let that happen. What I told Jasper was true. Our father was a different man when he was around Jeannie. We were so happy together that I thought that happiness would be enough to protect her from him. The morning I found her in his bed and in a coma, I cried so hard I thought for sure my heart would break. I made a promise to her that I would take care of her child, and I've tried to keep that promise ever since."

"You were only five, Tristan," I reason. "Odds are she would have just laughed off your warning and called you too imaginative. It's hard for someone who isn't aware of the world as we know it to understand how dangerous it is. Her death wasn't your fault. You need to let go of that guilt."

"I'm not sure you can understand what it feels like to be the reason your own mother is dead," he tells me, looking somewhat lost by the thought. "Not only have I had to live with that knowledge but I've also had to live with the guilt of Jeannie's death, too."

"You weren't responsible for either of their deaths, Tristan. I don't understand why you believe you were."

"When you're raised by someone who hates you because your existence is the reason the person they loved most is dead, you tend to start believing what you're told."

"I take it your dad told you that your mother's death was your fault."

"Ever since I can remember," Tristan confirms, looking haunted by the memories of his father's mental torture.

"Then he was wrong," I tell him in no uncertain terms. "He's the one who felt guilty over her death, but your father just wasn't man enough to own up to his mistake. He projected his own self-loathing onto you, Tristan. Can't you see that?"

Tristan doesn't say a word. He simply stands there and stares at me, but I get the feeling he isn't really seeing me at all. He seems lost in his own thoughts and memories. I can tell by the yearning in his eyes that he wants to believe what I'm telling him, but that after years of being brainwashed by his father he's having a hard time separating the facts from what his father has told him over hundreds of years.

"Would you mind taking me back to my cabin, Mae?" Tristan asks.

"Shouldn't we go after your brother?" I ask in return. "We know he's here, and your father is probably at the cabin you told me about."

"I just want to go home, Mae!"

I'm a little taken aback by Tristan's volatile outburst, but I try not to take it personally.

"I'm sorry," he immediately says, realizing that what he did was wrong. "I didn't mean to scream at you like that. Now isn't the time for me to try to talk to Jasper again. I need to get my head on straight before I do that. Even if my father *is* at the cabin, they'll be long gone by the time we get there. They'll find somewhere else to hide since we found them."

I take a couple of steps forward and grab hold of Tristan's right hand.

Without saying anything else, I phase us to his cabin. Once we're there, he immediately pulls his hand out of mine like he can't get away from me fast enough.

"Would you mind giving me some time alone to think?" he asks. "Maybe we can look for Jasper again tomorrow, but right now I would really just like to be alone for a while."

"I can stay," I offer.

Tristan shakes his head. "I don't think that would be a good idea, Mae. I wouldn't be very good company."

"We don't have to talk if you don't want to. We could watch some TV or read a book. I just don't feel right leaving you alone like this, Tristan."

"Please," he practically begs me, "leave, Mae. All I want to do is forget things for a while and the best way for me to do that is take a run through these woods until I'm exhausted. Just let me handle things my own way, and I promise you that tomorrow I'll be better. If you truly do care about me, do what I ask and just leave me alone for a while."

I don't want to go but I can't think of a good enough argument to put up, considering what he just said.

"Do you have that satellite phone here?" I ask him.

"Yes. Jered said he replaced the one my father took. Why?"

"I'll leave on one condition. If you change your mind and want me to come back, I want you to promise that you'll call me. Jered has my number."

"Okay. I promise I'll do that."

I sigh heavily—everything inside me is screaming that I shouldn't leave Tristan alone right now. Yet, he seems desperate for me to depart so he can sort things out his own way.

"If I don't hear from you later, I guess I'll see you tomorrow?" I ask hopefully.

Tristan nods. "I'll have Jered bring me over to your house in the morning. Then we can go from there and decide what we should do next."

Even though his body language is guarded, I go to Tristan and wrap my arms around his waist. I reason with myself that he's the one who needs the hug but, secretly, I know it's me who needs to hug him before I go.

Tristan doesn't return my embrace right away, but I don't let go until I feel his arms wrap around me.

"I don't like leaving you like this," I tell him, being as honest as I can about the situation.

"I know," he tells me. "And I'm sorry if asking you to go is hurting you, but this is the best way I know how to handle this, Mae. All I ask is that you be patient with me."

I squeeze Tristan one last time before stepping away.

"I'll see you later, then," I say, attempting to prolong the moment for a few seconds more.

"See you," he replies just before I phase back to the front porch of my mom's house in Colorado.

As I stand on the porch, I hear Uncle Malcolm's voice coming through an open window in the living room.

"I know what you've told me about the mission God gave her, Dearest, but I don't think now is the right time for her to start it. At least give me some more time to settle this situation first. Once we put Rolph down she can try to save as many souls as she wants, but he's still a threat to her."

From what Uncle Malcolm just said, I can tell my mom and dad haven't told him that I'm helping Tristan try to find his family. In a way, I'm grateful they haven't yet. If he knew, odds are he would try to talk me out of it. Besides, it's really something that I should tell him about myself.

"I'm just not sure we're doing the right thing," I hear my mother tell him. "Maybe she's meant to be there Wednesday night. Why else would God come now to tell her what she's destined to do?"

"I don't think a game of Bait is the safest place for her to start her work with the Watcher children, Lilly," I hear my father say. "They might end up attacking her during their frenzy."

"Brand's right," Uncle Malcolm agrees, sounding relieved that my father is taking his side in this argument.

It's a rare occasion when the two of them agree on something, and if the circumstances weren't so dire I would probably barge in and make a joke that we need to make a note of the date of such a miracle. Taking into consideration the subject of their conversation, I decide to stand stock-still and learn as much from eavesdropping as possible. I'm not proud of spying on their private conversation, but I have to believe me being here at this exact moment isn't just a coincidence either.

"Whether she saves them now or next week, it doesn't really matter in the grand scheme of things," my father says, presumably to my mother. "Mae is headstrong. She'll get the job done in her own time, and we'll be there to help her if she needs us. Right now, I think Malcolm has the right idea. We need to get rid of Rolph first, since he has the biggest grudge against her."

"And how do you plan to do that exactly?" my mom asks.

"I promised Mae I wouldn't kill him," Uncle Malcolm says, even though he never officially declared such a thing to me. He simply said he would think about it when I made my plea for him to spare the lives of Rolph and Jasper for Tristan's sake. "Therefore, I'm going to rip his head from his body and hide the two parts where no one but me can find them. After a few decades like that, maybe he'll be ready to talk."

"Or be driven completely insane," my mother says, sounding disgusted by Uncle Malcolm's plan. "That's barbaric, Malcolm! You can't do that to him."

"Would you rather I killed him, Dearest?" Uncle Malcolm says, sounding exasperated and on the verge of becoming angry with her. "These are the only two options I have, and what I plan to do isn't exactly what I want to do. I'm only sparing his life because Mae asked me to."

"Where is the game going to be taking place?" my dad asks. I get the feeling he asked his question to turn the conversation in a different direction before my uncle and mom got into a heated argument.

"In the woods near Tristan's cabin," Uncle Malcolm tells them. "I think Rolph plans to use the event to taunt his son. He may even be hoping that Tristan will join them and lose his soul all over again."

"But it's happening Wednesday?" my mom asks. "Tara told me that Ella invited Tristan to stay with us during the sleepover. We'll just have to make sure he stays here the whole time you're handling things over there. That way, he won't even be in his cabin while the game is taking place. He'll be here, safe with us."

"Do you plan on lying to Mae then?" Uncle Malcolm asks.

"It's not exactly lying if we simply don't mention it at all," my mother reasons, even though I'm sure she's aware how flimsy the line is between a lie and the truth in this circumstance. "We'll let you handle things, Malcolm. I'm going to trust you to use your best judgment in this matter."

"Good," Uncle Malcolm says, sounding satisfied. "Now, why don't we talk about more important matters? Is your team ready to play tomorrow, Brand?"

I know my dad and uncle will end up talking about the 'big' game for at least the next half hour. I debate with myself if I should go back to Tristan's cabin and try to find him, but since it's nighttime in that part of the world now I probably wouldn't be able to locate him even if I tried. When he said he was going to go for a run in the woods, he more than likely meant that he would do so in his werewolf form. It could be hours before he transforms back into a human, and I know I'll just have to keep what I've learned to myself for the time being.

Since I don't want my parents to know that I overheard their conversation with Uncle Malcolm, I decide to phase over to Caylin and Aiden's home on the other side of the mountain that my mother's house faces. I need to talk to someone who can give me some good advice about what I should do next to help Tristan. I've always turned to my big sister for help when I faced a problem I didn't want my parents to know about. She's one of the most levelheaded people I know who I also trust to give me constructive advice. I know she won't let me down in this instance either.

As soon as I phase into the foyer of the mansion Aiden built for Caylin, I call out both their names but end up being answered by another member of the Keles family. After Kate phases in front of me, she leans forward and gives me a hug.

"Hey, Aunt Mae," she says before pulling away. "Everyone is out back. Come on. I'll show you where they are."

"So how are things going with you and Luke? It seemed like the two of you patched things up last night," I say to my niece as we walk through the house together.

"Yeah," Kate replies, looking uncomfortable about the whole incident. "He might be younger than me, but in some ways he seems older. I'm not so sure I would have forgiven him if the tables had been turned, at least not as quickly. I would have made him squirm a little bit more first."

"I'm sure you would have forgiven him more easily than you think," I say. "Would you mind if I ask you something, Kate?"

Kate stops walking and turns to face me. "Sure, Aunt Mae. What's up?"

"When you're with Luke, how does he make you feel?"

"Like my world is complete," she tells me, without even having to pause to think about her answer.

"Do you feel like you could live without him?"

"Hmm." She looks thoughtful before answering my question. "I suppose if he dies before I do I would have to go on living without him, but the world would never feel the same again. I would always know a part of me was missing. Why do you ask?"

I shrug my shoulders. "I was just curious. You girls and your soul mates. It's all a bit of a mystery to me."

"I thought Tristan was your soul mate," she says, looking confused by what I'm implying.

I shake my head. "No. He isn't."

"Are you sure?" She questions, looking dubious about my answer. "From the way the two of you look at each other, it's obvious you're meant to be together."

"Thanks," I tell her, wondering if she's right or if the connection between me and Tristan is just wishful thinking on my part.

When we make it out to the backyard, I see Caylin sitting at the white-painted iron table on the veranda, calling out encouragement to Aiden and Andrew as they throw a football back and forth.

"You're doing great, Andrew!" my sister tells her son. "You'll be quarterbacking your grandpa's team before you know it!"

I hear Andrew laugh with joy at his mother's compliment. Right now, Aiden is the quarterback of my dad's team, but in another ten or fifteen years I can see Andrew taking over his father's position. My nephew may only be eleven years old, but he already looks like a miniature version of Aiden. I can only imagine how handsome he'll be when he comes of age.

"I still don't understand why I can't play in the game," Kate pouts, punctuating her words by crossing her arms over her chest and looking annoyed about the whole thing.

"The same reason I never could," Caylin tells her daughter as she motions for me to sit down in one of the three empty chairs at the table. "You're too strong, Kate. You might get excited and inadvertently hurt someone."

"If Grandpa and Uncle Malcolm would make Watcher teams instead of human ones, I could play. It's just not fair that Andrew will get to play in it one day and I won't."

"Kate," Caylin says, attempting to be patient with her eldest child, "you know Andrew doesn't have your powers. Only the first female descendant will, just like your daughter will one day. I didn't make the rules. It's just the way things are. If you want to argue about it, ask God why He decided it should be that way."

"Hey, Kate!" Aiden yells to his daughter. "Come play with us!"

This seems to break through Kate's pensive mood, as a reluctant smile graces her face and she runs down the steps from the veranda to the backyard.

"Kids." My big sister laughs as she centers her attention on me. "Now, tell me what's bothering you, Mae."

"How do you know something's wrong?" I ask, wondering if mind-reading has been added to Caylin's list of God-given talents.

"Because I know you," she answers. "And the look on your face tells me that you have a problem that you can't solve. What is it?"

"Tristan," I say. "Something happened a little while ago, and I'm not sure what I can do to help him."

I spend the next few minutes describing our run-in with Jasper in France, and his successful attempt at guilt-tripping Tristan.

Caylin sighs after she hears what happened. "Poor Tristan.

Honestly, Mae, I'm not sure there's much you can do to help him except just be there for him when he feels like talking about it."

"There has to be something," I say desperately. "I'm willing to do almost anything."

My sister considers my predicament for a moment, as if she's running through different scenarios inside her mind.

"Come to think of it, there might be one thing," she finally says, but sounds unsure about the outcome of what she's about to suggest.

I lean forward in my chair and ask, "What is it?"

"If Tristan is feeling guilty about what happened to his mom and Jasper's mother, they may be the ones who hold the key to freeing him from his guilt."

"But how do I..." And then it suddenly dawns on me what Caylin is suggesting I do. "You think I should go to Heaven and get their advice."

Caylin nods her head. "It's the only thing I can think of, Mae. You simply don't know enough about the situation to be helpful, but they know everything. I think they're your best bet right now."

I consider Caylin's advice and conclude that she's right.

"How exactly do I phase to Heaven?" I ask her. "How did you do it the first time?"

"Mom took me, remember? If you want to go there, I can take you."

"Thanks," I say. "I would appreciate that. Do you happen to have time to do it now?"

"Sure," Caylin says as she stands from her seat. "Let's go."

Caylin holds her hand out to me, and before I can even blink she phases us.

The moment I arrive in Heaven, I feel an unease permeate every cell of my body. I know what it is because I've heard my mom and Caylin speak of the uncomfortable sensation of the living visiting Heaven.

"Hello, Mae and Caylin," I hear God say.

I look to my right and see Him standing there, grinning at us.

146

"I suppose I could ask what brings you here, Mae, but since I already know, it would be a rather redundant question, wouldn't it?"

"Do you need me to stay with you?" Caylin asks, even though I can clearly see how uncomfortable she is on this side of the veil.

"No. I can take it from here," I tell her. "Thank you for bringing me."

"You know I would do anything for you," she says to me. Before she leaves, Caylin tells God, "It's been a while since we last saw You."

"I feel as though I'll be returning sooner than you think," he replies mysteriously, without giving away the reason He'll be coming back to Earth for a visit.

"I'll look forward to spending some time with You then," Caylin says before phasing back home.

I focus my attention on God and ask, "Do You know where I can find Tristan and Jasper's mothers?"

"I can take you to them," He says, "but what is it that you hope to gain by your visit?"

"I don't know exactly," I reply with a small shrug. "Maybe something that will help me figure out how to make Tristan feel less guilt. I really won't know until after I speak to them."

The scenery around me changes and I find myself standing on the rocky shore of a vast lake. God is no longer by my side, but I see the two people I want to talk to walking along the shore toward where I'm standing.

Both women are dressed in flowy white gowns with skirts that catch the wind, causing the fabric to billow out around them as if they were made of smoke. Each woman is beautiful in her own right, but it's blatantly obvious how strikingly similar they are to one another. If I didn't know any better I would have assumed they were sisters, considering their matching blond hair, pale white skin, and bright blue eyes.

"Hello," the one on the right says to me, quickly followed by the same greeting from the woman on the left.

"Hi. My name is Mae Cole," I say, introducing myself to them, even though what should be a normal formality seems awkward to do in Heaven.

"We know who you are, Mae," the woman who first spoke tells me with a distinct French accent. "And we know why you're here."

That definitely makes my quest easier.

"Can you help me, then?" I ask them both, uncertain which woman is Tristan's mother, and which one is Jeannie. "I don't know how to help Tristan work through his guilt over both of your deaths."

"Do you love my son?" the woman on the right asks, identifying herself as Tristan's mother with her query.

I have to say, I didn't expect to be asked such a question point-blank, but there's only one answer that I can give to her question.

"Yes," I reply.

"Good," Tristan's mother says as she holds out her hand to me. "My name is River, Mae, and I think both Jeannie and I can give you the information you need to help Tristan."

I slide my hand against River's, assuming that she wants to shake hands, but I soon discover that isn't her intention after all. Once we clasp hands, Jeannie places her hand over both of ours and again the scenery around me changes.

We're standing inside a cabin that's only composed of one room, but the interior has been lovingly decorated with fresh flowers, colorful curtains, and a large bed with what looks like a bear pelt for a comforter. A vision of a laughing River opens the front door as a man playfully chases after her. River is wearing a dress similar in design to the one she has on now, a crown of small white flowers encircling her head.

"I made it here first!" River declares to the man as she slowly backs into the cabin while watching him close the door behind him.

"That you did, my love," he says. "What do you claim as your prize?"

"A lifetime of happiness and love," River declares before throwing herself into the man's arms. "Can you give that to me, Rolph? Will you make my heart's truest desires come true?"

Tristan's father looks at River with the same depth of love and devotion I've witnessed my father give my mother ever since I can remember.

"I will always love you," he proclaims softly, but with conviction. "Never in my entire life did I believe someone as perfect as you could exist in the universe. I thank my lucky stars I found you, and I never intend to let you go, River. You are the light of my world, and I can't even remember what life was like before I met you, my sweet angel."

"Why do you call me that?" River asks, smiling at Rolph as if the world itself revolves around him.

"Because if angels truly do exist," he tells her, "you would have to be the sweetest one of them all."

"I think it's time you showed me just how much you love me," she whispers as she lightly brushes her lips against his.

The scene changes and I see River lying on the bed, looking so pale and gaunt she seems to be on the verge of death. When I see the bump at her belly I know Tristan is inside her, gestating until it's time for him to claw his way out of her body to be born. Rolph is kneeling beside her, his head resting on clasped hands. I can hear him praying to God to intervene and save River from certain death.

"You're wasting your breath," I hear a strange man say in a bored voice. "Your prayers are falling on deaf ears."

I look over at the small dining table in the room, and see the speaker sitting there with his legs crossed and propped up on the table as he watches Rolph's display of grief. I don't recognize him physically, but the way he holds himself tells me everything. This has to be Lucifer in one of his previous forms.

Rolph looks up at the man and confirms my suspicion.

"He may have abandoned you, Lucifer," Rolph says heatedly, "but He won't do the same thing to me. I just need to convince Him that I'm sorry."

Lucifer laughs, but it's an unpleasant sound. Instead of being filled with mirth, it's drenched with commendation.

"I never took you for a fool, Rolph, but you're proving me wrong in the worst way possible. Our Father doesn't care about you. He stopped caring the moment you started thinking for yourself. All He wants are lemmings to follow His every word and command. I'm surprised you haven't figured that out by now."

"Go away, Lucifer!" Rolph demands. "I know what you want. The others have already warned me about you."

Lucifer swings his legs off the table and leans forward slightly. "Oh, did they now? And what have the other little Watchers said about me?"

"That you promised them revenge against our Father for what He's done to our wives. I won't be so easily fooled by your games. You may be able to deceive them, but you don't fool me one bit. This is just a test of my faith. God will save my wife because my belief in Him won't falter like the others' did."

Lucifer snickers at Rolph's words. "Then I guess you won't mind me sitting here and watching your faith in Him crumble."

"You can sit there all you want," Rolph says defiantly. "It's only your time that you'll be wasting."

The scene changes again slightly, and I see Rolph holding a baby covered in blood and crying so loud his voice reverberates off the walls of the small cabin. Lucifer is still sitting in the same spot at the table, silently watching Rolph as he stares at Tristan.

"Are you ready to join me, brother?" Lucifer says. From the triumphant tone of his voice, it's obvious he believes Rolph is finally ready to denounce God and join his side of the battle.

"I thought He would save her," Rolph replies in a distant voice as he continues to stare at Tristan in disgust and disbelief. He seems to be refusing to look up. Perhaps he can't endure the thought of seeing River lying on their bed, her belly ripped open and the sheets soaked red with her blood. "I thought if I believed in Him enough, He would help me."

"Our Father is a selfish bastard, Rolph," Lucifer declares angrily. "You need to face that truth and do the only thing you can to avenge your wife's death."

Rolph looks over at Lucifer, a broken man. "And if I join your side, what will that gain me?"

"Revenge," Lucifer hisses, his eyes blazing with the promise of vengeance. "He doesn't deserve your loyalty or your praise. Look at what He allowed to happen to your wife, Rolph! All because you chose to love a human, His most precious creation. Tell me, how is that an act of a forgiving God? Even though you prayed and asked Him to forgive you for what you did, He still punished you. Join me and we'll make Him pay for what He's done to all of us. Fight by my side, and together we can avenge River's death. She was an innocent in all of this, yet He still used her to punish you. A God like that doesn't deserve your loyalty. He deserves your hate and loathing. He deserves to pay for His own sins."

Rolph stares at Lucifer a moment before standing to his feet, Tristan still cradled in his arms.

"What is it you want me to do for you?" Rolph asks Lucifer.

Lucifer smiles and the scene ends. I find myself back on the lakeshore with the two women as they continue to clasp my hand.

"From what you just showed me, it looks like Tristan's father was a devout man until he didn't get what he thought he deserved from God," I say to River.

"Rolph never forgave himself for what happened to me, so how was he ever going to forgive God for making it happen? He allowed Lucifer to dangle the notion of revenge in front of him like bait, and once he bit into it he lost his soul and became what he is today. I have to believe that there's still a part of him that can find redemption, but I'm afraid his time may be running out."

"I'm not sure how what you showed me will help Tristan," I confess.

"In order to understand a problem, you have to know where it started. The day Rolph pledged his loyalty to Lucifer is the day my husband lost who he was. Tristan was raised by a man who forgot he still had a soul, at least until he happened to meet Jeannie."

River looks over at Jasper's mother as if she's handing off a baton.

The scenery around us changes again, and I see Jeannie chasing a five-year-old Tristan through a meadow of lavender on the side of a hill. Tristan's joyous laughter is contagious, and I find myself smiling while watching the scene unfold.

"I'm going to get you!" Jeannie threatens playfully, and I notice her voice has a Scottish lilt to it.

"No, you won't! I'm fast like a wolf!" Tristan declares as he weaves back and forth while he runs and laughs.

Completely out of breath, Jeannie finally stops running to fill her lungs with some much-needed oxygen.

"You win!" she declares. "I can't keep up with you. You're just too fast for me."

Tristan runs over to her and wraps his arms around her waist.

"I love you, Jeannie," he proclaims. "I don't want to see you get hurt."

Jeannie looks confused by Tristan's words. She unwraps his arms from around her and kneels before him until they're eye level with one another.

"Sweetie, why would you say such a thing?" she asks. "Who would hurt me?"

"Daddy," he tells her. "You should leave us, Jeannie. He's not a good man."

Jeannie looks even more perplexed by Tristan's words of warning.

"Why would you say that? Your father is one of the best men I know."

Tristan vigorously shakes his head. He opens his mouth to say something else to her, but he's interrupted by his father calling out his name.

At the bottom of the hill I see Rolph standing there, waving a hand as if signaling Jeannie and Tristan to come join him. I can see from my vantage point that he has laid out quite a picnic for the three of them to enjoy.

"Come on, little man," Jeannie says, taking Tristan's hand in her own. "Let's go see what your daddy brought for our lunch. And let's just forget about what you said. We wouldn't want to hurt his feeling, now, would we?"

Tristan doesn't make a reply. He simply obediently follows Jeannie down the hill.

The scene ends. Once our surroundings go back to the rocky

shore of the lake both women let go of my hands, as if signaling that they've shown me everything they wanted to.

"Tristan *did* give you a warning," I say, finding this curious. "Why doesn't he remember doing that?"

Jeannie shrugs. "It could be that he was simply too young to remember such a brief encounter, but I want you to remind him about what he tried to do. I should have taken his warning seriously, but Tristan was only five years old at the time. How many adults actually listen to the advice of someone so young? Make sure you tell him that I don't blame him one bit for what happened. I was the adult. I should have seen the signs, but Rolph was so charming back then. I thought the sun rose just because he was in the world. Now that I think back on that time with him and Tristan, I should have known something was wrong. I believe he loved me in a way, but only for his own selfish reasons. He wanted another son to prance around, and unfortunately I helped him accomplish that goal by giving him Jasper."

"Tristan refuses to ask God to remove his curse until Jasper is willing to go before God with him," I tell the two women, hoping their combined experiences with Rolph and love for Tristan can provide me with a way to help him. "He's willing to waste his life on a goal that he may never be able to reach. I don't know what else to say to him to make him change his mind."

"I don't believe there is anything that you can say," River tells me. "Tristan will have to come to terms with things in his own way. If you try to force him to do what you want, it might just alienate him even further."

"I don't want that to happen."

"Then give my son the time and patience that he needs right now, Mae. I have a feeling you won't have to wait too much longer before things are resolved."

I can't say River's words are very comforting. She isn't telling me whether Tristan will eventually give up on his quest or if his brother will finally see the light.

"Mae?" I hear a woman say behind me.

I turn around to see a beautiful black woman standing on the rocky shoal, dressed in a white dress with a large red rose on the skirt. The clothing looks like something you would see in a movie set during the 1950s. Standing to the right of the woman is a blond-haired girl who looks like she's maybe four years old.

"Hello," I say to the woman. "Do I know you?"

"No, child, but I know you," she says with a kind smile. "I'm Utha Mae."

I walk over to my namesake and feel an instant connection to her. As we hug for the first time, I feel a sense of homecoming that comforts my soul. When I pull back, I look down at the little girl standing beside her.

"Hello," I say. "And what's your name?"

"River," the girl tells me as she tilts her head to the side. "You're really pretty."

"Thank you," I say. "And you're quite beautiful."

"That's what Utha Mae is always telling me," she says, looking bashful about the compliment.

"River, honey," Utha Mae says, "why don't you go see your grandma? It's been a while since you saw her last."

"Okay," River says as she carefully makes her way over to Tristan's mother.

I look at Utha Mae, feeling somewhat confused by what's happening.

"Grandmother?" I ask her. "I didn't know Tristan had a daughter who died. I thought Watcher children couldn't have kids of their own while they were still cursed."

"They can't, sweetie," she tells me. "River hasn't been born yet. She's a new soul."

"Then, I don't understand. Why is she with you?"

"God lets me spend time with the children who will eventually become a part of Lilly and Tara's families," she tells me.

It doesn't take a genius to understand what Utha Mae is telling me. I look back at River with newfound amazement.

"She'll be Tristan's and my daughter?" I ask her, just to clarify my assumption.

"Eventually, yes," she replies. "She's simply waiting for the two of you to sort things out on Earth and have her."

I look back at Utha Mae. "Then we *are* meant to be together?"

"Was there ever any doubt?" she asks, as if my question didn't need to be asked.

"A little," I admit. "When we learned we weren't soul mates..."

"Oh," Utha Mae says as understanding dawns. "Well, if you think about the way Tristan sees himself right now, don't you believe he would rather know you're with him because you want to be and not simply because he's your soul mate?"

"I suppose so..." I say, wondering where she's going with this until it dawns on me what's she's getting at. "Are you saying that he'll believe my love for him more if he knows I'm actually choosing him of my own free will?"

"That's exactly what I'm saying, child. Tristan has never thought too much of himself, and I can't say that I blame him for that. His father put him down so much, Tristan began to believe what Rolph told him. How a parent can do that to their own child is beyond me. If I could, I would put Rolph over my lap and give him a good spanking for what he did to his sons."

"Do you know Ella has found her soul mate?"

Utha Mae smiles. "Of course I do. There isn't much that gets past me up here."

"I got a little jealous of her over that," I confess.

"You're only human, child. It happens. But I think it's better that Tristan knows you choose him because you want to, not because you don't have any other choice."

The more I think about Utha Mae's advice, the more I realize she's absolutely right.

I look back at River as she talks to her grandmother and Jeannie.

"Does she know I'll be her mother?" I ask Utha Mae.

"I didn't mention that part to her," she replies. "I just told her that we were going to meet one of the babies I used to take care of."

I look at Utha Mae and ask, "You took care of me before I was born, too?"

"I sure did," she says proudly.

"I don't remember any of that."

"None of you do," she sighs disappointedly. "It makes me a little sad, but I guess it's for the best. Once you come here after your life on Earth is over, all the memories we made here together will come rushing back to you."

"If you don't mind, I think I need to make a lot more memories for myself on Earth before that happens."

"Yes, you do," Utha Mae agrees. "And I have no doubt whatsoever that it'll be a life filled with beautiful ones."

I silently agree with Utha Mae. I plan to live a life with no regrets, and now that I've met the daughter Tristan and I will have in the future I don't intend to let her down. I'll help her father work through his family issues and then show him what it truly means to be in a loving and supportive relationship, because after everything he's been through he deserves nothing less.

W hen I return home, I feel as though I'm being tortured. I can't go to Tristan and tell him what I learned in Heaven, because he's probably still running around in the woods near his cabin in wolf form. The rational part of my mind knows I just need to be patient. Unfortunately, patience has never been a virtue of the women in my family. I call Ella to see if she wants to go out and do something to help me fill my time that evening, but I don't get an answer from her until well after six that night. I should have known she would be attending the evening services at our church, and I suddenly realize I'll need to start sharing my best friend with David. I feel another small pang of jealousy at the thought, but it's not the first time Ella has had a boyfriend who needed to be incorporated into our lives. Although, David is more than just someone she'll date. He'll be the man she eventually marries and raises a family with.

The thought of family brings a clear picture of little River to my mind. I guess the mystery of what Tristan and I should name our daughter is solved for me. It seems fitting that we'll name her after Tristan's mother, and I wonder if making her first name River and her middle name Rayne, in honor of my own mother, is too corny. I quickly decide I don't care if other people think it is or not. My daughter should always remember the strong women who helped make her life possible in the first place.

I'm not exactly sure how much of my visit to Heaven I should tell Tristan about. Would the knowledge that our daughter's soul has already been made be too much for him to handle? I don't know the answer to that question. For me, meeting her was a joyous moment, but in view of everything that Tristan is going through right now, it might be better not to tell him of her existence just yet. Odds are it would only add to the pressure he's already feeling, and increasing his burden is the last thing I want to do to him.

I end up going to bed early that night, which turns out to be easier than I thought it would be. Having not slept that much the night before helps me fall asleep almost immediately.

When I go down to breakfast the next morning, I hear a multitude of voices emanating from the kitchen. I listen for Tristan's voice to be in the mix, but I don't hear him. I do, however, hear Jered speaking with Uncle Malik about the horses on his ranch. When I enter the room, I quickly scan the area for Tristan because I assume he simply isn't talking, but I soon discover that he isn't here at all.

"Where's Tristan?" I ask Jered, without even saying a good morning to everyone else first.

Jered stands from his place at the table and walks over to me.

"He asked me to send his apologies. He isn't feeling well after his run in the woods last night, so he thought it would be better if he rested up before tomorrow's game."

"Then he's sick?" I ask, wondering if this is the case or if Tristan is simply avoiding me this morning.

"That's what he told me," Jered says truthfully. "He did look tired when I left him."

"Where is he? At his cabin or your house?"

"My house."

"Do you mind if I go over there to see him?" I ask the question out of pure politeness, but whether Jered says yes or no is irrelevant. I fully intend to go there to see what's wrong with Tristan for myself.

"You can," Jered says hesitantly, "but I'm not sure he's going to be very good company."

"He doesn't have to say anything," I assure him. "I have enough to talk about all on my own."

Before any of my family can talk me out of going, I phase to the living room in Jered's house. There I find my quarry, lying on the couch, covered in a thick fuzzy grey blanket, and watching a football game on the holographic TV.

"What are you doing here, Mae?" Tristan asks in surprise, as if he's not sure if I'm real or a hallucination.

When I look at him, I can tell that he is indeed sick. His eyes look bloodshot, his voice sounds raw, and he looks as pale as a white sheet of paper.

"Did you catch a cold?" I ask him.

Tristan sniffs before answering. "I guess so. It's really odd, because I almost never get sick. I must have stayed out too long last night."

"Do you want me to get Rafe over here to heal you?"

"No. I don't want to waste his gift or time on a simple cold."

"Okay, then, stay where you are, and I'll be right back with something that should help," I tell him.

I phase to my bathroom and rummage through the drawer in my vanity that holds some of my Uncle Malik's Fae elixirs. I find the purple bottle for a common cold and the blue one for a stuffy nose. With medicine in hand, I phase back to Tristan.

Without me having to ask him to, Tristan lifts himself into a sitting position as I come over to stand by the side of the couch. I unscrew the top off the first bottle and use it as a cup to administer the right dose of medicine. After Tristan drinks medicine from both bottles, I set them down on the coffee table and proceed to tuck his grey blanket around him.

He doesn't say anything while I do this, but he does look at me like he's amused by my actions.

"Do you treat everyone you care about like an invalid when they're sick, or just me?" he asks.

"I treat everyone this way, so don't think you're special or anything," I tease him.

"I'll try not to get too big a head, but I might get spoiled if you keep this up."

"You should start to feel better in a couple of hours," I tell him. "So, enjoy this while you can."

"Wow. That's impressive. I assume that was Fae medicine that you gave me from Malik and Tara's company."

"Yeah. We have a lifetime supply of the stuff at our house." I look over at the football game Tristan is watching. "Trying to learn some new plays before the big game?"

"Right now, I would be happy to just learn the rules."

"Learn the rules?" I ask, assuming I misunderstood what he meant. "It's just football. We don't play it any differently in my family."

"I, uh," Tristan begins, but hesitates as he looks over at me sheepishly, "I don't know anything about football."

"How can you not know anything?" I ask in total shock. "It's been around forever."

Tristan shrugs. "I just never took an interest in it, to be honest. I mean, the basic rules seem pretty simple. Your dad said I would be the running back, so I'm trying to watch what other running backs do."

"I'll watch the game with you," I say as I sit down on the floor next to the couch near Tristan's head. He scrunches back underneath his cover to keep warm. "If you have any questions, just let me know and I'll answer them for you."

"How is it that you know so much about this sport?"

"My family likes to get together occasionally to watch games together and, of course, there's the annual Thanksgiving match-up. We've been doing that since I was little. Between my dad and Uncle Malcolm, it was pretty much impossible not to learn about football."

"Do you enjoy the game?"

"I would rather be at a live one than watch it on TV, but I still have fun this way. I have a lot of fond memories associated with it. Mostly because my dad and uncle would always choose to root for opposing teams. Watching them taunt each other always made it a lot more fun for everyone else. I think they just did it to entertain the rest of us."

"It must have been fun growing up in a family like yours."

I note a tinge of jealousy in Tristan's voice concerning the loving relationship I have with my relatives. I can't say I blame him for being envious of my close-knit family, considering the state of his own.

I grab the TV remote and turn up the volume.

"Let me know if you have any questions," I tell Tristan. "I can answer almost anything."

Tristan and I begin to watch the game together. By the two-hour mark, he tells me that he's feeling much better and attempts to leave the couch to go make something to eat. I push him back down and tell him to stay while I go to the kitchen to make him some food.

"Do you think that's a good idea?" he asks me, not trying to be funny, but to me the sincere worry on his face about me entering the kitchen alone is quite amusing.

"I'm just going to make you some sandwiches," I promise him. "Don't worry. I won't burn Jered's house down."

Tristan smiles and lowers his eyes guiltily, because that's exactly what he was thinking about my culinary skills. I don't blame him one bit, considering my family's track record of failed cooking attempts. I'm not sure why none of us can cook well. Perhaps it was God's way of making sure the men in our lives felt needed. By nourishing our bodies with food and our souls with love, they keep us physically and emotionally able to perform God's work and accomplish His plan for all of us.

After I make a stack of ham and cheese sandwiches, I return to the living room and promptly drop the plate of food on the floor when I discover we're no longer alone.

Tristan is now standing from his spot on the couch, facing his father.

I briefly remember my promise to my parents that if I ever ran into Rolph I would immediately phase away and seek help, but I can't leave Tristan with his dad. He's still in a weakened state from being sick and wouldn't be any match against a Watcher's strength.

When Rolph glances in my direction, I see him sneer as if the mere sight of me turns his stomach.

"I guess I should have known you would be with *her* now," Tristan's father says in disgust. "Since you left us for her once, it's not exactly a surprise that you would choose to disregard my offering to let you back into our family by killing her."

I gasp in surprise. Does that mean my death was actually supposed to be a test of Tristan's loyalty? If he killed me, Tristan's father would forget his son's previous transgressions and bring him back into the fold. Since Tristan didn't kill me, thereby refusing his father's offer to return to his side, what kind of punishment was he planning to exact on his son?

"River says hello, Rolph," I say, only telling a smidge of a white lie to distract Tristan's father from the real reason he came here this morning.

I witness Rolph wince, as if just the mention of his wife's name causes him pain. I begin to wonder if I've made a grave error in judgment when his gaze turns downright murderous.

"How do you know her name?" Rolph demands.

"Who's River?" Tristan questions as he looks between me and his father, a confused expression on his face, waiting for one of us to answer his question.

It never even occurred to me that Tristan wouldn't know his mother's name.

"She was your mother," Rolph answers as he keeps his gaze steadily on me. "What I want to know is how you know it when I never even told Tristan what his mother's name was."

"I talked with her yesterday," I reply, hating the fact that Tristan is learning about my trip to Heaven like this. I had planned to tell him after the football game on TV was over, but Rolph's unexpected presence is forcing me to talk about it now.

Both Rolph and Tristan remain silent as they allow the implications of what I just said to sink in.

"And what did she say to you?" Rolph asks, never questioning the fact that I did indeed speak with his dead wife. It tells me that he must know about my family's ability to phase into Heaven whenever we want. When I look over at Tristan to gauge his reaction to my statement, he doesn't necessarily look surprised about my ability to cross the veil over into Heaven. Instead, he seems to be as curious as his father is to know what his mother said to me when I spoke with her.

"It's not necessarily what she told me," I say. "It's what she showed me about you."

"And what was that?" Rolph asks tersely, as his already thin patience is quickly waning.

"She showed me how much you loved her," I tell him. "And she showed me the way Lucifer goaded you into abandoning your faith to God after Tristan was born."

"He didn't goad me into doing anything that I didn't want to do," Rolph defends.

"That's not exactly true," I remind him. "Up until the point River died, you believed God would save her life, even though her fate had already been sealed. I saw you praying to Him and asking Him for His help."

"Help that He never gave!" Rolph storms, making me second-guess my decision to even bring up my conversation with River.

"Is she happy?" I hear Tristan ask, drawing my attention away from his dad. "Is she at peace?"

"Of course, she's at peace," I tell him. "And she's very proud of you for standing up to your father." I look over at Rolph. "She's as proud of Tristan as she is disappointed in you. She's sad that you used her death as an excuse to turn your back to God. River never wanted you to do that. She wanted you to remain strong for her son, not drag him down with you into depravity by following Lucifer."

"If you're trying to shame me for the things I've done, I'm afraid that tactic isn't going to work on me, little girl," Rolph says condescendingly. "I don't believe that emotion is within my repertoire of feelings anymore. River can delude herself into believing whatever lies my Father is telling her, but I know the truth. He abandoned us for His own selfish reasons."

"You broke His one rule to you," I counter. "My father went through the same heartache you did, but he never turned his back on God. He protected my sister and kept her pure."

"None of our children is pure," Rolph says in disgust. "They're all a bunch of filthy mongrels who only live to serve whatever need we have for them. Tristan was lucky Lucifer was there the day he was born, or I would have ended his life almost as soon as it began."

Again, I gasp involuntarily. Rolph's words are filled with so much unmitigated hate that I know they're true. When I look over at Tristan, he doesn't seem the least bit surprised by what his father just said, and I can only assume that he must have heard the same exact words many times before. My heart aches at the thought of him as a child, having to grow up in a home where his father reminded him just how worthless he was every day of his life. I feel my eyes burn with unshed tears as I imagine Tristan as a little boy, enduring his father's unfiltered hatred of him.

"Your wife wasn't the only one I spoke with in Heaven," I tell Rolph. "I also saw Jasper's mother."

Rolph lifts a dubious eyebrow at this revelation.

"I have to say I'm somewhat surprised by that," he tells me. "I didn't think my Father allowed whores into Heaven."

My look of surprise at his use of the word makes Rolph laugh cruelly.

"Don't tell me Saint Jeannie didn't tell you she was a whore when I knew her on Earth," Rolph says, unable to contain his mirth. "When I found her, she was living in filth in a whorehouse. I cleaned her up because I couldn't stand her stench and presented her to my son as a temporary mother. Once I fattened her up enough to carry a Watcher child, I blessed her with my seed so she could give me Jasper. I'm glad I had the foresight to plan ahead and have another child as backup. Tristan turned out to be a complete failure, but his brother is staying true to me despite his brother's treachery."

"Not for much longer," Tristan growls, casting a gaze of pure loathing at his father.

"Jasper is stronger than you," Rolph declares, holding his head up a notch as if he's looking down on Tristan because he views him as being weak. "I don't care what this bitch says: your mother could never be proud of a son who would turn his back on his family."

"I turned my back on *you*," Tristan points out, "not Jasper. He knows I still love him, and I'll do whatever it takes to get him away from you. You're a hate-filled, spiteful person, Father. I was holding out hope that your soul could be saved one day, but now I'm not so sure that will ever be possible. I think your soul might be lost to Lucifer forever."

"I gladly gave Lucifer my loyalty because I believe in his cause!" Rolph storms as his face twists into a mask of rage. "God should be made to pay for what He did to us. He had no right to punish our wives for something that we did. They were innocents that He happily slaughtered to teach us a lesson in His own cruel way. How can you possibly think He deserves our loyalty? How can you blindly follow someone who would force you to kill your own mother just to be born into this world? If you're able to love a vengeful creature like that, then you're as much of a monster as I am."

With those parting words, Rolph phases away.

I stand there for a moment to see whether Rolph intends to come back and attack us, but nothing happens. I bend down to pick up the pieces of the shattered china plate and scattered sandwiches from the floor.

"Let me help you with that," Tristan says as he walks over to where I am.

"Why was he here?" I ask Tristan. "Did he say something to you before I entered the room?"

"He came to warn me to stay away from Jasper. It's an old argument. I honestly don't know why he even bothered," Tristan replies. He doesn't go into detail about what his father said exactly, and I don't push the matter. I can only imagine what my revelation about visiting Heaven is doing to him, because he certainly isn't telling me.

"I'm sorry you had to learn about my speaking with your mom and Jeannie like that," I tell him in way of apology. "I had planned to tell you after you ate."

"Why did you go to Heaven to talk with them?" Tristan asks with a great deal of hesitancy as he picks up the last shard of china from the floor, adding it to the small pile he has in his other hand.

"We should go throw away all of this first," I suggest. "Then I'll tell you why I went and everything that they told me."

I quickly phase us to the kitchen so we can dispose of our trash. I then proceed to make some more sandwiches while Tristan sits down on one of the stools at the kitchen island and watches me expectantly.

As I'm slathering a piece of bread with mayonnaise, I tell him, "I went to Heaven yesterday to find a way to end your guilt over your mother's and Jeannie's death. It was obvious yesterday that Jasper's accusations about his mother's death hurt you, and I was hoping she could tell me something about that time that would ease your mind. Turns out I was right about going, because she was able to tell me something that you must have forgotten."

"What do you mean?" he asks.

"She showed me a moment from your past when you warned her about your father. You told her she should leave him, but she didn't take your warning seriously. Jasper's accusation that you didn't tell his mother what his father planned to do to her wasn't correct. You tried to tell her but she didn't believe you because, in her eyes, you were only a five-year-old child with an overactive imagination. Considering what your dad just said about her past, I doubt she wanted to leave what must have been paradise for her. Not only was she fooled into believing he cared about her, but she was also tricked into thinking that he would eventually marry her and the three of you would live happily ever after. You did all that you could to save her, Tristan, and she knows that."

Tristan doesn't look as relieved as I thought he would that Jeannie doesn't blame him for her death, but I suppose that's to be expected. He's lived with the guilt of her passing for a long time now. It's going to take quite a while before what I said has a chance to take root in his heart and grow into self-forgiveness.

"I never knew my mother's name was River," Tristan tells me, sounding slightly awed by the sound of her name passing over his lips. "My dad wouldn't tell me what it was. I got the feeling it hurt him too much to even think about her."

"From what she showed me he loved her very much, and he truly believed that God would save her life."

"I didn't know Lucifer was present for my birth," Tristan says. "He chose to coerce my father into following him when he was at his most vulnerable. I wish my dad had been stronger back then. If he had been more like your father, I would have lived a much different life."

"Do you think it would help if Jasper knew how sad his mother is about his refusal to leave his father?"

"I'm not sure," Tristan sighs. "It might help, or it might just sound like a desperate ploy we're using on him to leave Dad's side. To be honest, I'm not sure what my brother is thinking right now. He was filled with so much hatred yesterday, Mae. The only other time I've seen him like that was when I first returned to the house after leaving them for you. He was so angry with me because he thought I had abandoned him. Then, when your sister's fight with the princes of Hell was over and I left him again, it was like that broke something inside him."

"Did you ask Jasper to leave with you that second time?"

"Yes, but he just called me crazy and said I would live to regret it. I think he's always believed that I would return home. When I didn't, it's like his resentment over me leaving grew exponentially."

By this time, I've made two sandwiches. I place them both on another plate and hand it to Tristan.

"You need to eat to build up your strength after being sick," I tell him.

"I wasn't really sick for all that long," he reminds me. "I can see now why Malik and Tara's organic remedies company does so well."

"Yeah, I think they're like billionaires now, but you wouldn't know it by looking at the way they live. Ella told me they give a lot of their money away to charities all over the world, just like my mom and dad do."

"I've always wondered why you and your siblings have jobs," Tristan says as he picks up his first sandwich. "I thought you all would have trust funds to live off for the rest of your lives."

"Oh, we do," I'm quick to correct. "We don't work because we have to. It's something we want to do. Take my parents for instance; they still teach their classes at Southeastern, even though they have enough money to live on for the rest of their lives and then some. Since we were kids, they've always instilled in us a sense of pride in giving back to society. But we also have the privilege of choosing exactly what we want to do with our lives. Most people aren't afforded that kind of luxury."

While Tristan eats his two sandwiches, I make one for myself because I realize I haven't had breakfast yet. I left my house in such a hurry that I didn't take a moment to grab something to eat.

Once Tristan is through with his and I'm halfway through with mine, I decide to ask a question that's been on my mind.

"Why hasn't your father tried to replace you by having another Watcher child?"

"They can't have children anymore," Tristan replies, as if I should have already known the answer to my own question.

"Oh," I say in surprise. "I didn't realize that."

"God granted the Watchers who asked for forgiveness the ability to have normal human children with their wives but he basically sterilized the others, like my father."

"I suppose that was a good thing," I say, unsure how Tristan will react to my statement.

"It was a good thing," he replies emphatically. "It was the best thing He could have done to them. No one should have to grow up like Jasper and I did. I just wish He had done it sooner."

I'm not really sure what to say about that. It's almost as if Tristan is questioning his own right to live.

"Maybe if you tell Jasper that you did try to warn his mom about his father, it'll make him change his mind about your role in her death."

"Maybe," he replies, sounding unconvinced. "To be honest, I would rather not talk about all of that right now. I would much rather just enjoy our time together today."

"Has your father ever been here before?" I ask.

"On occasion. It's not like this place is an anti-phasing zone, but normally he doesn't come here. He's only been here once before, and that was when I left him and Jasper for good. I thought he was going to kill me, but all he really did was yell and tell me what a worthless son I had always been to him."

"That's awful, Tristan," I say, feeling saddened by the hateful treatment he's received from his father all his life.

It makes me wonder if part of Tristan's problem stems from a sense of feeling unworthy to be loved by someone else. I can empathize with that sort of mental abuse. I just pray that it isn't irreversible. I wish I could tell Tristan about meeting our daughter's soul in Heaven, but it just doesn't feel like the right time to do that. I want to give him enough space to sort through his family issues first. Once he's done all he can for them, maybe then he can move on and start thinking about starting a family of his own.

"Why don't we go back and finish watching that game?" he suggests after I finish eating my sandwich. "Then we can take a walk around Jered's ranch, if you want. I feel like getting some fresh air."

"Sounds good to me," I agree. I'm just happy that he didn't suggest I leave after the game is finished. It at least shows that he wants to spend more time with me.

We go back to the living room and watch the rest of the football game together. Tristan is a quick study and instinctually picks up on the ins and outs of football. While he changes into clothes more fitting to wear out in the cold of a Montana autumn, I phase back to my bedroom and grab a coat. I make a slight detour downstairs to let my parents know that I'm all right and simply spending some time with Tristan. However, I neglect to mention my run-in with Rolph, because I know that would simply make them worry more and question my judgment about not phasing away as soon as I saw him. I silently promise to fess up about the encounter later, but right now I simply want to spend some quiet time with Tristan so we can continue to get to know one another.

After meeting his mother, I feel as though I know Tristan a little bit better now. He may view himself as a monster, but he's the exact opposite. I know he still feels burdened by the deaths he caused in the past, but there comes a time when you have to let such feelings go and find a way to move forward. I don't know the details about the atrocities he's committed and, to be honest, I don't want to know. All I want to learn more about is the man he is today, because it's that man who captured my heart the moment I met him.

Tristan escorts me around Jered's ranch after we watch the end of the game. I don't have the heart to tell him that I've been here quite a few times in the past. I suppose Uncle Malcolm and Jered made sure to coincide my visits with times Tristan wouldn't be around. When we reach the bunkhouse on the backside of the property, I'm suddenly struck by what I consider a brilliant idea.

"Does Jered use this place for anything?" I ask Tristan as I look around the spacious, yet mostly empty, dwelling. Almost everywhere you look there is finely-grained exposed wood that gives the place a rustic, yet polished, feel. Since it's a bunkhouse, there are six bunkbeds situated just off the small living room, three beds against each wall. A large kitchen is built just off the living room space, with matching stainless-steel appliances and a copper exhaust hood built over the stove in the kitchen island.

"Not that I know of. He doesn't like having people live on the property. That's probably because of me, though."

"Do you think Jered would let us use it as a place for the Watcher children we're going to be helping? Kind of like a halfway house until we can find them somewhere more permanent to live."

"I don't see why he wouldn't," Tristan says excitedly. "That's a great idea, Mae. It would certainly help to have a place we can bring them to." Tristan looks at the empty bunkbeds and sparse furnishings. "Although, it would be better if we fixed it up beforehand. We probably have some time to handle that after the holidays."

"I wouldn't be too sure about that. Yesterday, I overheard my Uncle Malcolm telling my parents that your father and a few of the other Watchers intend to have a game of Bait near your cabin this coming Wednesday."

Tristan's back stiffens after hearing the news.

"Malcolm's sure about that?" he asks in a grave voice.

"I didn't get to ask him if he was sure, because I was eavesdropping, but he seemed pretty confident that he would be able to capture your dad there."

"Capture him? How exactly?"

I hesitate before answering, not quite sure how he'll react to my uncle's plans.

"From what I overheard, he plans to separate your father's head from his body and hide each part separately for a while."

"Did he say for how long?"

"From what he said he plans to keep him that way for at least a few decades, if not more."

"Good," Tristan says, sounding pleased. "If Malcolm can take my father out of the equation, I'll have a better chance with Jasper. It might be exactly what he needs to see happen to force him to realize our father isn't indestructible."

"I was thinking we might also be able to help the Watcher children who will be there," I say. "If we're able to convince them to break their bonds with their fathers, then we need to have this place ready."

"Want to go shopping then?" Tristan says with a grin.

"You almost sound excited about going shopping."

"I like to buy things," he admits freely. "It's nice to go out and be with people, even if they're strangers. I spent years being isolated when I was with my dad. He only let me and Jasper out of the house when he needed us to do something for him. Besides, it means we get to spend more time together doing something constructive. What could be better than that?"

"Nothing," I agree as I take hold of Tristan's arm. "Let's go shopping then."

The first place we go to is a local furniture store because the living room area is in desperate need of chairs where people can sit and relax, and the beds need twin mattresses for people to sleep. We keep things simple and buy a brown leather set for the living room composed of a couch, two chairs, a coffee table, and two matching end tables. The easiest way to take the furniture back to the bunkhouse would be to phase all of it there, but to keep things looking normal we arrange to have the items delivered early the next day.

After shopping for furniture, we take time out to have lunch at a local burger joint. I opt for a simple grilled chicken salad, but Tristan goes all out and buys two of the special hamburgers with all the trimmings. He also asks for a rare cook on the patties.

"Is that the wolf in you craving the meat?" I whisper across the table to him.

"You know," he says, looking confused by how to answer my question, "I'm not really sure. It could be. I guess I won't know until my body is human."

"Your body?" I ask, finding his choice of words curious. "You make it sound like your body and soul are two separate things."

"They are," he replies, looking as if I should have already known about the difference.

"I guess I don't understand what you're getting at," I admit.

"Take your dad and Aiden for instance. Their bodies were made human, which means they age and they're mortal, but their souls never changed during the process. That part of them remained the same."

"I didn't realize there was a difference between an angelic soul and a human one."

"From what I understand, soul conversion would have taken a great deal of energy. Besides, all your dad and Aiden wanted was a chance to live out a normal life with your mom and Caylin. They wanted to grow old with them and sever their ties to what they were before, especially Aiden. He told me that he asked God to make his body human when he and Caylin were getting married, so he could pledge his mortal life to her and finally leave his past behind him. I can totally empathize with wanting to do that. There are things that I've done in the past that were just as bad or maybe even worse than what Aiden did. Hopefully, I'll have a chance to leave all of that behind me and have a fresh start at a new life."

"What's the first thing you plan to do after your curse is removed?" I ask.

Tristan smiles mysteriously, and sits back in his chair as he ponders my question.

"If I told you that," he says, "it would ruin the surprise, and I don't like spoilers."

"A surprise for me?" I ask, already feeling a sense of amazement that he's factored me into one of his plans for the future.

Tristan nods. "I hope so."

"You're not even going to give me a teeny tiny hint?"

"I'm not sure I can without giving it away." Tristan pauses, and looks down at the table as if he's trying to figure out if he wants to tell me what he's thinking. He finally makes up his mind and looks up to meet my gaze with his. "It's not just me, is it?"

"Just you what?" I ask, uncertain about what he's referring to.

"This thing between you and me," he says. "You feel it, too, right?"

"Absolutely," I reply without a smidge of doubt or hesitation. I smile when he starts to chuckle at how forthright I was with my answer.

"You're very honest," he comments, still grinning. "I like it. A lot of people try to hide their feelings, but you seem to wear yours on your sleeve and don't make any excuses for that."

"I don't like to hide things," I reply. "It doesn't make me feel good about myself. Considering that, I think we need to talk about something. I know I said I wanted to leave Uncle Malcolm out of our search for your family, but since he'll be there Wednesday night, I'm sure he and the Watchers who are going to help him will already have a plan set up to handle things. I think we should tell him we want to be there, too."

"You know he'll try to talk us out of going," Tristan warns.

"I realize that, but whether he approves of us being there or not we're still going to be there. He would be wiser to accept our help than try to work against us."

"I like this feisty side of you, too," Tristan says. "Remind me to never get into an argument with you, because I'm pretty certain I would lose."

"You most definitely would," I agree.

Tristan laughs. The waiter brings our plates to us, putting an end to our conversation for the time being.

After we finish our meal, we head to the mall and shop for bedding and a few knickknacks to make the bunkhouse feel like home for those who will be staying there. Tristan proves to be an excellent shopper, or maybe it's the fact that what he picks out is the same exact thing I would have if I had been shopping alone.

"Do you think we should have told Jered what we have planned before buying all of this stuff?" I ask Tristan as I place the new dishes we bought into one of the cabinets while he lays the silverware in a drawer.

"Told me what exactly?" Jered says unexpectedly as he walks into the kitchen of the bunkhouse with Ella.

"What are doing you here?" I ask my best friend, leaving my work for the moment as I walk over to give her a welcoming hug.

"I came to see what you were up to," she tells me. "I haven't seen you all day."

As I pull away from her, I say, "I assumed you would be spending the day with David."

"I did spend some of it with him, but he's not the only person in my life, Mae. I still want to spend time with you."

"What are the two of you doing to the bunkhouse?" Jered asks as he looks at the pile of store bags strewn across the large kitchen island. "Setting up house?"

"Kind of," I tell him.

I look over at Tristan with a questioning gaze, because I'm not sure how much of our mission he's told Jered about. Apparently not a lot, because Tristan proceeds to tell Jered and Ella everything, including our plans for the bunkhouse.

"I take it you haven't told Malcolm about your desire to be there Wednesday," Jered says knowingly.

"Not yet," I reply. "I will as soon as I can, though. He needs to know that Tristan and I intend to be there. It's the perfect opportunity for me to make contact with some of the Watcher children. According to what God told us, they need to be in wolf form to feel the full effect of my gift."

"You do realize Malcolm will argue that you should wait for him to handle Rolph first," Jered points out. "If you think about it, that would be the smart play here."

"I understand that," I say patiently, "but I'm not going to hide in a corner when I can help people now, Jered."

Jered doesn't say anything, and I can tell he's biting his tongue. He probably assumes Uncle Malcolm will talk some sense into me when I tell him about my plan.

Jered looks around the bunkhouse and says, "You're welcome to use this place as long as you want. I haven't had anyone stay here since I bought the ranch. It'll be nice for it to finally have a purpose."

"Thanks, Jered," Tristan and I say in unison.

"You're going to need some furniture, though," he points out, "and some mattresses for the beds."

"We went and bought some in town today," Tristan tells him. "They're supposed to deliver it tomorrow morning."

"Which furniture store did you go to?" Jered asks.

Tristan tells him the name of the store, and Jered says he can go get the items we bought and just phase them directly into the bunkhouse. Apparently, the store owner is a friend of his and knows he's a Watcher. Most of the world remembers the Watchers. They were famous for a time, but since the Tear was closed their infamy has dwindled. That's the way they wanted it, and none of them seem to miss being in the limelight.

With Jered and Ella's help, we have the bunkhouse ready for its new arrivals within an hour's time.

"I think this looks awesome!" Ella says once everything is in its place. "It's all so homey it makes me want to move in."

"I'm not sure it would be wise to live with a bunch of rehabilitating werewolves," I point out.

"What's your plan with that anyway?" Ella asks. "Do you hope to have them ask God to remove their curse right away?"

"I think it will depend on each individual case," I reason. "Some of them might be ready to go before God, and some of them might need more time to adjust. I'm sure we'll just have to play it by ear and see what works best."

"Personally, I think the two of you are off to a good start," Jered praises. "Would you ladies be interested in staying for dinner? I have some yummy ribeye steaks in the refrigerator just begging to be grilled."

"That's super sweet of you, Mr. Jered," Ella says, "but Mae and I need to get back home."

"We do?" I ask, not understanding why she's in such a hurry to leave.

"Tomorrow's game day, remember?" Ella says. "We've got to practice our routines."

"Oh yeah," I say, feeling foolish. "I totally forgot about that."

"Practice what routines?" Tristan asks, sounding intrigued.

"Our cheerleading routines," Ella says, as if it should have been obvious to him. "Everybody knows that the team with the best cheerleaders wins."

"Are you sure that's how it works?" I ask. "Because if that's the case, then we've been sucking at it for years. My dad hasn't won a game in a decade."

"This year we're winning!" Ella declares. "With my new svelte curves off the field and Tristan's moves on the field, we're a shoo-in for the golden turkey this year!"

"Golden turkey?" Tristan asks, looking perplexed by the mixing of the two words.

I have to laugh because the expression on his face is just too priceless. I can just imagine his thoughts right now. I'm sure the most prominent one is *What in the world have I gotten myself into?*

"It's the trophy," Ella says matter-of-factly. "Whoever wins gets to keep the golden turkey on their mantel until the next year. It gives the winner bragging rights until the next Thanksgiving."

"You guys really take this game seriously," Tristan says, fully realizing that the match-up he's competing in tomorrow isn't just a sports game. It's battle of the titans, as far as my family is concerned.

"While you girls are practicing your cheers," Jered says, "I think it might be a good idea if I take Tristan out back and give him some pointers about the game."

"That's a very good idea," I agree.

Even though I would much rather stay and have dinner with Tristan and Jered, it's a better idea if he practices his moves before tomorrow. I really want him to do well, and I know the reason isn't just because I want our team to win this year. If Tristan can help my father finally take home the golden turkey, it will go a long way in forging a relationship between the two of them.

Tristan walks over to where Ella and I are standing.

"I had fun with you today," he tells me. "Thanks for bringing over that medicine. It really helped a lot. And thank you for what you did for me yesterday. It meant the world to me that you would go all the way to Heaven just to get answers for me."

"I'm just glad it helped," I tell him.

"I guess I'll see you in the morning then," he tells me, sounding reluctant that we'll have to spend so much time apart.

"I'll see you later," I promise him. I have no intention of waiting until morning to see him again. As soon as my house goes to sleep, I plan to phase back here and stay with Tristan in his prison cell. He shouldn't have to spend the night alone in a place he detests. At least with me there, he can snuggle up to my warmth and know that someone who loves him is watching over him while he sleeps.

Tristan leans in and gives me a small peck on the cheek.

"See you later," he whispers in my ear, and I know he understands the hidden promise of my return later that evening.

I phase Ella and me back to my mom's house in Colorado, because that's traditionally where we practice with her and Aunt Tara. If my dad and Uncle Malcolm take their rivalry seriously, my Aunt Tara and Jess take their cheering to a whole new level on the insane scale. Jess' cheerleading squad consists of her, JoJo, Leah, and

Faison. Aunt Tara already warned me and Ella that she had a new cheer for us to learn for the game. It was one the cheerleaders used to do when she and my mom were in high school. I soon learn the good reason why it was retired from all cheerleading events.

"You're kidding, right?" I ask my aunt after she demonstrates what we're supposed to do.

"No, baby, I am not kidding," Aunt Tara tells me, with a slight swaying of her head to indicate she means business. "This is going to bring Jess and the others *down* this year."

"Down laughing, you mean," Ella whispers to me with a roll of her eyes.

Honestly, she really should have known better.

Aunt Tara lightly taps her on the back of the head.

"No sass from you, little Miss Ella," her mother says. "You will learn this routine and you will *love* it with all your heart and soul."

"Tara, I think you're taking this a little too seriously," my mother says as the voice of reason.

"And I don't think you girls are taking it seriously enough!" Aunt Tara complains. "Every year poor Brand has to suffer through Malcolm's gloating after he wins."

"Malcolm doesn't gloat," my mom defends. "He barely says a word."

"Exactly!" Aunt Tara says, pointing a finger at my mom like she hit the nail on the head. "He doesn't have to say anything. That smug expression on his face says it all. And every year Jess and JoJo show up in their cute little cheerleading outfits that JoJo makes them, cheering circles around us. Do I need to remind you what they did last year to one-up us?"

"Oh, that dance routine they did really was awesome," Ella says. "I hope they do another one again this year."

And again, Ella really should have known better. Her words earn her another light tap on the back of the head.

"Stop hitting me in the head, Mom! I kind of need my brain intact to make it through college!"

"Then stop sassing me, girl!"

"Okay, okay, okay," my mom says, quickly intervening. "Let's all learn Tara's cheer, so we can make her happy."

I cringe that my mother is taking my aunt's side on this particular matter, but we all know she won't let us go until we've learned her routine. Once the torture is over and Aunt Tara is satisfied with our efforts, she releases us back into the wild.

"Why don't you girls go inside while Tara and I go get some spaghetti and salads from Happy Howlers," my mother suggests to me and Ella.

None of us argue against her plan. It's an age-old tradition that we've done for many years. My mom and Aunt Tara decide to phase over to the franchise in Denver to wait for the order to be made, which gives me some girl time with Ella.

"What did you and David do today?" I ask her as we lounge in the living room in front of the lit fireplace.

"Talked mostly," she says with a smile, looking somewhat shy.

"You're so lucky," I tell her. "I can't believe you found your soul mate!"

Ella looks over at me in surprise at first, but dawning soon enters her eyes and an even happier smile graces her face.

"That makes total sense," she says, shaking her head like she can't believe how lucky she is. "I instantly knew he was the one for me."

"It looked like the feeling was mutual," I tell her as my heart swells with joy for my best friend.

When Ella looks back at me, she seems concerned. "Does it bother you?"

"That you found your soul mate and I didn't?" I ask. When she nods her head, I know I have to fess up. "Honestly, it did at first, but then I realized Tristan doesn't need to be my soul mate for me to love him."

"Has he said how he feels about you yet?"

"Not in so many words, but I know he at least likes me a lot. That much I can tell for sure. Whether he loves me or not, I can't really say, and I wouldn't presume to know what's going through his mind. I think he's so consumed by his quest to get Jasper away from their dad that he isn't able to think about much else. I'm hoping that after that situation is resolved, one way or the other, he'll have more time to figure out what it is he feels for me."

"I'll be honest, Mae, I think he's always loved you in his way. It probably wasn't a romantic love at first, because that would have been a little creepy since you were only a toddler when the two of you met, but he's always done whatever it took to keep you safe."

"I just can't believe God gave us such an important mission to complete together."

"I sort of figured there was something special about you, considering every animal you encounter obeys your every command, but I had no idea it was a gift from God. That's amazing, Mae! I can't say I'm too happy about your plan to go to that Bait game, though, but as long as Uncle Malcolm and the other Watchers are there you should be safe enough."

"Yeah, let's keep that between us for now, okay? I haven't exactly told my parents or Uncle Malcolm about that part of our plan."

"I would advise you to do it soon," she warns. "You know how protective Uncle Malcolm is when it comes to our safety. He might put up a fight and force you to stay behind."

"Tristan and I plan to go whether Uncle Malcolm wants us to or not," I state firmly. "He learned to let Caylin fight her own battles. He'll just have to learn how to do that with me, too."

Ella just looks at me like I'm crazy before she busts out laughing.

"What's so funny?" I ask her, not seeing how what I said would cause her so much unbridled mirth.

Ella finally brings her laughter under control and says, "Out of all us kids, you've always been Uncle Malcolm's favorite. He even loves you more than his own grandchildren."

"Oh, that's not true," I deny, shaking my head slightly.

"Of course, it's true," Ella replies. "Good luck getting him to back down, because you're going to need it."

As I mull over Ella's words, I worry that she just might be right. Uncle Malcolm and I have always shared a special bond for some reason. I remember Caylin saying it's because I always looked so much like our mother. Whatever the basis for his years of doting, he'll just have to learn that I'm not a child anymore. I haven't been for quite some time.

However, I do know my Uncle Malcolm quite well. He won't just lie down and let me walk all over him if he believes my life is in danger. It could be that we'll end up having our first real argument, and I'm not extremely confident that I'll win.

The rest of the evening passes by relatively peacefully. After we eat our supper, I tell my family that I'm tired and just want to go to bed to rest up for the next day. As soon as I enter my room I grab a thick wool coat, a pillow, and a blanket from my closet. I'm not sure why the room Jered built for Tristan doesn't have any sort of heating. Perhaps it's because Tristan is hot enough while in wolf form, but I'm human and need the added warmth.

I leave a note on my bed, just in case my mom or dad come looking for me during the night. I don't want them to worry unnecessarily over my whereabouts or safety.

When I phase into the cold, dark space where Tristan should be, I instantly feel his warm breath brush against the back of my neck.

"I need a minute for my eyes to adjust to the dark," I tell him.

I hear him whimper slightly behind me, but he doesn't move. He gives me time to get used to the surroundings. Just as before, the light by the door outside and the pin lights in the ceiling, which mimic the constellations in the sky, illuminate the space just enough for me to see by. When my eyesight has adjusted, I turn around to face Tristan in his werewolf form.

As I stare at him, I blurt out a question.

"Does it hurt when you transform?"

Tristan whimpers in response, telling me that, yes, it does in fact hurt him every night when his body is forced to transfigure itself into this form.

Slowly, I reach out with my right hand and caress the side of his face. He instantly tilts his head and mewls softly, as if my touch brings him comfort.

"I wish you could talk to me when you're like this," I say softly, just as I realize something. "Can you talk to me? I never even bothered to ask."

"Some," he replies in a deep growl. "Not much."

"But you can understand what I'm saying," I state, not having to ask since his answer shows me that he maintains at least some intelligence while he's a wolf. "Then I want you to know that I find you just as beautiful like this as you are in your human form."

"Ugly," he replies, lifting his head away from my hand.

"I'm not lying," I tell him. "I didn't say that to make you feel better about the way you look when you're this way. I said that to you because, in whatever form you're in, I can still see the magnificence of your soul. You're beautiful here," I tell him as I touch the spot on his chest where his heart should be. "And that's all that matters to me."

Tristan lifts one of his misshapen hands and places it over my chest, too.

"Mae beautiful here, too," he tells me. "Always."

I assume he's not only talking about how I am now, but also the way he saw me when I was a child.

Tristan lifts his hand from my chest and places it over the hand I still have over his heart.

"Never leave," he says as he presses my hand firmly against him. "Always stay."

If Tristan wasn't still in wolf form, I would have just kissed him. Instead of a kiss, I do the next best thing.

I drop the pillow and blanket I was holding in my left arm and raise my other hand to run it along the length of his snout. I feel a slight vibration underneath the hand that is still on his chest and realize that he's purring. To be honest, I'm not sure that's what it's called when a werewolf does it, but the effect is just the same.

After a while, I take both my hands away from him and find the spot on the wall where I slept before. Tristan follows my lead and lays down, resting his head on my lap and providing me with his added warmth. I gently stroke the side of his head until I hear his deep breathing, signaling that he's fallen asleep. I grab the pillow I brought with me and prop it against the wall to rest my head on. I can't say the position I'm in is the most comfortable, but at least I'm with Tristan. From what Jered told me, I'm able to bring Tristan some comfort simply by remaining with him through the night, and if a sore neck is all I have to suffer through it's well worth the minor discomfort. I would do anything to help him, and I hope he realizes that during these stolen moments we have together.

I feel a sadness envelop my body as I imagine Tristan having to endure the transformation every night. Does he view it as a justified punishment for the things he did in the past, and for leaving his brother with his demented father? I'm not sure, but it seems like something he would do as part of his repentance. Once again, I pray to God that we can resolve the discord between Tristan and his brother soon. He deserves to gain control over his fate for the first time in his life and live it the way he wants to. I know in my heart that we'll eventually be able to have a future together, because I've already seen the proof of our love while in Heaven, and I don't intend to let my daughter down before she even has a chance to be born.

Chapter 14

When I wake up the next morning Tristan is still asleep, his head resting comfortably on my lap, but he's no longer in werewolf form. I let myself study his handsome features for a few seconds and absently begin to run my fingers through his thick hair. It's just as silky as I imagined it would be.

"That's nice," Tristan says, startling me by his unexpected awakening.

I pull my hand away but he reaches up, takes hold of my hand, and places it back on top of his head.

"Don't stop," he says. "I've never had anyone play with my hair before."

"Never?" I ask, finding it hard to believe that in all the years of his existence, no one ever showed Tristan affection in this way. "I would have thought some past girlfriend would have done this at least once in your life."

"I never really had girlfriends," he says. "My father didn't allow me or Jasper to socialize much."

"Haven't you dated since you left him?" I ask.

"Not really. I have way too much baggage to burden someone else with, and it's hard to form a relationship with a person if you have to keep them in the dark about who and what you are. When you have to keep everything in your life a secret, it doesn't leave much to talk about on a date."

"Then I take it you at least tried to go out with girls?"

"Tried and failed miserably," he admits as he turns his body until he's lying on his back, so he can look up at me. Thankfully, the blanket I brought is serving a dual purpose. Not only did it keep me warm during the night, but it's also preserving Tristan's modesty since he has part of it draped over the lower half of his body.

"How about you?" he asks me. "Have you dated a lot of guys?"

"I wouldn't say a lot, but I've dated a few."

"Did none of them capture your heart?"

"One came close, but it's like you just said. It's hard to form a lasting relationship if you can't be completely honest with someone."

"Your sister-in-law, Amanda, she's human, isn't she?"

I nod my head. "Yeah, but she's the exception to the rule. She was made Jess and Mason's liaison to the president, so she already knew everything there is to know about our world through her job."

"Are Will and Amanda soul mates?"

"No. They fell in love the old-fashioned way: mutual attraction."

Tristan closes his eyes and smiles, making me wonder what he's thinking about. I don't ask, though. I simply keep playing with his hair as we sit in a comfortable silence for a while.

"Can I ask you something?" I say.

Tristan opens his eyes to look at me again. "You can ask me anything you want, Mae. You don't need my permission first."

"How much of last night do you remember?"

"All of it," he tells me.

"I didn't realize you could talk while you were in wolf form," I say.

"Some of us can and some of us can't. It all depends on how much our fathers wanted us to talk."

"What does that mean?" I ask hesitantly.

"With enough...physical motivation...you'll do almost anything to make it stop. Eventually, Jasper and I learned to say simple words to satisfy our father's need for us to respond to him verbally while in wolf form. It's not natural for us to speak, but when it's the only way to stop someone from torturing you it's something you work hard to learn."

"I'm so sorry, Tristan," I say, feeling my heart break over what he's had to endure during his life. "I can't even imagine what you've had to go through over the years."

"I don't really want to dwell on the past," he says. "I would much rather focus on the future."

"Speaking of the future, we should probably get up. Do you feel ready for today?"

"I think so. Jered helped me a lot last night when we practiced. He seemed to think I was a natural, but I guess we'll see. Did you learn any new cheers last night?"

"Only one new one that my aunt is insisting we do," I say in despair. "It's outrageous. Apparently, the cheerleaders at the high school she and my mom attended used to perform it. I can see why it's remained with her all this time, though. It's definitely memorable."

He grins at me. "Then I can't wait to see it."

Tristan stands to his feet, being careful to wrap my blanket around his waist as he does so. He holds a hand out for me to take and helps me off the floor.

"If it were up to me," I tell him as we stand face to face now, "you'd never have to witness me acting so silly."

"Well, now I have to see it," he declares with a toothy grin.

I reach out to grab a hold of one of his arms and phase us to Jered's living room.

"My dad usually makes a big breakfast and has everyone on his team come over to our house the morning of the game," I tell him. "Do you want me to come back and get you in a few minutes?"

"Jered can bring me over," he says, reaching out to take my hand and simply holding it between us, "but I wanted to ask you something before you go back home."

I wait for him to continue but he simply stares at me, looking uncertain if he should ask me whatever question it is he has on his mind.

"What do you want to ask me?" I prod him.

Tristan clears his throat before speaking. "I wanted to ask if you would like to go out on a date with me this evening."

I sigh with relief because he had me worried there for a second, but this question is an easy one to answer.

"I would love to go out with you," I tell him. "How should I dress?"

"Any way you want," he tells me with a happy grin on his face. "I thought I would cook for you here at Jered's house, if that's all right."

"It sounds perfect," I tell him.

"I've already spoken to Jered about it. He's agreed to watch the exterior while you're here, just in case my father decides to make another unexpected appearance."

"I'm sure Jered wasn't very happy about his visit here yesterday," I say.

"That's the understatement of the century," Tristan sighs. "He was pretty livid when I told him, but there's really nothing either of us can do about it. I just hope Malcolm's plan works so my dad is out of our lives for a while."

"We still need to tell Uncle Malcolm that we plan to be there tomorrow for the Bait game," I say. "In a way, I hope he wins today. It would at least put him in a good mood before we make him mad."

"About that," Tristan says hesitantly. "Please don't be angry with me..."

"That's never a good way to start a statement," I say. "What did you do that would make me angry with you?"

"Last night, Jered and I went to see Malcolm and told him everything."

I stand completely still, needing to let his words sink in.

"Why would you do that without me?" I ask him tersely. "I should have been with you when you told him."

"I wanted to take some of the pressure off your shoulders. I knew you were dreading having to tell Malcolm about our plan, so I did it for you. I was hoping you would be relieved more than angry with me, but now I can see that I made the wrong decision."

"You should have talked to me about it first," I say, feeling aggravated more than angry. "I'm not a child you need to keep protecting, Tristan. I'm a grown woman who can take care of herself and make her own decisions. This was something we should have done together as a team. God gave us both this mission, not just you."

"You're right," he replies, completely contrite. "I should have talked it over with you first. It just made so much sense to me last night to spare you from having to tell him. I'm sorry, Mae. I shouldn't have gone behind your back like that. It won't happen again."

I still feel annoyed, but I ask, "How did Uncle Malcolm react when you told him?"

"He definitely wasn't happy. That much I can say for sure, but after he got over his initial anger he seemed to accept it. I think he's just worried about your safety more than anything else, which is totally understandable."

"I should probably go to him before the game today," I say.

"I'm really sorry, Mae," Tristan says, squeezing my hand a little tighter. "Can you forgive me?"

The distraught look on Tristan's face forces me to let go of my irritation towards him.

"I will, as long as you promise never to leave me out of an important decision like this again, Tristan."

"I promise," he declares.

"Then I forgive you. Now, go get ready for breakfast. You'll want to be there when my dad starts making waffles. They're much better when they come right out of the waffle maker."

"Yes, ma'am," he says obediently as he lets go of my hand.

I just shake my head at him in exasperation before phasing back home.

When I look at the clock on my nightstand, I see that it's only 6:30 in the morning. I hop into the shower, using the time to mentally prepare myself for game day. It's always a little stressful for me because I hate seeing my dad lose all the time. The ending score of the game is usually close, but Uncle Malcolm's team always seems to pull off wins every year. I think it's because he practices with his grandsons once a month so they don't get rusty. His team functions like a well-oiled machine.

After my shower, I put on my Cole cheer squad maroon and white track suit. On the back of the jacket is embroidered the words 'Team Cole', but other than that the outfit looks pretty normal. Jess told me once that she hates wearing the uniforms JoJo makes for them each year. Not because they're ugly, but because they normally end up exposing more flesh than she cares to outside of the safe confines of her own home. I've always wondered if JoJo imbues their outfits with something that makes their cheers a bit more effective for their team, but that would mean that JoJo has stacked the deck in Uncle Malcolm's favor each year. I can't see her cheating in that way. I seriously doubt she has a devious bone anywhere in her petite French body.

When I go downstairs, I'm pleasantly surprised to see that Tristan has already beat me to the kitchen. The area is bustling with family and friends, making it truly feel like the holidays.

"Good morning, Mae," most everyone says when I walk in. It almost makes me feel like a celebrity, but I know it's how almost everyone in the room was greeted when they arrived. I just ended up being one of the last ones to show up.

After I say good morning to everyone, I go up to my dad as he's just pulling two waffles out of the maker.

"Hot and steaming, just the way you like them," he tells me as he slides them onto a plate for me.

"Thanks, Dad," I say, giving him a kiss on the cheek and small hug around the waist.

As I remain near my father to smother my waffles with some butter from a dish there, I notice we have a new addition to our gathering.

"What's David doing here?" I ask my dad in a low voice, noticing Ella's new man sitting beside her at the kitchen table.

"He's our new center," my dad informs me. "Malik said his back was hurting this morning and decided to inaugurate David into the family by throwing him into the game."

While my dad chuckles about Uncle Malik's initiation of David, his presence begs for a question to be asked. Since our church is back in Lakewood and this house is in Colorado, it must mean David has been told about the peculiarities of our family.

"Who told him what we are?" I ask.

"Surprisingly, your Aunt Tara did," he replies.

"And David just accepted it all?"

"It seems that being a man of God and having come through the Tear prepared his mind for all of this. He didn't seem too surprised to learn what makes us special, and I know we can trust him with our secret."

After I drench my waffles with some syrup, I walk over to the other side of the kitchen counter and sit on a stool beside Tristan.

"You were right," he tells me, finishing up his helping of waffles. "These things are like liquid gold when they're warm."

"Would you like some more waffles, Tristan?" my dad asks.

"If you're offering, I would love a couple more," he replies.

I feel a gentle hand rest on the center of my back.

"Good morning, Mae," my mother says. "There's someone in the living room who would like a word with you."

I don't need my mom to tell me who my visitor is. Even Tristan knows who it is without having to be told.

"Do you want me to come with you?" he asks me. "If he's still mad, I should be the one to take the brunt of it."

"I'll be fine," I assure him as I get up from my seat and slide my plate over to him. "Eat these and save me the fresh waffles Dad is making. I won't be long."

I walk into the living room and find a brooding Uncle Malcolm.

"I didn't know he was going to go to you without me," is the first thing I tell him.

"Yes, I gathered that last night when he and Jered came to me," my uncle says. "What I'm upset about is the fact that you didn't come to me right away, Mae. And eavesdropping on my conversation with your parents? That isn't like you at all."

"It wasn't intentional," I defend. "You just happened to be talking with them when I phased back home."

"Still, you should have made your presence known to us and we could have all discussed the two of you joining us tomorrow for the Bait game," he grumbles. "Besides, that would have been the perfect time to talk to me about your plans to find Tristan's family. If you haven't figured it out yet, I've been pretty useful to the women of your family when it comes to their missions for God and the ones they set for themselves. I'm not sure why you didn't think I would help you with yours."

"I knew you would help me with the mission God gave me, but I also knew how much you would worry about me helping Tristan," I tell him. "I guess I was trying to delay this argument."

"This isn't an argument, Mae. This is a discussion about what you should have done versus what you did. There's a difference."

I sigh. "You're right. I should have included you in on this the moment I told Tristan I would help him, and I should have let you and my parents know I was listening to your conversation. I'm sorry I didn't. Can you forgive me?"

"Of course, I can," he says, holding his arms out to me.

I go to my uncle and give him a hug. I feel him rest his cheek against the top of my head.

"I always knew you were special, Mae," he tells me. "I just didn't know how exactly. Now we all know, I guess."

"And here I thought I was just your favorite because I look like Mom," I jest.

"Oh, that's always helped," he agrees with a chuckle. "But no. There was something inside you that always drew me to you. It all makes sense now."

When I pull away from my uncle, I decide to change the subject.

"Is your team ready for the big game today?"

"Since most of my team is made up of my grandsons, I would have to say they were born ready."

"I heard Luke is joining your side this year. Isn't he a bit young?"

"That boy is built like a horse," Uncle Malcolm says, sounding totally unconcerned about Jess' young son's welfare. "Besides, I had to replace Linc with someone, and Mason offered him to me. I wasn't about to say no."

"I'm a little surprised Jess is letting both of her boys play for you," I say.

"Since Rafe will be there acting as the referee, she doesn't really have much to worry about. The moment one of them gets hurt, he can heal their wounds."

"Hopefully, there won't be any wounding going on," I say.

"Eh, you can never tell in these games," he says blithely.

"Why don't you remind your boys that this isn't the NFL, even though we're playing by their rules. They don't have to hit people so hard that they knock them out cold."

"Jasp only did that once to Will," Uncle Malcolm says, defending his eldest grandson. It's only then that I realize Abby's first-born child shares the same name as Tristan's brother. I guess it is indeed a small world after all.

"Still, let's try to play nice this year. We have a few newbies in the mix."

"Oh, I see," my uncle says knowingly. "You just don't want us to rough up Pretty Boy's face."

"Pretty Boy?" I ask.

"Tristan. You know, that pretty little face of his. I suppose you wouldn't want to kiss him if he has a busted lip."

"Unfortunately, we haven't exactly reached that stage of our relationship yet, but I'm hoping that will change later today."

"I really don't want to know about your romantic interludes with the boy, Mae," Uncle Malcolm says, looking slightly disgusted. "I would rather keep you in my mind as the sweet little girl I built a rainbow slide for."

"You can think of me that way if you want to, but I'm not a child anymore, Uncle Malcolm."

"Don't remind me," he says. "It already feels like the years are slipping through my fingers, and there's nothing I can do to stop them from escaping my grasp. Before you know it, this house will be empty and all of you will have moved on without me."

I reach out to my uncle because I know exactly what he's thinking about. I'm not entirely sure what the future holds for Uncle Malcolm, but I do know he will never ask to be human until at least after my mother's death. I suspect his destiny will have him living further into the future than he wants to admit right now, but I'm not a fortune teller. Only God knows what lies ahead, and I have enough faith to let Him handle things the way He sees fit.

Uncle Malcolm leans over and kisses me on the cheek.

"I'll see you on the field," he says. "Tell your dad I look forward to beating him again this year."

I have to laugh at his overconfidence. "You never know. We might have a couple of ringers this time," I tell him. "Tristan and David could be just what my dad has needed all these years."

"David?" Uncle Malcolm asks. "Do you mean Pastor David? What in the world is he doing playing in our game?"

"You don't know about him and Ella?" I ask in surprise. For some reason, I assumed my uncle would have already known about their relationship. He was, after all, the one who suggested David to the selection committee at the church.

After I tell Uncle Malcolm that David is Ella's soul mate he seems surprised, but not completely so.

"I guess I should have known something was up when my Father asked me to suggest him to the church's search committee," he says as understanding finally dawns on him.

"God told you to tell them about David?" I ask in surprise, until I think about it for a moment. "I guess that makes sense, though. If anyone would know who Ella's soul mate was, it would obviously be Him."

"Still, He doesn't normally interfere in human affairs, but considering David's past, perhaps my father thought he deserved to finally find some happiness in his life. I couldn't have picked a better man for Ella, even if I tried."

Uncle Malcolm leaves shortly after and return to the kitchen, to find Tristan still eating.

"I thought you would have finished the waffles from my plate already," I say, retaking my seat next to him.

"Oh, I did," he says like a confession. "These are another helping."

I just laugh at Tristan as I accept a new plate from my dad with a couple of fresh waffles.

After breakfast, we all phase to the football field where the game is to take place. It's the field at my old school in Lakewood, and the same one my Uncle Malcolm still teaches at. Since my family has donated a lot of money to it over the years, the school officials don't mind us usurping their field one day out of the year. Besides, all the kids are on Thanksgiving break so there's no chance of them seeing us here.

When we arrive Uncle Malcolm's team is already dressed and on the field, doing their warm-up exercises. Jess, JoJo, Leah, and Faison are busily filling water cups on a grey fold-out table for the boys to help keep them hydrated. On the last phasing trip that my mother makes from our house, she brings a similar table for her and Aunt Tara to work on for our group.

"Come on," my father tells the members of his team, "let's go over to the field house and get your uniforms on."

I spy Tristan standing on the side of the field, watching Uncle Malcolm and his team, which is mostly made up of his grandsons.

"You should probably follow the others," I tell Tristan, wondering what it is he finds so fascinating about Uncle Malcolm's players.

"I had no idea we would be in full football uniforms," he says, voicing his thoughts. "I thought this would just be us playing in our regular clothes."

I can't help but laugh at Tristan's naiveté.

"My dad and uncle don't do anything simple," I tell him. "You'll need to just expect them to go all-out if they ask you to do things with them in the future."

Tristan looks over at me and smiles. "I'll keep that in mind."

"Go on," I say, playfully pushing him on the arm towards the field house. "Go get changed so you can warm up before the game."

"Yes, ma'am," Tristan says as he backs away, with a slight bow in my direction and a smile on his face.

I turn around and walk back to the table where my mom and Aunt Tara are filling cups with water.

"Would you look at that?" Aunt Tara says to my mom as she waves to Jess across the field. "You would think they were entering a cheerleading competition considering how fancy those outfits are."

"Now, Tara," my mom admonishes her. "You let them be. JoJo gets so much joy out of making those uniforms for the girls every year. You need to keep in mind what she's been through. I think the least we can do is support all her hard work."

"Just seems a little overboard is all," Aunt Tara grumbles.

"I like the ones she made this year," Ella comments as she studies their black and gold uniforms. "They're a lot less skimpy than other years. And Mason certainly doesn't seem to mind it on Jess. I bet he'll be getting some matches later."

Reason would dictate that Ella should have learned not to say such things while she's within arm's length of her mother, but apparently not. As Aunt Tara proceeds to tap Ella on the back of the head, I can't help but laugh. My aunt's physical admonishments don't hurt. I've been the recipient of a few in my lifetime; they're just meant to get the victim's attention.

"And what in the Sam hill do you know about matches?" my Aunt Tara demands.

"Not much," Ella says wisely as she sidesteps away from her mother to the opposite side of the table.

Aunt Tara points a finger at Ella and says, "You better not know much about matches *or* marshmallows."

"What in the world are marshmallows?" I ask the two older women of our family, hoping to finally solve the secret behind the word. Tristan did warn me not to ask my mother such a question, but there's very little that I don't discuss with my mom. "Ella and I figured out what matches were years ago, but marshmallows are still a mystery to us."

"Could we please change the subject?" my mom says. "I don't think this is an appropriate conversation for us to be having since there are children running around."

"Oh come, Lilly, the child simply wants the itch of her curiosity scratched," a strange new voice with a slight Australian accent says from somewhere nearby.

My mother instantly turns towards the bottom of the steps leading up to the bleachers on our side of the field.

"I don't believe anyone invited you here, Lucifer," my mother says in a hate-filled voice I've never heard come from her before now.

Lucifer smiles at my mother, but there's zero friendliness attached to the action.

"When have I ever needed an invitation to crash a party?" he asks snidely. "Besides, Jess seems a bit preoccupied with Mason at the moment. You would think after all these years the two of them would be tired of one another like any regular married couple."

"They love each other," my mother tells him. "I don't find it the least bit surprising that you can't understand that."

"Why would he?" Uncle Malcolm says, right after he phases in right beside my mother to protect her. "You would have to have a heart to feel that kind of emotion, and we all know Lucifer lost his a long time ago."

Lucifer grins grimly at Malcolm and taunts, "How's the leg?"

"What do you want, you old devil?" my Aunt Tara demands, effectively diverting his attention. "You've never bothered us here before. Why now?"

"That's none of your business, Tara," Lucifer says, sounding annoyed by her question.

"Is it my business, Lucifer?" we hear Jess say as she and Mason walk across the field towards us.

"I've come to collect my day," he calls out to her.

"Are you serious?" Jess says incredulously. "You pick today out of the whole year to make me spend with you?"

"Would you rather I come back on Thanksgiving Day, or perhaps Christmas?" Lucifer asks, already knowing the answer to his question.

"You know I don't," Jess says in resignation.

"You don't have to go with him," Mason argues. "He isn't your lord and master, Jess."

"I don't break my deals with people," Jess tells her husband. "You know that."

Mason sighs, but doesn't try to convince Jess to refuse to go with Lucifer.

From what I was told, Jess made two deals with Lucifer while they were on alternate Earth. Each deal provided them with his help to solve a particular problem there. I know Jess agreed to spend time with Lucifer on her birthday, and she also agreed to spend a whole day with him on any day of the year that he chose. I'm not sure why Jess agreed to his terms, but there must have been a reason. Either she thought she would be able to help Lucifer change his ways by spending time with him or she simply enjoys his company, even though he's evil incarnate according to my family. I can understand Jess' need to try to save her friend. It's similar to Tristan's quest to save his brother and possibly his father. Yet, Jess' quest seems even more impossible. I fear it will take more than just her friendship to change how Lucifer views the world.

Jess turns to Mason and gives him a lingering kiss and hug.

"I'll see you tomorrow," she promises him.

"I'll be waiting," Mason states.

I've always loved the way Jess and Mason never shy away from showing how much they love one another, no matter who they have as their audience.

Jess walks over to Lucifer.

"Where are we going this time?" she asks him.

Lucifer scrutinizes her outfit and says, "Even though I find you rather fetching in that tight-fitting teenage boy's fantasy of a uniform, I'm afraid our first stop will have to be a clothing store. I doubt the people of the Louvre would appreciate you prancing around their museum in such attire."

Lucifer places his hand on Jess' shoulder and phases her away. Through their phase trail, I can see that he has indeed taken her to a Paris dress shop. In fact, it's one that JoJo owns because it has a House of Armand sign hanging above the door.

"I'm so sorry, Mason," my mom says, sympathizing with her friend's plight.

"Jess knew what she was agreeing to when she made the deals," he replies, sounding resigned to live with Lucifer's whims for the rest of his life. "There's not much any of us can do about it now."

Mason turns around and walks back to the other side of the field. Both Max and Luke walk over to their father, presumably to see how he's doing. They've lived with Lucifer's interruptions into their lives for a long time now, and each of them knows how much their mother's absence affects their father. Mason won't feel whole again until Jess is safely back in his arms, but he'll have to wait a whole twenty-four hours before that will happen.

Since the Devereaux cheer squad is down a member, and the ones who are left look dejected that they don't have their leader with them anymore, Aunt Tara extends an olive branch and suggests we all cheer together. JoJo, Leah, and Faison readily agree because cheering with Jess missing would have just been too depressing for them.

When my father brings his team out of the field house, I nearly lose my breath at the sight of Tristan running out onto the field in his tight-fitting white spandex pants and maroon and white jersey. The jerseys don't have numbers on them. They simply have 'Team Cole' silk- screened on the front.

"Ohh, look at my man!" Ella says excitedly as she receives a wink from David right before he bends down to the ground to start the twenty push-ups my father has demanded.

"Just remember that David is a gentleman," my Aunt Tara tells her daughter. "Keep your hands to yourself until there's a ring on both your fingers."

"Why are you telling *me* that?" Ella asks. "Isn't that what you're supposed to be saying to the man who's courting your daughter?"

"I ain't worried about him behaving himself," Aunt Tara declares. "You, on the other hand, come from my loins, and I don't have as much faith that your hormones won't go crazy."

Ella just shakes her head at her mother in dismay and doesn't reply, which is probably the smart move. Anything Ella might say in retaliation would only escalate the argument.

While Team Cole and Team Devereaux continue to warm up

before the start of the big game, I see Kate and Gabriel walk into the commentator's booth on our side of the field. They will be in charge of commenting on the plays and keeping everyone straight about what's going on.

When it's time for the game to begin, Rafe, dressed in his black and white referee outfit, stands in the middle of the field with my dad and Uncle Malcolm on either side of him. He asks my dad if he wants heads or tails. My dad says heads. Rafe tosses the quarter in his hand into the air and catches it.

"Heads!" Rafe announces. "Team Cole has the ball."

"And it looks like the Cole team is off to a fabulous start!" Kate says over the speakers in the stadium as she and Gabriel begin their commentary on the game.

"Come on, Kate," Gabriel says. "You and I both know that Team Cole has a lot to overcome. They're down two of their normal starting players and have substituted them with untried rookies."

"True," Kate agrees, "but maybe that's exactly what Team Cole has needed, some fresh talent."

"Well, I wish both teams luck, but let's face it. Team Devereaux has proven for the last ten years that they can hold their own. Say what you will about pack mentality, but for the Deveraux boys it seems to work."

"Speaking of packs, Team Cole has a real-life werewolf as one of their players this year."

I look over my shoulder and up at the box to glare at my niece. Of course, she's too high up to see my stare, but I hope she feels it.

"It could just be Team Cole's ticket to the golden turkey this year," Kate states. "Let's watch and see what happens as Aiden takes the field as quarterback for Team Cole."

While Aiden calls out the play, I keep my eyes on Tristan. I don't know why, but I feel as though this is a make or break moment for him with my family. Obviously, I know they won't intentionally judge him too harshly if he fails to help us win the game, but if he's the reason we lose they'll never forget it. I cross my fingers and watch the first play as it unfolds.

"Aiden has the ball," Kate says as the play begins. "He passes it to Team Cole's new running back, Tristan. Tristan has the ball, and he's running for a first down."

We all watch in amazement as Tristan runs passed the 40-yard line and avoids being tackled by Mason and Jess' eldest son, Max.

"Tristan's at the 30," Kate says in excited amazement, "the 20, the 10...touchdown Team Cole! Woohoo! Congratulations, Tristan and Grandpa! Team Cole has made history by scoring on their first play in one of these games. I guess the addition of my aunt's new boyfriend has really paid off!"

I cringe slightly at the use of the term 'boyfriend' spoken by my young niece over the loud speakers, but I'm sure that's exactly how she views my relationship with Tristan. To me he's so much more, but I suppose calling him my boyfriend is as good a way to put it as any.

Tristan comes running back to the sidelines with a smile on his face, the football cradled in his arms. I immediately hug him around the waist.

"Good job!" I praise him.

"Do you think I overplayed it?" he whispers to me. "It seemed a little too easy to dodge the people on the other team."

"Maybe you should let them tackle you a couple of times," I whisper back. "Just to make them feel like they're not total losers."

Tristan laughs, and I can't help but feel happy by the sound.

"Come on, girls!" my aunt says, waving Ella and me over to where she and my mom are standing.

"I think it's time for our special cheer!"

I look up at Tristan and beg quietly, "Please don't watch this or I'll be mortified forever."

Tristan looks amused and perplexed by my request.

"It can't be that bad," he says, looking sure that I must be joking.

"Come on, Mae," Ella says as she begins to pull me away from Tristan. "You know my mom won't be satisfied until we do this cheer she's all excited about. It's better if we just get it over with quick, like pulling off a Band-Aid."

I look at Tristan and mouth the words, '*Help me*', but he just laughs since he's convinced I'm exaggerating.

As I line up with my family, I decide to take Ella's advice and just rip through the cheer as fast as possible. When I flap my arms around like a chicken and ask how funky everyone else's is, I know I've descended to at least the first level of Hell. By the time I'm shaking my booty and telling our supporters to 'shake their caboose', all I want to do is run and hide underneath a rock somewhere because, by this point everyone, including Tristan, is laughing so hard that saving what little dignity I have left will take an actual miracle.

The game goes on for two more hours. I can tell that Tristan is holding himself back, but at least he's able to balance the game the way he wants to and makes it appear tense. By the time the last play rolls around the score indicates that the Coles will win the game, but Team Deveraux still has a chance to at least tie it if they can make another touchdown.

"I can see how this must be quite a quandary for you, Kate," Gabriel says to her over the speakers. "On the one hand you have your grandfather who is all but assured to win the game, as long as his team doesn't screw this play up, and on the other hand you have your boyfriend playing as running back for Team Deveraux. How do you pick a side in a situation like this?"

"I don't," Kate says quite simply. "I'll be happy for either team to win because, in the end, we're all family."

Everyone on the field claps and cheers over Kate's answer, and she stands from her seat in the box to take a bow.

"I have to say, I agree with you," Gabriel says. "Although, living with Uncle Malcolm for the next year without the golden turkey on his mantel won't be pleasant for those of us who spend a lot of time with him."

I see Uncle Malcolm glare up at the commentator box. I just hope Gabriel can't see that far down.

When Sebastian and Abby's son, Jasper, hands off the ball to Luke, I hold my breath to see if he does indeed make a touchdown for Team Deveraux. Luke evades tackles by both Aiden and Will. It looks like no one will be able to catch him as he heads straight towards the end zone until Tristan propels his body into the air like a corkscrew coming out of a bottle, just barely wrapping his arms around one of Luke's legs and pulling him down to the ground just shy of the goal line.

"The Coles win the golden turkey!" Kate screams into her microphone, causing feedback to fill the air.

Everyone, except for Team Devereaux of course, jumps up and down and cheers the victorious members of Team Cole.

I run to Tristan, who is still on the ground but rolled over onto his back. When I first approach him, I hear him making a noise that sounds like crying, but as I get closer, I realize he's laughing so hard that he's crying.

I kneel beside him, catching his attention.

"That was awesome!" he tells me, looking happier than I've ever seen him before. "I've never had that much fun in my life! Are you sure I have to wait a whole year before we can do this again?"

"Shh," I tell him, holding my index finger up to my lips. "Don't give my dad and Uncle Malcolm any ideas or they'll make us do this every holiday."

Tristan keeps smiling as he attempts to calm his exhilaration over the victory.

"Nice job, Tristan," I hear my father say as he comes to stand on the opposite side of Tristan. He holds his hand down to help his star player stand to his feet. Tristan readily accepts the offer of help, and I feel the two of them bond from the simple gesture.

"Thank you," Tristan tells my dad as he stands before him. "I had a good tutor yesterday." Tristan looks over in my direction to indicate who he's talking about.

"Mae has grown up watching the game," my dad says, looking over at me with pride in his eyes. "I couldn't imagine anyone else being a better teacher for you."

"The two of you make it sound like I'm the reason we won today, when all I did was stand on the sidelines and watch," I protest.

"Knowledge is power, Mae," my dad points out. "And you

certainly seemed to give Tristan the knowledge he needed to do well today."

"Besides," Tristan says, "you didn't just stand on the sidelines. I don't suppose you and the girls would be willing to do that special cheer for the champions again, would you?"

"Nope," I say resolutely. "That was a one-time show, so I hope you took a mental picture because it won't be happening again in either of our lifetimes."

"Brand!"

We all turn at the calling of my father's name by Uncle Malcolm.

Being true to the spirit of good sportsmanship my uncle is walking over to my dad, holding the treasured golden turkey in his hands. In truth, it's not that impressive a trophy. It only stands five inches tall, and that's including the pedestal but, in this case, it's not the size of the trophy that matters. It's the importance that each man places in possessing it that does.

Each team stands behind their coach as the golden turkey passes from Uncle Malcolm's hand to my father's.

"Make sure you polish it for me next year," Uncle Malcolm tells my dad. "I like the trophy shiny when it sits on my mantel."

My dad smiles, and nods his head affably. "I'm sure I'll be taking care of it for a while, so I'll remember to do that."

My mom walks up to them and takes both men by the hand.

"Come on, you two," she says. "It's time to go back home for those victory banana splits."

My mother phases them all back to the house in Colorado.

"I'll see you at your mom's house in a little bit," Tristan tells me as he takes off his helmet. "Will said he could phase us all over there after we shower in the field house. I'm sure your mom will appreciate us not entering her home all sweaty and dirty."

"Okay," I say. "I'll see you back at the house."

"Oh, and I told your dad about our date tonight," he informs me as he takes a couple of steps backward in the direction of the field house.

I'm about to ask him why he felt the need to do such a thing, but the expression on my face must indicate what I'm thinking.

"I wanted to get his permission to start dating you," Tristan explains with a slight shrug of his shoulders. "I'm old-fashioned that way."

Tristan turns around and jogs over to the field house.

I can't help but smile as I watch him leave before turning around to help phase everyone back home for the traditional banana splits.

The rest of the afternoon passes by so quickly, I don't even realize it's time for my date with Tristan until he tells me that he needs to leave to start preparing supper for us.

"If you can give me about an hour," he tells me after I phase him back to Jered's house, "I'll be ready for you."

"Okay. Do you want me to phase directly into the kitchen when I come over?"

"That would be great," he tells me. I feel the pad of his thumb slide up and down the side of my index finger as we continue to hold hands. I get the feeling he doesn't want me to go just yet. Finally, he drops his hand away from mine. "I'll see you later, Mae."

I phase back to my room and immediately start the process of getting ready for my first date with Tristan. I probably shouldn't feel as nervous as I do about this necessity of the courting ritual. It's not like Tristan and I haven't spent most of our time together since Friday night. As I begin to count the days I suddenly realize four days have passed since we were reunited, but it doesn't feel like that much time at all. I begin to wonder if it's too soon for us to start getting physical. I wouldn't think a kiss would be out of the question at the end of tonight. Has he even thought that far ahead yet? Surely, he's considered the possibility, too.

Wait, why am I having an internal monologue that makes me sound like a sixteen-year-old girl looking for her first kiss from a boy?

I shake off my insecurities and begin to disrobe so I can hop into the shower. What am I worrying about? Of course, Tristan plans to kiss me tonight. He would be a fool not to at least try. If he doesn't initiate it, I will. I'm a woman of the modern world. I can take matters into my own hands. Who knows? I just might.

After bathing, putting makeup on, and styling my hair, almost the whole entire hour has passed by. I quickly go through everything in my closet, but can't seem to find anything suitable to wear. I grab my bathrobe and some black high-heeled shoes before phasing over to Caylin's house.

"Caylin!" I call out.

My sister instantly appears in front of me.

"Is something wrong?" she asks worriedly.

"I'm about to go on my first official date with Tristan and I have nothing to wear," I tell her.

Caylin smiles at me and touches my arm. After she phases us to her large walk-in closet, she immediately begins to pull dress after dress from her massive wardrobe.

"What in the world is going on in here?" I hear Aiden ask as he walks into the room.

"Mae needs a new dress to wear on her first date with Tristan," Caylin tells him as she tosses my choices onto the table in the middle of the room.

"She should wear the red one you just got from JoJo," Aiden tells her without a hint of hesitation.

Caylin spins around and looks at her husband in amazement.

"That's perfect! I knew I married you for a good reason."

"I've been told that I have impeccable taste when it comes to fashion," he jokes.

Caylin phases to the other side of her closet and pulls out a black garment bag with JoJo's signature HA embroidered in hot pink on the front. She unzips the bag and reveals a dress that's not too revealing, but just tight enough to show off my figure.

Aiden leaves the room while Caylin helps me into the dress.

"Are you nervous?" she asks me while she zips up the back.

"Extremely," I confide, knowing my sister will understand my feelings. "Were you nervous on your first date with Aiden?"

"Horribly so," she tells me. "But it was one of the best nights of my life. I'll never forget it."

Once Caylin has the zipper secure, I turn around to face her.

"How do I look?" I ask nervously.

"Gorgeous as always," she says with a proud smile. "You're going to knock his socks off, Mae, but I don't mean that literally."

I giggle at her words of caution. "I'll just be happy to get a kiss tonight," I tell her, "much less knocking his socks off."

"Have fun," she encourages. "And just be yourself. That's the person he's interested in getting to know better."

"I will," I promise. "I'll bring the dress back in the morning."

"Don't bother," she tells me. "We'll see you at the sleepover tomorrow night. I can pick it up then."

I lean in and give my big sister a kiss on the cheek before phasing back over to Jered's home in Montana, where I enter a scene I didn't expect to find.

The kitchen is enveloped in flames and filled with smoke. I immediately start choking and feel my right calf begin to burn. I don't waste any time phasing myself back home.

I yell for help from my mom and dad as soon as I arrive. My mother phases into the living room and my dad runs out of the kitchen.

"Mae, what happened?" my mom asks, immediately kneeling in front of me when she notices the burn on my leg.

"Jered's house is on fire," I tell her urgently, trying my best not to scream from the pain of my injury. "I don't know if Tristan is still in there!"

"I'm going to get Rafe," my mom tells my dad. "After I bring Rafe back, I'll go get Malcolm," she tells me.

My dad kneels on one knee as he examines the burn on my leg.

"The whole kitchen was on fire, Dad," I tell him, just then noticing that I'm crying. "What if Tristan's dead? What if I never see him again?"

"Don't think like that, Mae," my dad consoles. "You'll only make yourself sick imagining the worst. Trust me, I know what I'm talking about. There was a time when your mother went missing, and I thought my whole world had just imploded. We'll figure out what's happened and get to the bottom of it. I promise."

"Do you think his dad set the fire?"

"I have no idea. At this point, it would just be a guessing game on our part. Let's get you patched up first and then we can figure out what needs to be done, okay?"

I nod because I know he's right. I'm no use to Tristan the way I am. My whole body begins to tremble because of the pain from the burn. My mom returns with Rafe a few seconds later, but each second felt more like a minute. With Moses' staff in hand, Rafe uses it to heal my leg in less than ten seconds. The skin is no longer blistered and red. In fact, it looks healthier than it did before I was injured.

While Rafe was healing my leg, my mother phased to Uncle Malcolm's house and brought him back to me. I quickly tell him what I found, and he phases over to Jered's house to search for Tristan.

"I have to go, too," I tell my parents.

"Wait a minute, Mae. We shouldn't go there unarmed," my dad says as he runs into his study, presumably to get his shotgun. My mom uses the time to call Mason and let him know what's happening. After the call, she tells me that he'll be meeting us there. She then phases Rafe back home, but asks him to remain on standby in case we need him again that evening.

As soon as my dad returns with his gun and my mom comes back from Rafe's house, I phase us to what I hope is a safe point on Jered's property between the main house and the barn. When we get there Jered's beautiful home has been to ashes, right before our eyes.

I begin to cry because I have no idea if Tristan is still inside the house. If he is, he's most certainly dead. Should I have toughed it out and tried to search for him inside the kitchen? I'm sure I would be dead from smoke inhalation if I had done that. My mom calls Uncle Malcolm to let him know where we are on the property.

"I wasn't able to search the house, for obvious reasons," my uncle says when he joins us. "There's no way we can save it. The fire's too widespread. We'll just have to let it burn itself out."

"What about Jered?" I ask him. "Tristan told me he was supposed to act as our lookout tonight."

Uncle Malcolm looks worried over this news. "I haven't seen him either."

"What do you think that means, Malcolm?" my mom asks.

Just then, Mason phases in not far from our location.

"What have you been able to find out so far?" Mason asks us.

Uncle Malcolm tells him what we know, which isn't much.

"Where could they be?" my mom asks worriedly. "They must have been incapacitated somehow, otherwise they would have contacted one of us by now. Has anyone tried to call either of their phones?"

"I didn't even think about doing that," I confess.

Mason pulls out his cellphone. "I'll call Tristan. Malcolm, you call Jered."

After they try to reach their designated party, we're met by disappointment when neither man answers his phone.

"I don't know about Tristan," Uncle Malcolm says, "but I know Jered always has his phone with him, even in the shower. If he's not answering, it's because he's not being allowed to, and that indicates to me that someone most likely has him and Tristan."

"But Jered should be able to phase to us no matter where he is or who he's with," my mom points out.

"Not if he's been injured in some way that renders him unconscious," Uncle Malcolm replies.

"I don't think we have to spend a lot of time guessing who has them, or who hates Jered enough to do this to his home," my dad says.

"Have you been able to find any leads on Rolph's whereabouts?" my mom asks Uncle Malcolm.

"Nothing more than what I told you concerning the Bait game they have planned for tomorrow night," he replies. "That was the last bit of intelligence we received. I wouldn't even know where to begin to look for him, Dearest."

"There has to be something that we can do!" I say hysterically.

"Mae," my mom says, placing her hand on my shoulders and

staring straight into my eyes, "right now you need to calm down, so you can think straight. You've been with Tristan the most lately. Can you think of anything that might help us figure out where Rolph took him and Jered?"

I force myself to take in two deep breaths to calm my nerves and concentrate on what I know versus what everyone else knows.

"Rolph was here yesterday," I say, realizing that's something no one else here knows.

"What did he want?" my dad asks. I'm surprised that he isn't mad at me for not telling him earlier about the visit from Tristan's father, but time is of the essence. He can chastise me later.

"As far as I know, he just came here to warn Tristan to stay away from Jasper," I say. "That's what Tristan told me."

"Is there anything else that the two of you did that can help lead us in the right direction?" Mason asks.

"When we went to France, we saw Jasper," I tell them. "There's a cabin there. It's the one Rolph used to live in with Tristan's mother. It's the only place I can think of that might have a clue where they might be now."

"Then phase us there," Uncle Malcolm says, gently placing his hand on my arm as everyone else does the same thing.

I phase the group to the farthest spot in the forest that I went with Tristan. We never actually made it to the cabin, and now I wish I had asked him to take me to it. If there's a clue to be found about where Rolph is hiding out now, it could very well be there. I inform everyone else that I don't know where the cabin is exactly.

"I recognize these woods," Uncle Malcolm says as he looks around the area. "I used to hunt here, back in the day. There's a stream not too far away. If Rolph built the cabin, he would have wanted it near a water source. Keep an eye out for anything along the way that looks out of place."

We all follow Uncle Malcolm in the semi-darkness to the stream he mentioned. Those who have their cellphones with them use the flashlight apps to help light our way through the woods. I wish I had worn sensible shoes for my date with Tristan when the high heels start to sink into the ground as we walk deeper into the forest.

After about fifteen minutes of walking beside the stream, we finally come to the cabin in the woods. It's a quaint dwelling, and you can tell that someone who loves it very much has taken care of the cottage over the years. I find it hard to believe that Rolph would take such painstakingly good care of an inanimate object, yet treat his sons with such cruelty. It seems a bit illogical to me, but I'm not a psychopath either.

When we step into the cabin, I immediately smell the scent of something unpleasant burning. Our eyes are drawn to the fire in the small hearth on the back wall of the structure. I stifle a scream when I see the head of a person sitting on the top log of the fire, completely burnt to a crisp. The features are still present, and the flesh hasn't been burnt off. Uncle Malcolm rushes over to the fire and grabs a set of tongs hanging on a stand with a few other fireplace tools. He pulls the head out of the fire and rests it on the small kitchen table in the room. We all gather around to look at it with morbid fascination.

"Is that Jered's head?" my dad asks as he examines the features.

"Yes," Uncle Malcolm replies in disgust.

"Does that mean Jered is dead?" I ask. I've been told that Watchers can pretty much regenerate from almost anything, but this looks like something not even one of them could come back from.

"No. He isn't dead," my dad assures me. "It'll just take him a while to regenerate after we reunite his head with the rest of his body."

The door to the cabin suddenly slams shut, and we hear the howls of at least three or four Watcher children fill the air.

Uncle Malcolm looks over at Mason. "Did we honestly just walk into a trap?"

"Appears that way," he says as each man walks over to the two windows at the front of the cabin to peer outside.

"Shouldn't we just phase out of here then?" I ask them, not seeing any point in staying in a place Rolph obviously wants us to be for his own wicked reasons.

"Not until we hear the ultimatum," Mason says. "Rolph knows we could either call for help or go get it ourselves. Odds are he has something else up his sleeve. We need to stay and find out what he's up to before we leave."

It doesn't take long before Rolph yells to us, making his demands known just like Mason said.

"If you want to protect those you love most, promise to leave me and my sons alone, Malcolm!" Rolph calls out. "All I want to do is live in peace with my children by my side."

"Tristan's alive," I cry in relief as my mother places a comforting arm around my shoulders. It's obvious now that Rolph kidnapped Tristan and set Jered's house on fire.

"And what happens if I say I can't do that?" Uncle Malcolm responds. "It's not like you can do anything to us, Rolph. We can all just phase out of this cabin. What's to stop us from doing that?"

"Wait here just a moment," Rolph replies, "and I'll be happy to show you."

"He just phased away for some reason," Uncle Malcolm says as he continues to look out the window. A few seconds later Uncle Malcolm's demeanor becomes even more tense, and he curses underneath his breath at something he sees outside.

"Malcolm!" I hear Aunt Tara scream just before her voice is muffled by something.

The rest of us run over to the window that Uncle Malcolm is looking out of, to see my aunt struggling in the clutches of Tristan's father. The light is dim outside the cabin, but even in the moonlight I can see the fear in my aunt's eyes. Her hands are bound in front of her with rope, and a piece of dark fabric has been tied around her mouth.

"All you need is a promise from me and you'll let her go?" Uncle Malcolm says, ready to do anything to ensure Aunt Tara's safety.

"That would be a good start," Rolph says as he tugs on the fistful of Aunt Tara's hair that he's using to keep her in place.

"Fine!" Uncle Malcolm thunders. "Let Tara go, and I promise I won't search for you and your boys."

"For some reason, I just don't believe you're very sincere in that promise," Rolph says. "I think that as soon as I release this human you care about so much, you'll back out of this deal of ours and search for us anyway."

"Then what the hell do you want, Rolph?" Uncle Malcolm asks, becoming visibly frustrated by the whole predicament.

"I intend to prove to you that I'm not someone to be trifled with. If you come for me and my sons I will slowly kill everyone you care about, starting with the humans you seem to love so much. You can have this one," he says, shoving Aunt Tara to the ground in front of him. "Good luck finding the other one the children are chasing right now, though. For her sake, I hope you reach her before they do."

Rolph phases away.

I grab hold of my dad's arm and the rest of us phase outside to free Aunt Tara from her bonds.

As soon as Uncle Malcolm removes the gag from around her mouth, she shouts, "Ella is out there!"

"Do you know where she is exactly?" Mason asks in a rush as we all become infected with Aunt Tara's panic.

My aunt shakes her head and continues to cry hysterically. "I don't know! I don't know where he took my baby!"

"Lilly," Uncle Malcolm says, "take Tara and Brand home and wait for us there."

"I'll take them home, but I'm coming back to help search for Ella," my mom says stubbornly.

"I'm not leaving Mae," my dad states defiantly.

"Dad," I say, "it would be better if you stayed with Aunt Tara. Mom and I can control the Watcher children. You would just be another human they would want to eat. Your presence with either one of us might cause us even more problems."

My dad sighs, knowing I'm right.

"I'll stay with Mae," Uncle Malcolm promises my dad. "I won't let anything happen to her."

My dad nods his acquiescence, even though he doesn't like having to leave us.

My aunt does something I consider odd. She quickly takes off her tennis shoes.

"Wear these," she says, handing her shoes to me. "Those heels you're wearing won't get you anywhere fast."

While my mom phases Aunt Tara and my dad back home, I change shoes. By the time my mom comes back, I'm ready to go.

"Mason," Uncle Malcolm says, "you go with Lilly and I'll go with Mae. If you find Ella before we do, call to let us know."

"Wouldn't it be better if we all split up?" I say. "We could cover more ground that way."

"It's safer if we go two-by-two, Mae," Uncle Malcolm replies patiently. "Both you and your mom can control the wolves, but if their fathers are with them Mason and I are better equipped to handle them."

I can't argue against his logic, because he's absolutely right. Neither my mom nor I have the physical strength that he and Mason do as Watchers. Of course, if any of the Watchers tried to kill us we could end their lives first, but that's definitely a last resort.

"Mason, you and Lilly go northwest, and Mae and I will go southeast," Uncle Malcolm says.

"Be careful!" my mom tells me before she and Mason run in their designated direction.

I follow Uncle Malcolm through the woods, and feel grateful that he seems to know them so well. We both take turns calling out Ella's name in hopes that she'll hear one of us. Even if it's just a Watcher child who hears us, it would be progress of some sort. At least it would be one less ravenous werewolf chasing my best friend through the woods like prey.

After ten minutes of searching, we finally hear a sound that stops us in our tracks.

"Did you hear what I just heard?" I ask my uncle, wondering if the wind blowing through the trees is playing tricks with my mind.

"If you just heard a tiger growl," he says, looking as puzzled as I feel, "then yes."

"As far as I know, France doesn't have tigers."

"It shouldn't," my uncle agrees as he holds up a hand to make sure I don't say anything else. We listen intently to the sound of the forest.

We hear the roar of a tiger again, but this time it's even louder and more aggressive.

Uncle Malcolm starts running toward the sound because it can only mean one thing: Ella has found her animal form.

When we reach a small clearing in the forest, we come upon a scene my imagination couldn't have conceived of even if I had let it run wild. Standing in the middle of a circle of three werewolves is a white tiger.

"Stop!" I yell to the Watcher children, causing all three of them to cease their advance towards Ella. "Kneel!" I order. Amazingly enough all three of them kneel to the ground, whimpering as they look in my direction.

"Take Ella home, Uncle Malcolm. I can handle them from here," I say.

Uncle Malcolm runs to Ella, places his hand on her head, and phases her out of harm's way. Just as I walk into the circle of werewolves, I notice Uncle Malcolm return to watch my back in case there are any Watchers lurking nearby.

Systematically, I stare into the eyes of all three of the werewolves. When I do, they immediately lower their heads and whimper in submission. Slowly, I approach the one who's closest to me and place my hand on top of its head. Almost instantly, I sense the creature gain a sense of calm. It's almost as if it regains an awareness of who it is in human form, and isn't acting on animal instinct alone anymore. I turn slightly and hold out my hand to one of the other wolves. Hesitantly, it nudges the palm of my hand with its wet nose as if urging me to slide it along its smooth, hairless snout. I hear the third one whimper behind me, but the sound is no longer fearful. There's a note of yearning in the cry, and I know it wants me to touch it like I have the others.

When I raise my hand from the first werewolf I touched, it whimpers and crawls onto its stomach until its head is resting on top of my right foot. It seems as if at least some contact with me is better than none.

Once I have all three werewolves under control, I look over at Uncle Malcolm.

"I'm going to phase them to the bunkhouse on Jered's property. Tristan and I prepared it as a halfway house for the children who break their bonds with their fathers."

"Are you sure the bonds have been broken?" he asks as he eyes the wolves with great suspicion.

"I probably won't know for sure until they return to their human form," I say. "I need to stay with them tonight, though. I get the feeling that it's crucial they be with me for a little while. I need you to find Mason and have him follow Rolph's phase trail. Maybe it will lead him to Tristan."

"I'll do that," Uncle Malcolm volunteers. "Rolph was right about one thing: I don't feel any allegiance to him to keep the promise that I made."

"No," I say resolutely. "You can't go, Uncle Malcolm. We can't give him a good reason to start attacking other members of our family. There are other Watchers who can track him down for us, so please don't go yourself. Come to the bunkhouse after you've spoken to Mason. I may need you with me tonight to help take care of them."

My uncle doesn't look pleased by my request, but he doesn't try to put up an argument either before I phase the three werewolves under my control to Jered's property.

I decide to take them to the living room area since it has a large open space. When we get there, I slowly sit down on the floor with my legs crossed. Without even having to tell them what to do the three werewolves lie down around me, forming a circle. Slowly, I begin to run both of my hands over them and sing the same song I sang to Tristan the night he broke his bond to his father. I don't neces- sarily believe it's important that the song be "Over the Rainbow". I could probably be reciting a poem in a sing-song voice and the effect would be same. The wolves simply need to hear my voice to feel at peace.

A few minutes later my uncle phases into the bunkhouse, but he's not alone. My father is with him, still carrying his loaded shotgun. Neither of them says a word. They've seen this scenario play out before, and know that there isn't anything they can do to assist me. Helping the children of the Watchers break their bonds to their fathers is my God-given mission, and I've taken the first step towards fulfilling the destiny He has planned for me. I only wish Tristan was here to share in this experience, and I pray that he's safe wherever he might be.

Chapter 16

Sometime during the night, I end up falling asleep while I'm still sitting in the circle of werewolves. When I wake up the next morning I find myself curled into the fetal position, my head resting on something soft and warm. I open my eyes, first seeing one of the rust-colored comforters that we bought for the bunkbeds. As I raise my head, my gaze is soon met by another pair of brown ones.

"Hello," the pretty young woman I'm leaned up against says to me. "I didn't want to move until you woke up."

I quickly raise myself to a sitting position, and stare at the stranger whose stomach I was apparently using as my own personal pillow.

"Good morning," I say to her, self-consciously smoothing the back of my hair since it's probably rather disheveled. "What's your name?"

"Tracy," she tells me as she also sits up, holding the comforter to her chest with a hand.

I notice that Tracy is shirtless, which tells me she's more than likely completely naked underneath the comforter. I assume either my dad or Uncle Malcolm placed the blanket over her when I decided to use her to prop my head against. I look around the bunkhouse, first smelling the intoxicating aroma of bacon cooking and then hearing my dad's voice as he talks to someone in the kitchen. I soon hear two strange voices speak back to him, and assume they must belong to the other two Watcher children from last night.

"Shawn and Andie are already in the kitchen," Tracy tells me.

"They woke up a little while ago. You looked so peaceful while you slept that I didn't want to wake you."

"Thanks," I say, wondering just how long Tracy laid on the floor watching me sleep. The thought is a bit disconcerting, but not completely unexpected.

"How do you feel this morning?" I ask Tracy, wondering if she did indeed severe her tie to her father last night.

"I feel..." she says, pausing, as she seems to be trying to find the right word to describe her emotional state.

"You feel free," a female voice chimes in. "That's what you're feeling, Tracy. Freedom."

I look towards the kitchen and see a very statuesque brunette walking towards us, followed by a young man with black hair and striking hazel eyes.

Andie and Shawn retake their positions on the floor around me.

"Hi," Andie says, holding out her hand to me, "I'm Andie, and this is Shawn."

I shake her hand and say hello to them both.

"Your dad told us what you did for us last night," she tells me. "He also explained that it's a God-given gift. We all wondered how Tristan broke his bond to Rolph. I guess we now know."

"And how do you all feel about that?" I ask.

"I can't speak for anyone else," Shawn says, "but I feel strange."

The others agree, but none of them explains what they mean.

"You feel strange in what way?" I ask, curious to understand the process.

"It's like..." Andie begins, but pauses to gather her thoughts. "Well, I guess I can only speak for myself, but it's like having a part of you missing but not missing it at the same time."

"That's a pretty accurate description," Tracy says. "For me, it was like my father was always inside my head even when he wasn't around, and now I can't seem to sense him at all. I feel like this is the first time in my life that I can make my own choices."

"Exactly!" Shawn says. "I can't even remember a time when my father wasn't deciding everything for me. I like this new feeling, but it also scares me a little. I'm not really sure what to do with myself."

"You can do anything," I tell him. "And you don't have to decide what that anything is right this second. This place," I say, looking around the bunkhouse, "is your home for as long as you need it. Once you decide what you want to do with your lives, we'll do everything we can to help you achieve your goals."

"We sort of assumed God would be expecting us to ask for His forgiveness first," Andie says, looking at her two counterparts.

"I think He wants you to do that when you feel ready," I say. "My ability to help you break your bonds to your fathers is simply step one of the process. You're the only ones who control your destiny now."

"Our fathers will want us to come back to them," Tracy says with certainty. "Just like Tristan's father has all these years."

"Why hasn't Tristan asked for God's forgiveness by now?" Shawn asks. "He's had years to do it."

"You know why, Shawn," Andie says. "It's because of Jasper."

"Do any of you know where Tristan is right now?" I ask, holding my breath as I wait for their answer.

"I don't know where he is now," Andie says, "but I do know where he's supposed to be later."

"Where?" I ask urgently.

Andie looks between Shawn and Tracy hesitantly, and I realize this is information that they all possess. Andie continues to remain silent, which leads me to assume I'm not going to like the answer she has to give me.

"Rolph said he was going to make an example of Tristan to the rest of us," she finally tells me.

"And how exactly was he planning to do that?" I ask, already knowing I won't like the answer.

"He was planning to torture him in front of us, then kill him so he couldn't interfere in his life anymore."

"Where is this supposed to take place?" I ask right away, feeling as though time may be running out to save Tristan from his father's plans.

"In the woods in Russia, where Tristan's cabin is," she tells me.

"That's what he has planned for tonight? We thought it was supposed to be a game of Bait."

"That's what was originally supposed to happen," Andie says, "but Rolph changed it last night after he kidnapped Tristan. He wants us all to watch Tristan be put to death for disobeying him. I think our fathers thought it would help motivate us to remain loyal to them."

"Do you know exactly where in the forest this is going to take place?"

Andie shakes her head. "No. We were never told that part because it wasn't important enough for us to know."

I quickly stand up and smooth the skirt of my dress.

"I need to take care of a few things," I tell them, "but I'll be back soon."

I run into the kitchen and get my dad's cell phone so I can call Uncle Malcolm. I tell my uncle what the others just told me about Rolph's plans for Tristan.

"What can I do to help?" I ask Uncle Malcolm over the phone. "There has to be something."

"I'm not sure there's anything you can do right now, Mae," he tells me. "And I doubt Rolph goes through with his plan now that you've got three Watcher children on your side. The fathers of the ones you helped last night will be angry with Rolph for causing them to lose their own children. I suspect he's laying low somewhere for the time being."

"Do you think that means he'll change his mind about killing Tristan?" I ask hopefully. If anyone knows the mind of a Watcher like Rolph, it would be my Uncle Malcolm.

"I'm not sure, Mae," he replies, but I can hear the loss of hope in his voice. "I'll see what we can find out about his whereabouts and get back to you."

"Are you just saying that, or will you actually tell me what you discover?" I ask.

"I promise I'll tell you. Right now, just do what you need to do today. We'll find Tristan, Mae. You have my word on that."

When the call ends, I realize my uncle didn't exactly promise that we would find Tristan alive.

"I need to go home and change clothes," I tell my dad. "Will you be safe here with them?"

"I'll be perfectly fine," my dad assures me. "Malcolm has Brutus and Desmond stationed outside to keep an eye on things. Daniel will be back in a little bit, too. I had him go grab a few more groceries so I can feed your new friends."

"Keep them safe for me, Dad, and I'll come back as soon as I can."

"Just keep yourself safe," he tells me. "We can handle things here."

I phase to my bedroom first, to quickly change out of the dress Caylin let me borrow. I doubt she'll want it back now since it smells like smoke and is singed in spots. Once I have a pair of jeans, boots, and a sweater on, I phase downstairs to the kitchen to see if my mom knows where Uncle Malcolm is right now. When I get there I find my mom, Aunt Tara, and Ella sitting around the table, having breakfast.

Ella stands from her chair as I walk over and give her a hug.

"I was scared to death you would get hurt last night," I tell her, hugging her even tighter.

"Me too, girl. Me, too."

"At least we know you're a white tiger now," I say as I take a step back. "That's pretty cool."

"I know, right?" Ella says with a proud smile. "I guess all I needed was to be literally scared out of my britches to find my animal form. I can't say I ever want to be put in that position again, though, but I also hope it isn't the last time I'm able to change. My dad said it should come easier now that I've done it once. Eventually, I should be able to do it whenever I want."

"I can help you practice that later," I tell her. "Right now, I have to go back to Montana. I have some people there who need me."

Instinctively I know Tracy, Shawn, and Andie need to remain close to me, just like Tristan did when he first broke his bond to his father. I'm also hopeful one of them will think of something that will help us find Tristan. One of them might hold a secret piece of knowledge that they don't even realize is important.

To pass the time, the gang and I decide to take care of Jered's horses and clean the barn for him. My dad told me that Mason and Jess were working on finding Jered's body, but they thought the best way to do that would be to find Tristan first.

"Why is that?" I ask.

"Tristan and Jered have a bond that's very much like the one between Watcher children and their fathers. Tristan may be able to locate the body for us by tapping into that connection. Apparently, he did it when they were on alternate Earth, and they don't see any reason why he shouldn't be able do it again."

"I knew they were close, but I had no idea they were that in tune with one another."

"I've never heard of it happening before, either, but Tristan was also the only Watcher child to ever break his bond to his father and yet remain a werewolf."

I look in the barn and see Andie feeding a red apple to one of the horses. Tracy is carrying a fresh bale of hay into one of the stalls, and Shawn is leaned up against the closed door of a stall, watching the other two with a smile of contentment on his face.

My phone beeps, alerting me that I have a text message.

When I look at my phone I see that the message is from an unknown number, but I immediately know who sent it after I read the text.

TRISTAN NEEDS YOUR HELP. *You need to bring back the three Watcher children you took. If you do, my father will trade my brother for them. Meet us in the desert in two hours. Don't bring any backup or Tristan will die right before your eyes.*

I IMMEDIATELY SHOW my father the message.

"What should we do, Dad?" I ask, seeing this as an opportunity to save Tristan.

"I'm not sure, but it's obviously a trap," he automatically says after reading it.

"Even if it is a trap of some sort, I have to go. You and I both know Rolph will more than likely kill Tristan either way, but I'm not sure I can ask Andie, Tracy, and Shawn to go back to their fathers," I say as I look at the trio still inside the barn. "They just got free of them!"

"It could be that Rolph is trying to smooth things over with the other Watchers by getting their children back for them."

"Are you agreeing that I need to go, then?"

"It would be pointless for you to go without the others, and only they can tell you whether they're willing to help you get Tristan back or not," he tells me as his gaze travels to the three inside the barn. "I think you need to ask your new friends what we should do. Maybe they can think of something that will help us get Tristan back alive, and also keep them safe from their fathers."

I sigh because I know he's right. If I don't take this opportunity, I may miss my one and only chance to save Tristan's life. But if I ask Tracy, Andie, and Shawn to go back to their fathers, I may be dooming them all to a fate worse than death. I cross my fingers and pray that there's another alternative, and know that there's only one decision I can make.

When I tell the others about the text message from Jasper, none of them says a word at first. They all look a bit shell-shocked by the situation.

"I don't want to go back," Andie says, voicing what I assume is what Shawn and Tracy are thinking, too.

"But we have to," Shawn says, looking resigned to his fate.

"Yeah, we do," Tracy agrees, "but we don't have to go without a fight. I think I have an idea that might not only solve our problem, but give you an opportunity to save Tristan."

"I'm all ears," I say, desperate for whatever hope Tracy might be able to offer me. After I hear her plan, I remain dubious that it will work.

"You're going to have to trust me on this," Tracy says. "I'm confident it will work. No one else knows our fathers like we do. This is a good plan, Mae, and it's really your only chance to get Tristan back unharmed."

I look at Andie and Shawn; they nod their agreement.

"It's your best shot at saving him, Mae. Let us do this for you," Andie says.

"But why are you willing to risk your lives like this? You barely know me."

"To be honest," Shawn tells me, "this is the first time in my life that I feel like I'm in control of my future, no matter how long or brief that might end up being. Everything inside me tells me that we need to do this, not only for you and Tristan but also for ourselves. We've all done things that we're ashamed of and disgusted by. If you want to think of this as our penance, it might be easier for you to understand."

"If all of you agree that this is the best course of action, then we'll do it your way. I'll gather everyone and let them know what it is you want to do."

"Don't look so worried," Andie tells me as she drapes a comforting arm around my shoulders. "We'll get Tristan back for you."

"I appreciate that, but it doesn't stop me from worrying about all of you, too."

"We've lived a long time," Shawn tells me. "If this is the end for us, then it's the end. At least we'll go out knowing we did something good for once in our lives."

"Thank you," I tell them all as I send up a silent prayer that their idea works.

Once everyone is filled in on the plan it's decided that Uncle Malcolm, Mason, and Jess will accompany us to the desert, even though the message warned me not to bring backup.

"I hate to state the obvious," Shawn says, "but there's nowhere for the three of you to hide in the desert, which is probably why Rolph chose that spot."

"They'll be wearing outfits made by JoJo that will make them invisible," I explain to them.

"We're only there in case things go sideways," Uncle Malcolm tells them. "I think your plan will work, but nothing is guaranteed to go the way you think it will. We'll only show ourselves if it looks like you're in trouble."

"I think you're one of the few of us who doesn't believe this is a suicide mission," Tracy jokes, even though I can tell there's a part of her that views it as a real possibility.

"Have a little faith," Uncle Malcolm tells her. "I don't think God would send Mae to you only to have you all die the next day. I mean, He can have a twisted sense of humor, but even that seems a bit extreme for Him."

"That's true," Mason agrees. "I don't think you kids have anything to worry about. It's a solid plan. It'll work."

"You know," Andie says as she looks between Mason and Malcolm, "I don't remember the two of you being so nice or optimistic before. Especially you, Malcolm. What happened to the snarky, know-it-all, blood-thirsty creature who bet against me during my first game of Bait?"

"Long gone," Uncle Malcolm assures her. "Though the snarky part lingers on, but I don't really see that as a character flaw. If anything, I think it showcases my witty repartee."

"Okay, Mr. Witty," Mason says sarcastically, "why don't we go get ready while Mae helps the kids with the first part of their plan." Mason turns to me and says, "Just phase to the spot I showed you earlier at the time the text message said. Malcolm, Jess, and I will already be there when you arrive. You won't be able to see us, but we've got your back."

"Thanks," I say, giving him a brief hug in gratitude.

It doesn't take us very long to finish the first part of the plan, which leaves us with an hour to wait. I end up pacing around the furniture in the living room of the bunkhouse until it's time for us to finally leave. My mom and dad try to calm me, but it's no use. I'm too nervous that something unforeseen will happen, and I'll lose Tristan forever.

Finally, it's time for us to meet Rolph in the desert. Before we do, my parents hug me and wish me luck. I can see the worry for me in their eyes, but they also know that Uncle Malcolm, Mason, and Jess are already positioned in the desert to ensure my safety. They did suggest that I use the leather outfit Jess let me borrow to go there invisible as well, but Jasper's message clearly stated that I needed to be there for the exchange to take place.

"Just get out of the way when things start to get messy," my dad advises me.

"And if it looks like the situation is about to get out of hand, phase home," my mom practically orders.

"I will," I promise.

I turn to Tracy, Shawn, and Andie, and we form a circle by holding hands.

"Are you guys ready?" I ask them. Ready or not we have to leave, but it seems more polite to ask first.

"I think we all just want to get this over with," Shawn says for the group.

"Here we go," I warn them, right before I phase us to the spot in the desert where the Watchers first came to Earth.

"I wasn't sure you would come," Rolph says to me when we arrive.

I see him and three other men I don't recognize, standing in a line behind a kneeling and gagged Tristan. Standing directly behind Rolph is a Watcher child already transformed by the night here in the desert. I assume it's Jasper. Tristan is able to delay his transformation, which must be why he's still in human form even though it's night-time in this part of the world.

"Well, no, I take that back," Rolph says. "I wasn't sure these cowards would accompany you here to face the wrath of their fathers."

"I guess you shouldn't have underestimated us," Shawn says defiantly. "We're a lot stronger than any of you ever gave us credit for."

"Shut your insolent mouth!" one of the strangers says angrily. I presume he must be Shawn's father, in view of his temper. "You filthy dog! I should whip you right here and now, then leave you in this desert to rot for a few days to punish you for what you did!"

"Do what you want to, Father," Shawn tells him as he holds his head up high. "My soul is prepared for whatever you want to do to this body."

The anger on Shawn's father's face soon transforms into a mask of realization.

"Why are you still in your human form?" he questions Shawn, briefly looking up at the moon as if to make sure it's still in the sky. "You should have transformed the moment you got here. All of you should have..."

"Took you long enough to catch on," Andie mocks. "What do you think, Father?" she says to one of the other strangers standing with Rolph. Andie holds her arms out and spins around. "How do you like the new me?"

"You're human?" Andie's father asks in shock.

"Thanks for noticing, Dad. The fact of the matter is, we all are."

Phase one of the plan was to bring God down from Heaven so Tracy, Shawn, and Andie could ask for His forgiveness and have their curses lifted. Now that we're facing phase two of their plan, I'm worried that it won't work out like they thought. In fact, it might even backfire, and we'll all be ducking for cover.

Luckily, phase two starts to unfold just like the others imagined it would as the three Watchers who just lost their children to humanity turn their anger towards Rolph.

"You said this trade would get us our children back!" Shawn's father yells furiously. "Now, all we're left with is a bunch of worthless, stinky humans!"

"Wow, that's harsh," Tracy comments as she quickly smells her armpits. "I don't think I stink."

Shawn's father throws the first punch, hitting Rolph so hard that he falls to the ground. The other two Watchers descend on him, but he phases away before they can physically make contact. All three

Watchers phase, presumably to follow Rolph and take their anger out on him.

I quickly run over to Tristan and pull the gag out of his mouth. Without even taking the time to think about it, I kiss his lips in a desperate attempt to prove to myself that he's really alive and safely in my arms. Everything around us fades away as we share our first kiss in front of all those who are present. I don't care if they're watching us because, as far as I'm concerned, this first kiss is long overdue. Since Tristan has such a tight hold on the front of my sweater and is keeping his lips pressed to mine, I can only assume he doesn't care about our gawkers either.

Even though I don't want to, I force myself to pull away from Tristan when I hear his brother whimper in the background. I know that this might be my one and only opportunity to help Jasper, and I need to take it while I can.

Before I focus my attention on Jasper, I pull away and look into Tristan's face. There is a mixture of emotions in his expression, ranging from exhilaration to worry. The first one I'm hoping is because of me, and the second one I know is due to his brother.

"I can help him," I tell Tristan, hoping my reassurance will ease his anxiety over his brother's welfare.

I rise to my feet in the sand and face Jasper. He's standing on his backward legs, looking confused and distraught now that his father has left him all alone.

"Jasper," I say as I slowly walk around Tristan to stand closer to his brother, "don't be frightened. I'm here to help you."

Jasper whimpers in fear, but he doesn't try to run away. Even if he did I could stop him with one word, but I don't want to do that with him. I want him to feel free to come to me, if he wants to. It would be better for him in the long run if he accepts what I'm offering him and doesn't try to fight it.

"I want to be your friend," I tell him soothingly as I hold out my right hand, palm up. "Take my hand and I can help you begin to see things more clearly."

Jasper whimpers again, and looks from side to side as if he's contemplating escape.

"I won't hurt you," I promise. I keep my hand out, praying that he'll accept my gesture of friendship.

Jasper takes a tentative step forward and lowers his nose to my hand to sniff it. When he lifts his head, and takes a step backward, I fear he'll run, but he ends up doing the exact opposite. He places one of his hands into mine and instantly stops whining. I tighten my grip on him to make it a more secure hold, and to show him he has nothing to fear from me.

Tristan walks over to stand beside me while removing the last remnants of the rope his father used to tie his wrists together. He doesn't say anything to his brother. He simply lets me take the lead and deal with him.

"Would you like to go home with us?" I ask Jasper.

When he steps a little closer to me like a lost puppy, I take that as a yes and place my hand on Tristan's arm before phasing us all to the bunkhouse. I do what I did the previous night and sit down on the living room floor. Jasper, who is still holding my hand, curls up on the floor in front of me and closes his eyes against the bright sunlight shining through the windows. I begin to sing to him, and he promptly falls asleep. Tristan grabs a comforter off one of the twin bunkbeds and lays it over his brother's body. Within a matter of minutes Jasper is asleep, and slowly changes back to his human form now that he's in a part of the world where daylight reigns.

Tristan sits down beside me and takes my free hand with both of his. I continue to sing to Jasper as I lean my head against Tristan's shoulder for added comfort. I feel him place his left arm around my back to bring me in closer, and he lovingly kisses the top of my head.

I've led a charmed life. One filled with love, laughter, and happiness, but in this moment as I sit beside the man who stole my heart so many years ago, I find that my life has finally come full circle, completing a journey that started so long ago.

Chapter 17

Tristan and I let Jasper sleep while we go outside to talk about what happened the night before.

"I was making you supper," he tells me as we sit side by side in the rocking chairs on the front porch of the bunkhouse, "when my father just appeared out of nowhere and hit me on the head as hard as he could. I don't remember much more than that except for waking up on the beach of an island."

"An island?" I ask. "Is that where they've been hiding out all this time?"

"I guess so," he replies with a shrug. "It was deserted and small from what I could tell. Well, I say deserted. There was one other person there besides us."

"Who was it?"

"Did your mother ever tell you about a Fae named Izzie?"

"I don't think so," I say, trying to remember if my mother ever mentioned her before.

"When your mom and dad first got together, she tried to kill your mom."

"No way!" I say, wondering why I was never told this story.

"Yep," Tristan says with a nod. "She almost succeeded, but your Uncle Malik saved your mom with some of his medicine. He exiled her to live out the rest of her life on the island for what she did. Anyway, she was there, but I barely spoke to her. I never liked that woman. She was always too full of herself. Besides, she was running around naked all the time."

"Oh, she was?" I ask, finding this interesting. "Are you telling me you don't like to look at naked women?"

Tristan smiles at me. "I wouldn't say I don't like it, but it all depends on the woman."

"I can understand that," I say.

"Tell me what happened last night. How did you convince Tracy, Shawn, and Andie to ask for God's forgiveness so quickly?"

I go on to tell Tristan everything that transpired after his abduction. He's heartbroken about Jered's house, which isn't visible from bunkhouse, and instantly stands up when I tell him about Jered's dismembered state of being.

"We have to go find him!" Tristan says, looking panic-stricken. "Why didn't you tell me this before now?"

"I know we need to find him," I say calmly, "but we can't just leave Jasper here alone. He's going to need the both of us when he wakes up. In fact, he might even be our best way to find the rest of Jered's body."

"I might be able to find it on my own," Tristan protests. "At least let me try. Take me to the woods in France first; my dad may have left his body out there somewhere. If he is, I can track him in wolf form. It's nighttime there."

"I don't think that's a good idea," I say. "We don't know what the other Watchers did to your dad yet. He might figure you'll try to find Jered's body and be waiting for you. Why don't we wait a little while to see if Jasper wakes up? I think that would be the smartest thing to do right now. Your father could have stashed Jered anywhere in the world, for all we know."

"I'll wait thirty minutes, but after that we do things my way."

"Fair enough," I agree.

Tristan sits back in his chair, but I can tell he would much rather be out searching for Jered. I decide to try to take his mind off what's going on by switching the subject.

"After things get settled, I would really like for us to spend some time with Ella and David. I want to get to know him better since he's going to become an integral part of our lives."

S.J. WEST

"How do you feel about Ella finding her soul mate?" he asks, looking quite interested in my answer.

"I'm happy for her. I can't think of anyone else who deserves to find happiness like that."

"I can think of one," Tristan says meaningfully. "Yours is still out there somewhere, Mae. Have you ever thought about searching to find him or her?"

"Actually, no," I say truthfully. "I honestly thought you were my soul mate for years."

"And now that you know I'm not, do you want to try to find that person?"

"I don't need to," I tell him, realizing this is my opening to lay to rest any foolish thoughts he might have that he's not good enough for me. "I was told by two very important people in my life that choosing who I give my heart to is just as important as, if not even more special than, being paired with my soul mate."

"Are you sure you can truly be happy without experiencing that type of connection?"

"I know who I want, and I know who can make me happy," I say, staring straight at him, hoping he takes the rather large hint I just laid in his lap.

"So, that kiss..." he says, leaving the word hanging in the air for me to grasp.

"Yeah, that kiss..." I reply, looking over at him and smiling.

"Was that a one-time thing, or can I expect more kisses like that in the future?"

"The answer to that question depends entirely on you," I tell him.

"Then it wasn't a one-time event, and I look forward to you kissing me some more."

I can't help but laugh at him, especially while he's wearing such a cheeky grin on his face.

"Am I the only one who will be doing the kissing in this relationship?" I ask. "You know, sometimes a girl likes to be swept off her feet."

"Hmm," Tristan says, seriously pondering my words for a

moment. Suddenly, he hops out of his chair and grabs my arms to pull me out of mine. Before I can protest (not that I actually would) he lifts me into his arms.

"Was that unexpected enough for you?" he asks, smiling happily at me.

"Yes," I laugh as I loop my right arm around the back of his neck and place my left hand on his chest to play with the buttons of his maroon-and-blue-plaid shirt. "Girls also like being kissed by the guy they're interested in like they're the only person in his world."

"That'll be easy," Tristan whispers to me. "You are the only person in my world, Mae. You're the only woman I want to wake up to every morning and say goodnight to every evening. I can't imagine kissing anyone else's lips but yours, because I've never tasted anything sweeter than your mouth. You fill my heart with so much happiness that sometimes I feel like it might burst out of my chest. I love you, Mae Cole, and I hope to hear you say those words to me one day."

"Why don't you kiss me, so I have some time to think that part over?" I tease him.

"I guess I'd better make sure it's a good kiss then," he says, letting my legs slip from his arm until I'm standing in front of him. "Apparently, my happiness will depend on it."

Tristan gently pulls me in closer until I'm pressed up against him. The first touch of his lips against mine is tentative. He seems almost shy, and I don't want him to ever feel that way with me, so I take matters into my own hands. I begin to move my lips against his more urgently, silently signaling to him that I'm not breakable. He doesn't have to treat me like a china doll when he kisses me. Tristan seems to be a quick study, as he leans against me even further until my back is pressed up against one of the large polished logs holding up the front porch.

I'm not sure how long we stand there kissing, but at some point we both hear a man clear his throat. Tristan instantly pulls away and turns to face his brother, who is standing in the doorway of the bunkhouse. Jasper has the top two ends of the rust-colored comforter tied together so that the blanket is draped over his right shoulder like a toga, hiding his nakedness.

"Jasper," Tristan says, sounding relieved that his brother is awake so soon. "I can't tell you how good it is to see you."

"I'm not quite sure what happened," he says, sounding confused as he looks between me and Tristan.

"How are you feeling?" I ask him.

"A little disoriented," he confesses, "but also more clearheaded than I've ever been."

When Jasper looks over at Tristan, I see a plethora of different expressions cross his face.

"I honestly don't know why you never gave up on me," he tells Tristan. "I was horrible to you just because I could be. How did you keep yourself from hating me after all the nasty things I said to you?"

"You're my brother, Jasper," Tristan says, walking over to his brother and giving him a hug. "I'll always love you, no matter what."

"Thanks for never giving up on me," Jasper says, his voice sounding as if he's on the verge of tears. "Now I understand why you wanted me to break my bond. It's like I've regained control over not only my soul, but also my mind."

I allow the brothers to just hold each other for a while, but I know I need to interrupt their family reunion to ask an important question.

"I'm really sorry I have to ask this," I begin, "but do you happen to know where your dad put Jered's body, Jasper?"

Tristan pulls away from Jasper, so his brother can respond to my question.

"His body?" Jasper asks, answering my question with confusion. "I'm sorry. I don't know what you're talking about."

Tristan sighs, and looks over at me as if to say Plan A is obviously a dead end. It's time for Plan B.

"That's all right," Tristan tells Jasper as he places a reassuring hand on his brother's back. "We'll sort it out."

During the moment of silence, we all hear Jasper's stomach growl.

"Are you hungry?" Tristan asks, with a smile because he already knows the answer.

"I'm starving," Jasper confesses.

Tristan turns to me and holds out his hand for me to take.

"Then let's go inside," he tells his brother. "There's probably some food in the kitchen. I'll make us all something to eat."

Jasper and I sit on the stools at the kitchen island while Tristan rummages around in the refrigerator to find something to cook.

"Daniel was supposed to bring some fresh groceries over," I tell Tristan. "Did he make it here with them?"

"Looks like it," Tristan replies, pulling out three steaks and potatoes. "We have the makings of a good meal."

"I would offer to help," I say, "but it's probably best if I stay away from all things uncooked and let more capable hands turn them into something edible."

Tristan laughs, but Jasper just looks confused by my joke. I go on to tell him about the curse which affects the cooking ability of the females in my family.

Jasper finds it amusing. "You're in luck, then, because Tristan is an excellent cook."

"It's pretty much a requirement for all the men who marry into my family," I say, only realizing after the words are out of my mouth that it sounds like I'm expecting Tristan and me to get married one day. I am, but I probably shouldn't have said it so blatantly.

"Then I guess it's a good thing that I can cook," Tristan agrees with a smile.

I smile back at him, happy to see that I haven't scared him off.

"It sure is," I agree whole-heartedly.

I see Jasper looking around the kitchen like he lost something.

"What's wrong?" I ask him as Tristan seasons the steaks.

"Where is everyone?" he asks. "I thought the others would be here."

"Tracy, Shawn, and Andie?"

"Yes. I thought they would be coming back with us."

"Honestly, I'm not sure where they are right now, but I assume they were taken somewhere safe. Uncle Malcolm probably thought it would be a good idea to give you some time to get used to things around here first. Are you doing okay?"

"I feel a little lost," he admits in a low voice. "And..." Jasper swallows hard and glances up at Tristan, as if he doesn't want his brother to hear his next words. "For some strange reason, I feel like I need to be close to you."

"It's natural," I tell him in my full voice, because this isn't something that needs to be hidden from Tristan. I place my hand on the kitchen island, palm up, and wiggle my fingers at Jasper. "Come on. You know you want to."

Jasper laughs and places his left hand on top of mine. I entwine our fingers to make him feel more secure.

"Do you feel better?" I ask him.

Jasper nods before saying, "I do. What is it that makes me want to be around you?"

"To put it into terms you can understand, Mae's like our pack leader," Tristan explains. "That's probably the easiest way to think of it."

"That makes perfect sense to me," Jasper says. "And if I ask God to have the curse removed like the others, will I still feel this way about you?"

I shake my head. "I don't think so."

That thought brings a question to mind. Will becoming human alter the way Tristan feels about me? As I think through the time we've spent together recently, he has wanted to hold my hand through most of it. Could it just be the wolf inside him that feels a need to be so close to me? I don't know the answer to that question, and I doubt Tristan does either until he has his curse removed.

I end up finishing my meal first because Tristan and Jasper have years of each other's lives to catch up on. I excuse myself so I can call my Uncle Malcolm to see what we need to do about finding the rest of Jered's body, and to see if anyone followed Rolph's phase trail. I would feel better knowing his fate at the hands of the angry Watchers.

Instead of answering my questions over the phone Uncle

Malcolm simply phases over, so he can talk to all three of us at the same time. He also happens to remember to bring over a fresh set of clothing and shoes for Jasper to wear.

After we tell him that Jasper doesn't know where his father hid the rest of Jered's body, Uncle Malcolm agrees with Tristan that we should put his bond to Jered to the test.

"And as far as Rolph goes, we're not sure what happened to him. The phase trail split off too much and just ended up leading us on a wild goose chase. But, considering how angry the other Watchers were, I don't think they just let him go. We may never know what became of him. I suggest we focus our attention on finding the rest of Jered's body."

I find it strange, and gruesome, to be speaking about such things, but I should realize by now that it's simply part of the world I live in.

"I think we should start in France near the cabin," Tristan tells Uncle Malcolm.

"I agree," my uncle replies. "It's the most logical place to search first."

Before they leave Tristan pulls me back out onto the front porch, saying that he needs to ask me a favor.

"Can you take Jasper home with you?" he asks me once we're out there.

"Of course. I was planning to do that anyway. Since he'll be staying with us for a while, I thought he might enjoy being at the family sleepover."

"I hope I can make it there before everyone goes to sleep," Tristan says.

"If you can't, there's always next year," I say optimistically. Hopefully by this time next year Tristan will be human, and we'll be well on our way to a lasting relationship with the promise of marriage sometime in the future. I don't particularly want to get married before I graduate college, though. I think trying to juggle everything all at once would be too hard on me, but if we're destined to spend the rest of our lives together I'll definitely want a late spring wedding.

Tristan takes me into his arms and kisses me on the lips.

"I wish things were different," he tells me. "I would much rather stay here and kiss you all day than search for a friend's body."

"I know it's a gruesome task, but the sooner you find it the sooner Jered can get back to normal. It was weird to see his head sitting in the fire of that cabin last night. I can't say that I've ever seen anything that horrible in my life."

"I'm just glad you weren't hurt in the housefire."

I remain mute on that subject because I don't want Tristan to know that my leg was burned. I'm about to change the subject when he lifts his eyebrows questioningly.

"Mae," he says seriously, "did you get hurt and decide to omit that part from your story?"

"My leg got burned, but it really wasn't anything. My mom brought Rafe to heal it so fast I barely had time to feel much pain."

Tristan's happy face soon turns murderous. "I hate my father. I don't know why I thought he could change, because it's obvious to me now that he never will. I won't let him hurt you again, Mae. Once Jered is put back together, I'm going to help Malcolm find out what became of my father and cut his head off myself if I have to."

"You might not have to do anything," I point out. "The other Watchers looked mad enough to take him out of the picture for us."

"I hope they did, but I'm not going to assume they've taken care of my dad. It'll be handled one way or another, though. You have my word on that."

"What should I do with Jasper when he needs to transform tonight?"

"Malcolm has a cell that he kept Sebastian in when he was still cursed. Have you ever been inside it?"

I nod. "Yes. He showed it to me once."

"Just take Jasper there when he needs to leave the party. He should be safe enough. I'll have Malcolm station a couple of Watchers at his house to watch over him."

I lean in and kiss Tristan one more time.

"Keep safe, and watch your back while you're out there," I tell him. "Don't run off from Uncle Malcolm, either. If you happen to run into your father while you're looking for Jered, you're both much safer together than you are apart."

Tristan kisses me again before saying, "I promise not to do anything boneheaded, Mae Cole. I have too much to live for right now. This is the first time in my life that I feel as though all the stars are aligned and fate is working in my favor instead of against me. You must have a forcefield of good luck around you or something. Since the moment you re-entered my life, everything seems to be coming together for me."

"Just come back to me in one piece," I beg. "You're not the only one here who feels happy."

"I'll be back before you have a chance to miss me," he vows.

"I don't think that's possible, unless you can find Jered in less than a second after you leave."

"Why, Mae, I never realized what a sappy romantic you are," he teases as he tightens his arms around my waist to bring me even closer to him.

"I never have been before but there's just something about you, Puppy, that makes me all ooey-gooey on the inside."

Tristan laughs. "I haven't heard you call me that since that night I found you in the woods. I thought maybe you didn't like the nickname since you haven't used it since."

"I've thought of you as my Puppy for so long, it's what I call you inside my mind sometimes."

"I kinda like it," he tells me with a smile. "It brings back good memories for me."

"Are you ready to go, Tristan?" Uncle Malcolm asks, sticking his head out the open door.

Tristan kisses me one more time before letting me go.

"Let's get this done," he tells my uncle.

"We'll leave as soon as Mae phases Jasper home," Uncle Malcolm says. "I don't want her to be here alone."

I'm not sure if my uncle is worried about me being here in the bunkhouse, or if he doesn't want me to be alone with Jasper. I don't ask because, in the long run, it simply isn't important.

As I phase Jasper and myself to my mom's house in Colorado, I pray that Tristan is able to find Jered's body easily. The faster he does, the sooner he can return to me.

I'VE HEARD the term 'a fish out of water' used before, but I never saw a real-life example of it until I saw Jasper trying to integrate himself into my family. The annual Cole sleepover is a tradition that was started the year Caylin went to college. I think my parents were feeling the empty nest syndrome with her gone, and wanted to make sure their eldest daughter was home for Thanksgiving. Since then we've all come together under the same roof and enjoyed each other's company, until real life intrudes and everyone has to return to their normal lives the following Monday.

One of the basic requirements for the evening is food. My father and Aunt Tara split the responsibilities of feeding us each year. Aunt Tara is in charge of making the snacks and sweets for sleepover night, and my father prepares the Thanksgiving meal the next day. When Jasper and I arrive my aunt already has Ella and David hard at work, making the three different varieties of fudge that she requires each year. As soon as she sees that she has two more willing hands to put to work, Jasper and I are placed in charge of forming the popcorn balls.

"Where're Mom and Dad?" I ask Aunt Tara as Jasper and I sit at the kitchen table together, working on our designated project.

"Your folks took Tracy, Shawn, and Andie out for a run," she tells us. "They wanted to test out their new human bodies."

I suppose that makes sense. I couldn't imagine going through such a drastic physical change and not wanting to make sure everything still worked like it should.

"Jasper, honey," my aunt says as she stands at the kitchen island, stirring up the dough for a batch of her famous chocolate chip cookies, "are you planning to go through the change soon, too, now that you've broken the bond to your dad?"

Jasper clears his throat nervously. "I'm not sure yet. I think I need some time to adjust to things first." Jasper looks over at me and asks, "Is there some sort of time limit? Do I need to do it soon, or can it wait?"

"God never said anything about a time limit, so I assume He wants you to do it when you're ready," I tell him. I don't say it, but I hope Jasper doesn't take too long to make his decision. The longer he waits, the more I fear his father will try to convince him to return to his side. Until we discover what happened to Rolph, that possibility still exists.

It takes us most of the afternoon to make all the sweets and other treats that will satisfy our hunger during the next few days. By the time we're finished, other members of my family start to arrive. Abby and Sebastian's family is the first to show up, heartily welcomed by my three reformed werewolves since Abby was in charge of bringing pizza from their local franchise. Considering the way they descend on the pizza like a pack of wolves I begin to wonder if God really did make their bodies totally human, or if He left a little bit of the wolf inside them just for kicks. My Uncle Malcolm always said that God had a twisted sense of humor. In any case, we end up ordering in more pizza to make sure everyone gets their fill.

Being with my family during this time of year has always been special to me. There's nothing like having your whole family together under one roof. The energy given off by so much love and happiness in one place is intoxicating. Even though he isn't a true member of my family, I can tell that our gathering is affecting Jasper. He seems a bit overwhelmed by it all. As dusk approaches and everyone is playing Pictionary, I quietly ask him if he's ready to retire for the evening.

"I would appreciate that," he tells me, sounding relieved to go somewhere a bit quieter.

"Okay, just let me call Desmond and Brutus," I tell him. "Uncle Malcolm asked me to get in touch with them when it was time to phase you over, so they can watch the house while you're there."

I call Desmond first; he says he'll call Brutus for me, so I don't have to worry about anything else, and that they should both be at Uncle Malcolm's house in just a few minutes.

I take Jasper's hand and phase him directly into the iron room underneath Uncle Malcolm's house. It's pitch-black inside the room, but I can physically feel Jasper relax as we stand there together. I can't see his face, but I hear him breathe a sigh of relief. Unfortunately, his moment free from anxiety is short-lived.

"Hello, son," we hear Rolph say in the darkness. "I thought I might find you here."

J asper instantly places me behind his back to shield me from his father. I fumble to get my phone out of my back pocket and turn the flashlight app on to pierce the darkness. When I shine the light in the direction Rolph's voice came from, I gasp in horror. It's evident the Watchers who attacked him earlier were out for blood, considering his current physical state.

Rolph's right arm has been detached from his body, leaving behind flesh with ragged and bloody edges. The skin that once covered his chest has been completely stripped away, and I can literally see the glistening of red muscles and white sinew. Rolph's handsome face is now blood-spattered pulp, and he has a gaping hole where his left eye used to be.

"How can you protect that bitch when she's the reason this was done to me?" Rolph demands of Jasper. "What kind of spell has she cast on you, son? Why have you abandoned me like your brother did?"

"I should have left you a long, long time ago," Jasper tells his father. "And don't blame any of this on Mae. The only thing she did was help me think for myself for the first time in my life. I let you fill my heart with all your anger and hatred for so many years that I lost myself by being blindly loyal to you. Now, I see you for who you truly are, and I understand now who really cares about me. You brainwashed me into thinking Tristan was to blame for my mother's death, but he wasn't the one who killed her. You did that all on your own. You never loved me. You only saw me as a way to elevate your standing among the other Watchers. Do you realize how twisted you are, Dad? None of the other Watchers ever had a second child, because even the worst ones couldn't stoop that low again. Yet, your petty greed and need to prove just how heartless you are led you to make the same mistake twice."

"You weren't a mistake," Rolph says. "I wanted you."

"You wanted me so badly you sacrificed my mother's life to have me," Jasper accuses. "I would rather have never been born than come into this world, clawing my own mother to death from the inside out. How could you do that to her, when you watched Tristan do it to your first wife?"

"River was my world, and God took her away from me to teach me a lesson!" Rolph storms. "Who exactly is the monster in that scenario? No one seems to demand that my Father answer for His crimes against us and the human women we loved. How can you take His side against me?"

"I don't know that I can," Jasper answers honestly. "But I do know that you aren't worth my loyalty anymore. All you've ever done is use me, but I was too deluded to understand that until now."

"If I kill that bitch who's hiding behind you I bet you'll come crawling back, begging me to forgive you."

"Mae," Jasper says to me, "phase and get help."

"If she leaves, I'll just follow," Rolph promises, "and I'll kill whoever happens to have the misfortune of being present at the time."

"I can take care of myself," I say as my hands burst into blue flames for the very first time in my life.

"Well, well, well. Are you telling me you would kill the father of the man you supposedly care about?" Rolph mocks. "For some reason, I don't see that happening. How do you think Tristan will react if you use your powers against me? Do you think you'll have enough time in your puny human existence to wait for his forgiveness?"

"He would understand that I was only defending myself and his brother," I argue, but Rolph's words have already taken root in my heart. Tristan has spent years trying to convince his brother and father to seek God's forgiveness and leave their past behind them. With one thought, I can kill Rolph and dash any hopes of him ever finding redemption. What would Tristan think of me if I sentenced his father to eternal damnation?

"Come with me now, Jasper," Rolph says, holding out his remaining hand to his son, "and I'll spare her life and the lives of those she loves."

"And if I refuse to go with you?" Jasper says defiantly.

"Then I'll kill you both."

"River would be so disappointed if she could see you right now," I say, using the only leverage I have against Tristan's father. I just hope he has enough of a heart left to feel guilt.

"Stop talking about her! You aren't good enough to say her name!" he roars.

"I think you've forgotten that there was a time you could love someone other than yourself. Why didn't you use the love you had for her to be a better father to Tristan? Instead you mutated your love for your wife and transformed it into unending hatred. What part of that do you think honors River's legacy?"

"Shut up!" Rolph screams, beginning to limp forward. "Shut up, you..."

Rolph's words are suddenly cut short. As if I'm watching some horror movie, I see an unseen force twist his head completely around until it snaps away from his body. While his torso slowly sinks to the ground, his head remains floating in the air like a macabre balloon without a string.

My Uncle Malcolm materializes out of thin air, holding Rolph's head in his hands.

"Are the two of you all right?" he asks me and Jasper.

"We're fine," I say, taking in Uncle Malcolm's black leather outfit. It's the same one he wore to the desert, making him invisible at will.

"How did you know we were in trouble?" I ask him.

"I didn't," he says. "I just came down here to make sure Jasper was settled in to ease Tristan's mind while he keeps searching for Jered's body. I didn't want to startle him, so I decided to phase in invisible. I have to say, I'm glad I did now. This certainly helps solve one of our biggest problems."

"What are you going to do with my father's body?" Jasper asks. The way Jasper is looking at his father's mutilated body tells me that he still cares about him. He wasn't the best father by any means, but even an abusive parent can leave their mark on your heart.

"I'll take care of your father, Jasper," Uncle Malcolm promises. "And when you and Tristan decide to give him another chance to change, I'll put him back together for the both of you."

"I think it's going to be a long time before that happens," Jasper says.

Uncle Malcolm nods his head, indicating that he completely understands and agrees.

"Mae," Uncle Malcolm says, "why don't you take Jasper to the woods near Tristan's cabin? I think he would prefer to be outside during his transformation rather than stuck in here while I'm cleaning up this mess. There're still a few hours of nighttime left in Russia. It should be enough to satisfy his need to change."

"Okay," I say, wholeheartedly agreeing with Uncle Malcolm's suggestion.

I phase us just outside Tristan's cabin. It is indeed still nighttime in Russia. It's also extremely cold, and I begin to shiver.

"You should go back home," Jasper tells me as he starts to unbutton his shirt. "You'll catch a cold if you stay out here."

I look out into the woods in a vain attempt to catch a glimpse of Tristan, but there's no telling where he is since the forest he lives in is so vast.

Jasper takes his shirt off and neatly folds it before placing it on the front porch of Tristan's cabin. He stands there staring at me, and I realize he's waiting for me to leave so he can take his pants off before his body forces him to change into his wolf form.

"I'm sorry about your dad," I tell him, feeling a need to talk about what we just experienced together before I return home.

"He's always been his own worst enemy. Maybe a little time to cool off is what he needs. I guess we'll see in a few decades."

"Do you think he needs that much time before he's willing to listen?"

"Honestly, I'm not sure if he'll ever be able to change the way he is, Mae. Sometimes people just are the way they are, and there's nothing you can do to make them see reason. All we can do is offer him a different path. If he decides not to take it, we'll just have to accept that and move on."

I know Jasper is right. You can't make someone change who they are just because you want them to. They have to choose to change for themselves, or it will simply be an empty gesture.

I hear the howl of a wolf at a great distance, and know that it's Tristan.

"It's been a long time since we ran together," Jasper says, sounding eager to join his brother.

"Then go," I encourage. "Be free and have fun. I'll see you guys later. Remind Tristan that you're both expected to join us for Thanksgiving tomorrow."

"I'll make sure he remembers," Jasper promises.

Just before I phase home, I hear Tristan's plaintive howl again. Now that I know Jasper has no intention of asking for God's forgiveness anytime soon, I have to wonder how long it will be before Tristan does it. He mentioned to me once that he always dreamed of doing it alongside his brother, but what if it takes Jasper years to get ready for that moment?

My mother has often told me that the future will take care of itself, and it can never be rushed. With a little bit of patience and a mutual devotion that is just as sweet now as it was the first time Tristan and I met, I know I won't have to wait too long for that momentous event to take place and for the rest of my life to begin.

"Are the two of you ready?" I ask Tristan and Jasper. As they both stand up from the swing on my mother's front porch, I can't help but smile at how nervous they look.

"Is He here?" Tristan asks.

"He's waiting for you in the living room," I tell him. "Chop, chop, you two! It's not nice to keep God waiting."

Tristan smiles, because he knows me well enough by now to understand when I'm teasing him mercilessly.

It's been a whole year since we were reunited, and during that time we've grown closer than I could have ever imagined. We've been working hard to save the souls of other Watcher children but, just like God warned us, it will indeed be a slow process. Although it was easy to show Tracy, Shawn, and Andie the right path, they had been ready to change their ways for a very long time. All they needed was someone to nudge them in the right direction and encourage their desire to improve their own lives.

"Wait," Jasper says, placing his hand on Tristan's chest to stop his forward motion before he reaches me in the doorway, "you brought it, right?"

Tristan dips his right hand into his pants pocket, searching for something.

"Yeah," he says in relief. "I've got it."

The boys continue to walk towards me, wearing grins that seem a bit on the mischievous side, making me wonder what they're up to.

"I don't suppose you're going to tell me what that was all about," I say to Tristan as he takes hold of my hand before walking into the house.

He leans in and kisses me sweetly on the lips.

"Not yet," he whispers to me. "You'll know soon enough."

"You're such a tease," I complain.

"It'll be worth the wait," he promises, with nothing to back his words but a charming smile.

As the three of us walk into the living room of my mother's Colorado home, God stands before the lit fireplace. He's patiently waiting for two of His children to formally ask for His forgiveness and cleanse their souls of their sins and their bodies of the curse that has plagued them since the moment they were born.

My whole family is gathered in the room to support Tristan and Jasper in their choice. Ella smiles at me as she stands next to her husband, David. They got married the previous May in a simple wedding at our church, which God officiated. I couldn't be happier for my best friend, because I know she will enjoy a love that will last beyond her time spent here on Earth.

As I watch Tristan and Jasper kneel before God and formally ask for His forgiveness, I look over at Jered and see unshed tears in his eyes. Luckily, Tristan located the rest of Jered's body not long after I left Jasper in the woods by his cabin in Russia. I later learned that when I heard Tristan's howls that night, he was signally his discovering of Jered's body. It took a few days for Jered to regenerate enough to reattach his head but he never complained about his ordeal, because everything that happened helped bring Jasper back to Tristan. That was all Jered ever wanted for the man he had basically adopted as his own son.

After Tristan and Jasper ask for forgiveness, God places His hands on their heads.

"I wish you both happiness in the lives you have chosen to lead," God says. "Now, please stand and feel the weight of your curses lift from your bodies and forever be forgotten."

When Tristan and Jasper stand back up, they look at each other and smile. Everyone in the room cheers as the brothers embrace for the first time in fully human bodies.

Jasper pulls away from Tristan and says, "I think it's time."

Tristan nods, and turns to look over at me.

Between the words Jasper just spoke and the odd question he asked Tristan out on the porch I have a feeling I know what's coming next, but I don't want to jinx things by being over- confident. Tristan told me once that after he went through the process of having God remove his curse, he would have a surprise for me. I believe I know what that surprise will be now.

Tristan leaves his brother's side and walks straight in my direction. Once he's standing in front of me, he gets down on one knee while taking my left hand in his. When our eyes meet my heart starts beating wildly, and all I can do is smile and wait breathlessly for him to ask the one question I feel like I've been waiting forever for him to ask me.

"Mae Cole," he begins, "this day has been a long time coming. I knew the moment you re-entered my life last year that there would never be anyone who could match not only your physical beauty, but also the pure joy you bring to my soul with your love. I can't imagine my life without you in it, and in front of our family and friends I humbly ask you to become my wife." Tristan reaches down into his pants pocket and pulls out a simple solitaire diamond ring. "Mae, will you agree to marry me and make a second one of my dreams come true today?"

I feel the eyes of everyone in the room on me as they wait for my answer, and tears of joy slip from my eyes while moments from the last year flit through my mind. I suddenly realize how complete my life has felt ever since Tristan and I were reunited. When he first left me as a child I instinctively knew something was missing, and now that I have him back I can't even imagine living the rest of my years without him by my side.

I squeeze Tristan's hand when I see how worried he is by my show of tears, and smile down at him. I fear if I try to put into words exactly how I feel in this moment it will come out a jumbled mess of gibberish, so I decide to keep my answer to him plain and simple.

"Yes," I tell him, "I'll marry you."

As Tristan slides the ring onto my finger I feel as though I've just been placed on a new path, one that will be filled with the love of my husband and the laughter of the children we'll have in the future. I look around the room at the happy faces of those I love and cherish the most in the world as they begin to cheer and congratulate the start of a new adventure for me and Tristan. I know that I'll always remember this one perfect moment as the beginning of the rest of my life.

THE END

.

AUTHOR'S NOTE

Thank you so much for reading Sweet Devotion, Ma & Tristan's Story.

If you have enjoyed this book please take a moment to leave a review. Please visit:

Sweet Devotion http://a.co/fHu4roO

The next book I will be working on is Requiem (Book 4, Vampire Conclave). After that is finished, I will start working on the second book of the Everlasting Fire Series which I have decided to call Between Worlds.

Thank you in advance for leaving a review for the book.

Sincerely,
S.J. West.

NEXT FROM S.J. WEST

VANKARA ,
THE VANKARA SAGA BOOK 1

Vankara, an island nation founded by runaway mages, finds itself besieged by a series of mysterious plagues which decimate half the world's population.

When the Queen of Vankara falls ill from one of the plagues, she calls upon the talents of Sarah Harker. As a shifter, Sarah is physically able to transform into another person but only if she is touching them at the moment of their death, gaining not only their physical form but also some of their memories.

Queen Emma Vankar entrust Sarah with the responsibility of protecting the people of Vankara from the ever growing greed of those in parliament and from the ambitious hands of Aleksander Chromis, dictator of the Chromis Empire and ardent suitor for the queen's hand in marriage. To help Sarah become the ruler Vankara needs, the queen enlists the help of her trusted political advisor, Gabriel, and her estranged lover, Captain John Fallon. Sarah soon finds herself at the center of a mystery when she discovers the cause of the plagues, uncovering a diabolical conspiracy to conceal the truth of their origins.

Exclusively on Amazon, Free on KU!
http://a.co/7ujpWky

ABOUT THE AUTHOR

Once upon a time, a little girl was born on a cold winter morning in the heart of Seoul, Korea. She was brought to America by her parents and raised in the Deep South where the words ma'am and y'all became an integrated part of her lexicon. She wrote her first novel at the age of eight and continued writing on and off during her teenage years. In college she studied biology and chemistry and finally combined the two by earning a master's degree in biochemistry.

After that she moved to Yankee land where she lived for four years working in a laboratory at Cornell University. Homesickness and snow aversion forced her back South where she lives in the land, which spawned Jim Henson, Elvis Presley, Oprah Winfrey, John Grisham and B.B. King.

After finding her Prince Charming, she gave birth to a wondrous baby girl and they all lived happily ever after.

As always, you can learn about the progress on my books, get news about new releases, new projects and participate on amazing give-aways by signing up for my newsletter:

FB Book Page: @ReadTheWatchersTrilogy
S.J. WEST
FB Author Page:

https://www.facebook.com/sandra.west.585112 **Website:** www.sjwest-.com **Amazon:** http://bit.ly/SJWest-Amazon **Newsletter Sign-up:** http://bit.ly/SJWest-NewsletterSignUp **Instagram:** @authorsjwest **Twitter:** @SJWest2013

If you'd like to contact the author, you can email her to: sandrawest481@gmail.com

Made in the USA
San Bernardino, CA
17 February 2020